THE CIRCLET
Half Drawn

Jessie Biggs

Cover art © 2016 Ashleigh Rahel Dunne
Editor: Stephen Parolini

To my family and friends
who believed I had stories worth sharing,
to brilliant authors like Sanderson and Rothfuss
who will always inspire me to reach higher,
and to God for...well...
everything.

To Eva,
I hope you enjoy the story,
friend! May these adventures
fuel your own :)

Love,
Jessie

CHAPTER ONE

"Ambry, *please* don't set yourself on fire."

"Will you relax, Prewitt? I'm not that inept," I said as I crouched, holding out the flickering match. I cupped my hand to form a shield around the wind-tossed flame.

"Experience would suggest otherwise," Prewitt muttered, running a hand through his mop of tawny hair. The full moon overhead cast his face into shadow, but I could hear a distinct smirk in his voice.

Ignoring his last remark, I began lighting the candles decorating our *krathong*. It was rather pathetic; broken flowers and a few poorly-constructed origami cranes littered its surface, but at least we'd made an effort.

"If you're going to worry about anything, your time would be better spent worrying about us getting caught," Gemma said. Her shoulders were tensed and her arms folded. The wind whipped up her hair so that thick, dark curls obscured her face. She swatted them away to reveal a deep scowl.

I sighed. Gemma had been cross ever since we left London, even though she'd volunteered to come along on our unsanctioned little outing. For the past decade, the Global Government had been on a slow campaign to stamp out any cultural practices which created "unnecessary cultural boundaries rather than striving toward global unity." This festival in Chiang Mai was one of the last left, and though Gemma would probably rather suffer a botched manicure than admit it, I could tell it intrigued her. "Honestly, Gem, who would recognize us here?" I asked.

"Well, you don't exactly blend in," she pointed out.

"Thank you for the unnecessary reminder." I swept agitated fingers through my long waves of steely-blue hair. "You know I can't help it that my hair sticks out like a sore thumb." It was true, too. I had no control whatsoever over the hue of my hair.

"It might actually help in this scenario," Prewitt said. "With all the Dregs milling around this place, there'll be dozens of people with every hair color."

I gritted my teeth. He had a point. Still, I hated the term. *Dregs*...as if the lower class were just the gritty sediment coating the bottom of Society's proverbial tea cup.

2

But I had long given up hope that my friends would abandon their use of the degrading label.

"Even so," Gemma was saying, "there's still a chance we might run into somebody from the Academy, or even someone who knows our parents."

I shook my head. "We're seven or eight thousand miles from home, Gem."

"Which is the equivalent of a nanosecond-long trip through the nearest Telepoint," she reminded me.

She had a point. "Still, that's a needle in a haystack since we didn't tell anyone where we were going," I argued. "What are the odds that out of every Telepoint-linked city in the world, someone would run into us here in Chiang Mai? And I don't think I did anything suspicious enough to make my parents request my tracker reports." But beneath the light reply, my confidence flickered not unlike the third match I had just lit. My father had always possessed an annoying habit of finding out what people were up to. Especially me, no matter where in the world I tried to escape his prying eyes.

Chiang Mai was the capital city of Thailand's northern province, and tonight the locals were celebrating their annual *Loi Krathong* festival—along with about fifty thousand eager outsiders, making the place feel like a wonton stuffed with bull elephants. I yanked our little leaf-boat out of the path of several drunken Australians, one of whom bumped into me with such force that I was nearly pitched into the dark river. Thankfully, Prewitt caught my sleeve before I wound up taking a rather dirty river bath. But even as the Aussies staggered away singing at the top of their lungs and swinging their bottles of contraband *lâo thèuan,* I knew it would be hypocritical to grumble too much about the influx of tourists. After all, I *was* one of them.

I rolled my eyes as Prewitt helped to stabilize me. Such large-scale population traffic was the direct result of the Telepoint system, which had been in operation since before I was born. However, it was also thanks to the Telepoint system that my friends and I could slip away to Southeast Asia for a quick excursion now and then and still be back before dinner. For that, I was grateful.

I refocused my energy on coaxing the candles on our *krathong* to ignite. Once it was lit—if I could ever get it lit — we would send the small watercraft down the Ping River along with thousands of other (more sturdily constructed) boats.

Prewitt crouched down to inspect my slow progress. "You know the Thais do this to worship their water goddess?"

"Since when do you know so much about Thai culture?" I asked, glancing up at him.

"I... did a little research," he mumbled.

"Huh." I struck the matchbox once more. "Was that before or after you said this was the most outrageously stupid idea I've cooked up yet and that you would never support it, not ever in a million years?"

"All right, fine," he retorted. "I was *curious.*"

"You were *excited*."

He glowered at me. "Well either way I'm here, aren't I?"

"And I'm grateful for the company," I said with a grin. Though I would have been more than willing to come on my own, my adventures were always more fun when Prewitt and Gemma could be coerced into tagging along. It also made for a water-tight alibi if I were to find myself in need of one.

The last candlewick lapped up the match's flame. "Oh, look! I think I finally got them all! Quick, let's get it in the water before the wind picks up again."

I allowed Gemma to do the honors. This perked her up, if only for the moment. She bent down and gingerly picked up the little boat, careful not to singe the silken sleeves of her new blouse, then set it in the opaque water. It bobbed and floated downstream, bumping into several other tiny vessels on their collective voyage to lands unknown. Their minuscule flames reflected a thousand pinpricks of light across the surface of the river.

Prewitt tugged my sleeve. "Come on. They're about to start sending off the lanterns."

We hurried through the crowded streets, pausing only to purchase three sky lanterns and a carton of pad thai to share. I shoveled mouthfuls of tofu and rice noodles into my mouth as we walked; I tried not to make a mess, but attempting to eat with chopsticks while being jostled by dozens of passersby was easier said than done.

All throughout the streets, people were beginning to congregate in small clusters with their own lanterns. "We've probably got about five minutes," Prewitt said with a glance down at his phone.

"Think we can make it to that roof?" I asked, pointing at the top of a nearby building. "The view would be incredible."

Gemma shrugged. "Worth a shot, I suppose."

We threaded our way through the multitude until we reached a dilapidated apartment complex. The white paint on its walls was chipped and cracked with age and neglect. So many people were coming and going that I doubted anyone would notice us slipping inside. After all, it was hard to look out of place in a world united by teleportation. Anywhere you looked there were people from every race, culture, background, and style.

Leading the way up the well-worn stairs, I decided to take them at a run. I hurtled past one floor after another until I finally reached the top. When I shoved through the heavy door at the top and alighted on the roof, I was rewarded with a spectacular three-hundred-and-sixty-degree view. We must have been about twelve stories up from the ground.

Prewitt and Gemma appeared panting behind me a few seconds later. "How do you do that?"

"Do what?"

"Move—so—fast—" he heaved, clutching a stitch in his side.

"It's called 'exercise.' You should try it sometime," I said. Prewitt was slender and relatively strong, but the only real workouts he ever got were those academically prescribed at Honoratus, such as the weekly self-defense course. And although he was proficient enough at that, sprinting wasn't his forte.

"No. It's called socially-acceptable masochism." He leaned against the doorway, panting. "Normal people don't enjoy running the way you do."

"At least I can make a quick getaway when I need to," I said. "Here, hand me those."

Gemma snorted and held the matchbox out of reach. She appeared winded, but not so much as Prewitt. "After your last performance, I'd say that unless we want to be lighting sky lanterns for next year's festival, maybe Prewitt or I should take it from here." She pointed at my hand.

I glanced down. Three of my fingertips were still soot-blackened from my earlier efforts. She made a fair point. "Have it your way," I conceded.

Prewitt set to work lighting the lantern while Gemma and I held it up, allowing its papery belly to fill with warm air. It looked as though it were taking a slow, deep inhale of breath and holding it in anticipation of its long-awaited flight.

As we waited, I stared out across the rooftop. All across the city, tens of thousands of lights began flickering to life. They speckled the streets and neighboring rooftops as tourists and natives alike came together in one enormous, corporate celebration.

I turned back to the *kom loi* suspended from mine and Gemma's hands. The cream-colored cylinder was almost ready to hover on its own. The locals believed that these lanterns would carry their troubles up into the black ocean of sky. This idea puzzled me. Laden with the cares of so many, how could they find the strength to rise? I had enough trouble getting out of bed most mornings with my own troubles.

"All right. It's ready to go," Prewitt said, straightening up. "Let her fly!"

As one, the three of us raised our arms and released the lantern. It struggled for several feet, tipping in a dangerous wobble from side to side. Just when I was starting to worry that it might set itself ablaze, a gentle gust of wind caught it up in its invisible arms and it rose with new purpose to join its siblings in the sky.

I looked back out over the rooftops. All across the city, thousands of other lanterns lifted into the air like ribbons of spotted light, threading up through the night sky.

None of us could speak. It was without question the most marvelous thing I had ever witnessed. Words seemed petty compared to such indescribable beauty. The aerial kaleidoscope continued to grow and undulate with every change of wind. On a nearby rooftop, I could make out people laughing and pointing, raising cameras and phones to capture a tiny piece of the spectacle. A few children gawked in amazement. It was incredible to think that across

8

the city, thousands of people from every age and race were all suspended in a single moment in time.

My heart swelled in my chest. How could the Global Government possibly find something like this dangerous or divisive? From my perspective, watching as citizens from every corner of the world joined together to create a visual masterpiece, I saw only unity.

But those were the kinds of thoughts the G.G. had branded dangerous.

Better left unspoken.

It was with deep regret that I finally trudged after Gemma and Prewitt to start our descent back down the rickety staircase. We still had one last item on our agenda: a concert in the market district. A popular Thai band was playing, though I couldn't pronounce their name to save my life—I had always been terrible with Asian languages. The other fifty-some thousand guests must have had the same idea because throngs of animated tourists and Thais alike were all slowly drifting in the same direction.

Several teens passed us. One of them had sculpted her hair into the shape of a *krathong* and decorated it in a similar manner. Banana leaves and colorful tissue paper stuck out at odd angles from her fiery red hair.

Prewitt would definitely have something sarcastic to say about that. I turned to point out the phenomenon to him, but he was nowhere in sight. "Gem," I said, trying not to panic. "Where's Prewitt?"

"He was right here just a minute ago," she said. Lines

of worry etched themselves into her forehead.

I laughed, trying to put her at ease, but I couldn't quite suppress the nervous edge to my voice. "If he's gotten himself kidnapped…"

"You'll what? Alert the Officials?" said a voice in my ear.

I swiveled to find Prewitt chuckling behind me. He held three colored lanterns suspended from wooden sticks. "You scare too easy, Croft!" he said.

"I wasn't *scared*," I corrected. "But if I were, it would be an understandable reaction when your friend disappears in the midst of thousands of other tourists." But I was too relieved to be angry at him. If we'd lost him and had to resort to asking the Officials for help, the Globe only knew what kind of fresh hell would be in store for us back home.

"Here," he said, holding out me one of the lanterns like a peace offering. The blue sphere was almost the same shade as my hair. "I just went to get us each one of these hanging lantern things. Only cost me two merits each—can you believe that?"

"Ooo! Can I have the purple one?" begged Gemma.

Potential crisis now averted, we continued on our way to the concert. It wasn't hard to find; we followed the screams and cheers of ten thousand fans to an outdoor amphitheater that could easily have held six of Rome's Colosseum. Many of the other people at the concert had hanging lanterns as well, causing the audience to sway in colorful waves as the crowd moved in rhythm with the melody.

"This is *amazing*!" cried Gemma. She waved her fat purple lantern back and forth with an expression of childlike delight. "Remind me, have I ever had this much fun before?"

"Doubt it." I beamed at her. "I told you this was a great plan!" I yelled to Prewitt over the music.

Prewitt opened his mouth to reply, but shouting nearby diverted his attention. He turned to look over my shoulder just as I was shoved from behind.

I stumbled forward. Prewitt caught me before I could fall headlong, but more people were immediately pushed into us as a fight broke out several yards away. It looked like the result of a mosh-pit that had gotten out of hand.

"Gemma, watch out!" Prewitt yanked Gemma out of the way just as a teenage boy came flying toward her. The boy hurtled to the ground but was up and cursing within seconds.

"We should get out of here," Prewitt said, still holding a protective arm around my shoulders.

I nodded and began searching for an escape route, then blanched. "Oh, you've got to be kidding me…"

Several men dressed in silver uniforms were shoving their way towards the source of trouble. A random spotlight swept over them, illuminating the globe and the letters *G.G.* emblazoned over their chests.

Next to me, Gemma clapped a hand to her mouth. "Officials!" she yelped.

"We have to move before they see us," said Prewitt. "Any Official could recognize Ambry by her hair alone."

"Told you you should've worn a hat," Gemma snapped.

I rolled my eyes. "No time for 'I-told-you-so's. Hurry!" I pushed Prewitt forward into the crowd and stumbled after him, dragging Gemma behind me.

I chanced a glance back as the crowd closed in behind us. Just as my eyes fell on the closest Official, another spotlight swept over me, blotting out the familiar face with a series of dancing white spots. When my vision cleared, I was startled to find his eyes on my own. He looked as shocked as I was. I watched him raise both hands to his mouth in an effort to shout over the din. *"Ambrosia Croft?"* he yelled.

My eyes widened. I grabbed Gemma and Prewitt by the arms. "Move it!" I cried, shoving them forward into the dense crowd. We pushed and squeezed through the melee of people. Irritated shouts of *"Hey!"* and *"Watch it!"* blended with similar exclamations in Thai, Spanish, and a handful of other languages as we shoved our way through. Elbowing our way out of one last cluster of tourists, we reached the open expanse of the market street and hurtled eastward toward the square.

I rounded a corner and grinned triumphantly at Telepoint archways gleaming in the distance. "They're up ahead!" I shouted to Prewitt and Gemma several strides behind me. "I think we can make it!" I chanced another glance back and saw that the officers were a good hundred meters behind us.

Turning to look forward again, I skidded to a halt just before ploughing into the silver sheen of a uniform.

Prewitt didn't slow as quickly. He ran straight into me, pitching me forward to the ground. He landed unceremoniously on my back, knocking the wind from my lungs. "Wait," he wheezed as he scrambled to let me up. "He, I mean you——" he spluttered, shaking his head at the Official. It was the same hardened man who had identified me in the crowd. "You literally just appeared out of thin air! But there's no way..." He trailed off as a look of dawning comprehension stole over him. His face was the picture of pure, unadulterated shock. "Did you seriously open a *time capsule* just to catch us?"

My stomach did a backflip. If the Officials had opened a time capsule, our situation had Officially gone from bad to catastrophic. My own father, Titus Croft, was a Timekeeper, one of twenty-four people in the entire world chosen to oversee and dictate the usage of the world's precious supply of time capsules.

"Those are reserved for world crisis situations!" Prewitt went on, more to himself than anyone else. "Well, that and maybe to cover up the odd political scandal..."

The Official who had first caught sight of me must have opened a freeze capsule. It had probably only required less than twenty seconds worth of power for him to catch up to us, but it was amazing the difference that less than half a minute could make. I recognized him from one of my dad's

Elite social functions as a Russian Official who had recently transferred to the European division. "Good to see you again, Miss Croft," he said with a curt nod. "I would recognize that lovely hair of yours anywhere."

His sarcasm was evident in the way he spat the word "lovely." It made me nauseous... to think that he had waltzed right by while I had been trapped immobile in mid-stride. This was a perfect example of why the Timekeepers were necessary; time capsules ripped away all control from anyone not in possession of them.

I found myself shaking uncontrollably. "Kozlov," I muttered, my eyes fixated on his black military boots. I knew that if I looked him in the face, there was a significant chance that I would sock him in the jaw. *Then again, I thought, with his reckless attitude toward the capsules, he might just open another and turn me around so I wind up punching Prewitt instead.*

"I wouldn't have expected to see you quite so far from London," said Kozlov.

"We were just trying to get some extra credit," Prewitt interjected. Prew had always been quick on his feet. His clever excuses had gotten us out of a number of close scrapes. "You know, for our Cultural Anthropology course at Honoratus."

Kozlov raised a heavy eyebrow. "I see." He took a calculated step closer. "Then I'm sure you won't mind if we escort you home? I'd say the evening's festivities are coming to a close."

14

My shoulders slumped. That was it then. There was no getting out of this one.

Kozlov and two of his fellow Officials marched the three of us through the square. Forty or fifty arches stood sentinel around the edges of the square—*far* more Telepoints than any one location would normally have. They probably rented some in anticipation of the crowds. Kozlov led the way to the nearest one, his hand clamped tightly around my upper arm.

As I stepped up to the gateway, my eyes traced the flight of one particular lantern as it rose into the sky. It continued onwards and upwards until, with one final wink, its distant flame went out. Had it fulfilled its mission of carrying its owner's troubles up into the black abyss? I found myself shaking my head. More likely it was hurtling through the darkness even now, its long-awaited journey nothing more than a free-fall toward inevitable destruction.

Kozlov nudged me forward into the archway. As the familiar tingling sensation of the Telepoint washed over me, I felt that I—like the lantern—was careening downward as well.

And the landing wasn't looking so good.

CHAPTER TWO

I stepped through the exit portal into a chilly London twilight. Appreciating the brief moment of solitude, I took a deep breath, but the crisp autumnal air had barely settled in my lungs when Kozlov materialized behind me. He stepped forward and planted a firm hand on my shoulder. "Yes, I get it… you caught me," I said under my breath. "Bully for you."

Prewitt and Gemma appeared a moment later. Each was trailed by a grim-faced Official, both looking less than thrilled with the task they'd been assigned. I doubted their normal patrols included shepherding reprobate teenagers. Together, our odd troupe marched down the street to an awaiting car, which Kozlov must have called ahead for while we were still in Chiang Mai.

I ducked my head and slid across the wide leather seat, followed closely by my fellow accomplices. Unfortunately, the driver must have just taken his dinner break. The overwhelming smell of mushrooms and onions assaulted my nose. Gagging, I immediately went to roll down the window, but found it to be locked. *figures*, I thought. Kozlov shut the door firmly behind us before sliding into the front seat next to the driver. But in spite of the horrific smell and less than pleasant company, I sent up a silent prayer that we would hit traffic. Anything to delay the homecoming that awaited me.

"What are you going to tell your parents?" asked Prewitt, leaning over to whisper to me across Gemma's lap. As usual, he had read my mind.

"I doubt I'll have to tell them anything really," I said. "My dad will most likely be too busy yelling to ask questions."

"Ever the optimist," said Prewitt, the corners of his mouth twitching.

"You're lucky you don't care what your parents think," said Gemma. "I, on the other hand, will have to go home and listen to how disappointed my mum and dad are with my behavior and how they expect better of me."

"Yeah." I twisted a blue lock of hair between my fingers. "My parents expect exactly this sort of thing from me, so I'll be facing exasperation more than disappointment."

"Hampstead Heath," announced the driver.

"Thank you," said Kozlov. "Miss Mellette? I believe this is your stop."

Gemma heaved an exacerbated sigh, looking crestfallen. "Nice knowing you both. I don't suppose we'll be seeing much of each other this weekend."

"It will be a miracle if we see anything more of each other over the next few weeks than the backs of one another's heads during class," said Prewitt. "Good luck!" he added.

Gemma shot him a scowl as she scrambled past him and out the door of the car. The driver waited until she was safely within the gates of her family's compound before zipping off again. We sped northward, and my heart sank as I realized that mine would be the next stop.

"They're going to realize I've been off my meds," I whispered.

Prewitt's head swiveled toward me, his expression alarmed. "You mean you haven't been taking them?"

I shook my head. "Not for the past three weeks." Prewitt still appeared stunned. "But how did you manage to get away with it? I thought your parents had started making you take them while they watched?"

"They do," I replied, "but I've gotten really good at hiding the pill under my tongue until I can slip away and flush it down the toilet."

Prewitt rubbed a hand over his face. "Ambry, you know I don't often agree with your parents. Most of the time… practically never, in fact. But regardless of that, this is one time when I believe they are truly doing something for your own good. It's *dangerous* to skive off taking your medication," he insisted. "The pills are to keep you healthy."

"They're to slow me down," I retorted, narrowing my eyes at him. "Prew, you've known me for six years. You've seen me on and off the meds, and you *know* that I can barely think straight when I'm drugged. I can't get a solid night's sleep, everything feels fuzzy, I'm depressed…" I trailed off, shaking my head. "I can't live like that anymore. Honestly, I'm surprised you and Gemma have tolerated me all this time when I can barely function as a human being, let alone a friend."

"You are a *wonderful* friend," Prewitt insisted, clapping a hand on my knee. "Who else could drag us halfway around the world and get us incarcerated by Officials in under three hours? Our lives would be downright boring without you." His grin was teasing.

A smile forced its way onto my face. Between the Croft manor and the Academy, Prewitt and Gemma were the only things that made life tolerable. Well, at least mildly tolerable.

"Regent's Park," barked the driver.

I tugged the collar of my jacket tighter around my neck. "Wish me luck…"

Prewitt gave my knee a final squeeze. "Call me tonight if you need to."

19

"I will," I assured him. "Thanks, Prew. See you Monday."

Kozlov held the door open for me as I slid across the leather and stepped onto the smooth cobblestone street. The car door slammed shut behind me. I turned, hoping for one last glance at Prewitt's encouraging face, but the car was already speeding off again into the encroaching twilight.

I swiveled on my heels and marched toward the wrought-iron gates. Veering to the left, I approached the hewn stone wall. Since the sun's light was beginning to fade, it took me a moment to select the correct stone, but in the end I found it: a roughly-hewn gray oval that sat slightly deeper than its surrounding neighbors. I placed my finger at its base and traced its shape along the pale mortar. When my finger arrived back to where it had begun, the stone emitted a faint glow. A mechanized female voice spoke as though from behind the wall. *"Retinal scan, activated."*

"Good evening, Meredith," I said dryly, addressing the scanner by the name I'd bestowed upon it as a ten-year old when we had first moved to London. I had long since abandoned any hope of receiving a response to my greeting. I leaned forward so that my eyes hovered in front of the glowing stone. Standing there for what seemed like an eternity, awaiting its approval, it felt as though even the compound's security system was judging me.

Finally, its computerized voice echoed again. *"Identity confirmed. Welcome home, Ambrosia Croft."*

"You've known me for six years now, Meredith.

You'd think it would take less time to figure out whose eyes you're staring at," I said as I stalked toward the gigantic house.

The manor jutted up from the sloping landscape like an accidental stroke of gray paint, the only modern blemish on an otherwise timeless canvas. And although I couldn't see any movement, I knew that there would be at least two highly-trained snipers positioned somewhere on the roof, ready at a moment's notice to defend the Croft family. My father found this a comfort.

I found it disturbing.

Rather than watch the manor growing closer with every step, I watched my boots as they created soft dents in the freshly-cut grass. I had always preferred taking the more direct route across the lawn rather than winding my way around the paved driveway—to the eternal dismay of my mother, who despaired of my shoes ever lasting more than a few months.

When I looked up again, the elaborate oaken front doors loomed before me. I took the front stairs two-at-a-time, took a steadying breath, and knocked sharply.

The doors opened to reveal an aged butler in full coat and tails. This caught me a little off guard. Though the staff always adhered to a strict dress code, the attire wasn't normally so formal. I blinked twice before realizing that he must be dressed for the Gala. Was that tonight? Just what I needed—a houseful of Timekeepers, Globe employees, Officials, and every other manor of Elite drone. *Well,* I thought, *at least their posture will be flawless since they'll be dancing with those ramrods of steel shoved up their…*

The butler's kind brown eyes widened in surprise. "Miss Ambrosia!" he greeted me. "I was told you were at a school function and wouldn't be returning for at least another hour!"

"Change of plans, Charlie," I said with a grateful smile. Breaking all sense of propriety, I threw my arms around him. Though I dwarfed Charles by almost four inches, his presence gave me a momentary sense of security.

Charles was easily my favorite person in the manor. I loved his salt-and-pepper hair; his warm, friendly eyes; the way he always smelled of the pipe he smoked during his infrequent breaks. He was more like a grandfather than a butler—sneaking me fresh-baked cookies from the kitchens when I was younger, covering for my absences when I needed time alone—and I hugged him now as though the pressure might somehow magically cause him to trade places with my father.

Charles patted my back, sounding flustered. "Dear girl, whatever is the matter?" he asked, his affection mixed with concern.

But my reply died on my lips as another voice echoed down from above. "That's quite enough, Ambrosia. I'm sure Charles doesn't enjoy being suffocated." My mother had appeared on the third floor landing and was looking down with disapproving eyes expertly painted with liner and mascara.

Calista Croft was a great beauty, known for her impeccable taste and immaculate appearance. Tonight was no exception. Her silver evening dress hugged her slim figure, accentuating every graceful curve. It was littered with elegant swirls of diamonds, which matched the diamond clusters suspended from her ears. Her chocolate-brown hair was pinned to perfection in a low French twist at the nape of her neck. "Your father and I would like to see you in the study."

It was a command, not an invitation.

"Yes, Mother," I replied, my voice feeling as mechanical as Meredith's. Charles relieved me of my backpack and coat, and I began the ascent up the wide, winding staircase.

Reaching the landing on the first floor, I was assaulted by a hundred mouthwatering aromas. The chefs were obviously in the middle of preparing a host of delicacies for the Gala. My stomach growled. I hadn't eaten anything since the piece of toast I'd scarfed down for breakfast that morning—other than a few hurried mouthfuls of pad thai.

Deciding to take a quick detour, I made a beeline for the kitchen doors. If my parents were going to reprimand me for the next hour leading up to their ridiculous soiree, at least I would have something to chew on while being berated.

The kitchen was abuzz with activity. At least a dozen master chefs were hunched over their simmering pots, pans, and trays, slaving over four dozen different hors d'oeuvres.

My parents must have hired a substantial amount of extra help for the evening. I watched as servants dressed in white button-down shirts and black pants flew in and out of the doors leading into the ballroom. Some carried silverware, others trays of elaborate delicacies.

Slipping my hood up to stifle my incriminating blue hair, I ducked around the nearest kitchen island and hurried toward the first edible thing I saw—a plate of sandwiches stuffed with something akin to egg salad. Shoving one in my mouth and grabbing three more, I turned and made for the exit, glancing over my shoulder as I went to make sure nobody had noticed.

I was ploughing through the double doors when I felt the heavy wood connect with something on the other side. There was a deep cry of alarm, followed by a thudding sound and an earsplitting *crash*.

I froze, my hand still braced against the door. Now what had I done?

When the moment of shock had passed, I hurried out to assess whatever damage I'd caused.

A young servant was sprawled on the floor of the hall, gaping in bewilderment at the carnage of hydrangeas and broken porcelain that surrounded him. Recovering from his shock, he began scrambling to retrieve the flowers and the remnants of their shattered vase.

"I'm so sorry," I said, dropping to my knees to help.

"You don't have to do that," the servant boy replied stiffly.

"I know, but I want to," I insisted, using a large hunk of porcelain to sweep the smaller particles within a more manageable distance. "It was my fault anyway."

No reply came. When I looked up from my growing pile of porcelain, it was to find the servant boy staring at me, the expression in his brown eyes unreadable. He looked as though he might be two or three years older than me. His frown was set in a handsome, angular face framed by shoulder-length auburn hair, which might have been deemed unpresentable by my mother were it not slicked back in the modern Elite fashion. Even so, a few loose curls hung rebelliously across his face, probably dislodged in his fall.

I paused mid-swipe as he continued to stare. "What?" I asked,

"Nothing," he said. He pushed several of the rogue curls aside. "It's just... you're a Croft, aren't you?" From his accent I guessed that he, like myself, was native to America.

"Ye-es," I said, drawing out the syllable. "Your point being?"

He gave a half-shrug. "I don't know. I suppose I wouldn't have expected you to..."

"Apologize?" I guessed, raising my eyebrows. "Even though I was the one who barged through the doors and knocked you over?"

The corners of his mouth quirked upwards. "Well, I heard from Trevors that another servant got sacked once just for bumping into your sister."

"Ah," I grimaced. "With Orelia, that wouldn't surprise me. But I'm not my sister."

"No, you're not," he murmured. Something about the way he said it suggested a far deeper knowledge of me than he could have acquired in the two minutes since I bowled him over. He searched my face, but I wasn't sure what he hoped to find there. For a moment his eyes held mine, and I forgot about the mess on the floor and my parents waiting for me upstairs.

But the sharp pressure of a broken piece of porcelain against my palm reminded me of where I was, and that I ought to be self-conscious under the gaze of a stranger. "I'm sorry, I never introduced myself." I held out a hand. "I'm Ambry."

He hesitated. "Henry," he replied, taking my hand after a moment's pause.

"Henry," I repeated, frowning. The name didn't fit him at all. Henry was such a safe, clean-cut name. Perfect for a butler such as Charles maybe, but utterly unlike the boy in front of me. He seemed about as familiar to his server's uniform as my father would be to a pair of black leather pants and a tongue piercing. This clearly wasn't his normal day job. "Are you just here for the Gala, Henry?" I inquired.

He nodded and began gathering more flower stems in the fold of his apron. "Seems like a big deal."

I shrugged, turning a piece of porcelain between my fingers. "I've suffered through a dozen of them. One is pretty much like the next."

"So you're not a big fan of these parties?"

I made a face. "Of being forced into some gaudy monstrosity of a dress and having to parade around with a bunch of my dad's stuck-up colleagues? Not exactly my thing."

Henry held out the apron. I shoved the vase's remains in to commiserate with the broken hydrangea stems. "At least you don't have to serve them," he reminded me as we both got to our feet, his apron clinking softly. "I'm afraid that if I spill something on someone I might be sentenced to death by guillotine."

"No need to worry," I said cheerfully. "They only pull out the guillotine on Wednesdays, so I'm sure it would just be a simple hanging."

"Oh, fantastic," he said with a chuckle. "Thanks for the encouragement."

I laughed. "But in all seriousness, don't worry. I'm sure you'll do a great job. It'll be over before you know it."

Henry opened his mouth to reply, but froze. His eyes were fixed on something behind my shoulder. Turning, I found Orelia standing outside the door to the library with an open book in hand.

Her waist-length hair was set in soft, golden curls, offsetting the navy sheen of her low-cut gown. Unlike my soft, rounded features, Orelia's high cheekbones and strong jaw made her beauty striking and fierce, like a lightening storm. It was a beauty which, combined with Orelia's fickle attentions, had turned many a dashing young man into desperate, pining fools, tripping over themselves for her attention. For years, I had watched as suitor after eligible suitor had pursued my sister, competing for even the smallest glance from her bright blue eyes.

Bright blue eyes—so like my own—that watched Henry and I with unabashed interest. "Wreaking more havoc, are we dear sister? I heard about your little escapade to Thailand this afternoon." She closed the book with a snap. "I'm sure Father is dying to hear all about it. Speaking of which, didn't I hear Mother call you to the study?"

"Just getting a snack," I said. I turned back to Henry. "I've got to go. I'm so sorry again for running into you."

"Don't worry about it," he said, the corner of his mouth lifting in a lopsided grin. "The benefits outweighed the inconvenience."

I felt a blush creep into my cheeks. "Well, good luck tonight. It was nice meeting you Henry."

"Nice meeting you too," he replied. Casting one final wary glance at Orelia, he turned and headed back into the kitchen. Its heavy doors swung in his wake. I caught a fleeting glimpse of his auburn hair in the background as another server emerged with a platter of miniature quiches.

"He's cute," Orelia said from directly behind me, causing me to jump.

I scowled and swiveled on the heels of my combat boots to face her. She was only an inch or two taller than me, but her pumps lent her a bit more height. Or perhaps it

28

was just her ego. "I knocked him down, Orelia," I said coldly. "It was an accident, not some carefully-constructed scheme to run off with one of the waiters."

"Well accident or not, don't get any ideas," she said. "Unless you want Father to have him teleported to Siberia."

"It was my fault he dropped the vase," I pointed out. I could feel the tension build as our gazes met like a collision of twin tidal waves. "I was just helping him out, like any decent person would do." I found myself leaning into the insinuation.

"He *is* the help, Ambry," Orelia said, her blue eyes flashing. "The sooner you get that into your head, the better it will be for all of us." With that, she tucked her book under one arm and sauntered off down the hall, her copious skirts swishing behind her.

Marveling that I should be chewed out for a simple conversation with one of the staff, I clenched my fists and stalked back down the hall, muttering words that might be deemed mutinous at best. I'd had more than enough of my family already, and I hadn't even reached the study.

Might as well get it over with quickly, I thought. I trudged up the stairs as though my feet were slogging through two feet of mud rather than an inch of velvet carpet, winding my way to the third floor. I turned left and jogged down the long corridor, coming to a halt at a solemn-looking door on the right. I knocked twice and took a measured step back.

The door immediately swung open. "Ah, Ambrosia. At long last," my mother said, ushering me inside with a wave of her bejeweled hand.

My father's study had always been a place of fascination for me, full of dust-sheathed books and peculiar objects. As a little girl, I would sneak in whenever he forgot to lock the door before leaving for work and pretend I was a detective, like the legendary Sherlock Holmes.

Our family had lived in Washington DC until I was ten, then moved to London so that my father could be closer (in actual proximity, not travel time) to his work at the Forum—the gathering place of the Timekeepers. Yet in all that time, I had never gained entrance to the study by actual invitation. Father would come home and head straight for his private sanctum, shutting himself away from the rest of the world. Away, in particular, from his youngest and most bothersome daughter.

He stood by the fireplace, his elbow propped upon the ornate mantelpiece. His icy eyes seemed lost in the dancing flames, but the trance was broken at the sound of the door closing behind me. "The world traveller returns."

"Hello, Father," I said.

He didn't turn to look at me. His eyes followed the tongues of flame. I, in turn, followed the lines of his profile, hard and sharp as his manner tended to be. In all the many books I had read in a futile attempt to escape my suffocating life, the father figures were often presented as warm and caring, willing to lay down their lives for the sake of their children. They had always mystified me, being so contrary to my own father. He'd been too consumed with his work at the Forum and perfecting his social standing to bother building a close relationship with me. "Tell me Ambrosia," he asked in a quiet voice. "Did you really expect your little field trip to go unnoticed?"

"Tell me, Father," I shot back. "Did you really expect your Globe stooge's use of a *time capsule* to go unnoticed? What, did you have the International Time Accords amended to include teenage curfew reinforcement?"

Time capsules were limited in number and beyond priceless due to their power, not to mention their scarcity. Some years after teleportation had been unleashed into the world, a Swiss physicist by the name of Bastian Imhoff made a discovery that had blown the Telepoint system out of the water. Somehow, inexplicably, he managed to create a machine that could harness the power of time itself. It had defied all previously prescribed limitations on quantum physics and the space-time continuum.

The "harness" that Imhoff had invented could encapsulate the power of time into storage units, aptly named "time capsules," of which there were two varieties. The first to be created by his singular contraption were the freeze capsules. These had the ability upon opening to bring time to a halt, freezing everything within a certain radius save for the person or persons who had opened it. The second type—the extension capsules—could "stretch out" time like one might a rubber band. There's still the same amount of rubber… it's just been forced to extend beyond its normal form. So it was with time when an extension capsule was opened. Everything would appear to go on as usual for the duration of its usage, but no time would have actually passed. The sun wouldn't move in the sky, the clocks wouldn't progress in their normal numeric rituals. If it were possible to create an extension capsule that could remain open for a year, one wouldn't age a day. Well, perhaps things would progress extremely slowly, but I doubted this theory would ever be tested as there was such a limited supply of capsules in existence.

Titus turned from the fire. "The usage of the capsules is none of your concern," he said sharply.

"It is when I'm trapped by one!" I retorted. "Do you have any idea how powerless that made me feel?"

"Hopefully as powerless as you *should* feel." He took a step toward me. "You're seventeen years old, Ambrosia. By the law, you're a child. And so long as you remain in this house, *we* have the final say in anything concerning you. Unless of course you'd rather throw away the privileged life you've been blessed with and live in squalor with the rest of the Dregs," he added.

"A girl can dream," I mumbled.

"You see," he said, bringing a hand down against the wooden mantle with a *smack*. "That's what appalls me above all else. Not that you would risk your own safety and that of your closest friends— "

"I didn't force them to come," I interjected.

"—but that you would carry out your plans with such a careless, negligent attitude," he drove on, "not giving a thought to how your mother and I would feel if something were to happen to you!"

"This isn't about my safety," I snapped. "You're just upset because I might have tarnished your precious reputation!"

"And why shouldn't that be a concern as well?" he asked. "A Timekeeper's daughter frolicking around a blatantly culturalist spectacle teeming with Dreg society? Our family is supposed to lead by example in uniting our world's cultures, not celebrating the eccentricities that prevent that unity!"

"For Imhoff's sake, it was just a festival!" I said, throwing up my hands. "It's not like we were off robbing a bank or vandalizing some historical monument!"

Titus smacked the wall. "Don't waste my time with pointless comparisons. The fact remains that you told us you would be at Honoratus for the remainder of the evening. Instead, you went gallivanting off across the globe to a dangerous and only marginally-legal festival. You *lied* to us, Ambrosia, and such deception will not be tolerated in my house!"

"So what? You're going to ship me off? Send me somewhere far away, where I can't blemish the Croft family name?"

"And reward you for your recklessness? No. We'll have to come up with some more imaginative consequences." He reached into his pocket. "For starters, you will take this," he said, holding out a hand. "Right now."

I looked at my father's proffered hand. A single lavender pill sat neatly in his palm.

"It should help to calm you down," he said.

He might as well have offered me candied arsenic. "I'd rather swallow that tea cozy," I said, nodding toward his desk.

"Nonsense, Ambry," said my mother, speaking up for the first time. "Don't you have any idea how *dangerous* it is for you to be shirking your medication?"

"Apparently not, because it's been three weeks since I took a pill and I feel totally fine. That doesn't give much credit to your theory," I replied as her hand rose to cover her mouth. "Do you know that I once went off the pills for two months? *Two whole months*," I continued, despite the looks of horror this admission produced on my parents' faces. "I can't remember ever feeling so good! I could think clearly for once. It was like someone blew away the fog that normally surrounds my brain. Not once did I feel depressed or anxious…I felt *alive* for the first time in years! And now you're telling me it's for my own good that I get back on those soul-sucking drugs?"

"You feel fine now, darling, but it only takes an instant for your heart to overreact," Mother said. "Don't you remember what happened when you were four?"

"*You* remember. You know I don't," I retorted. My boots dug into the carpet. I hoped they would leave a mark. "And even if I did, why should I spend the rest of my life drugged and miserable because of one attack as a kid?"

"Because I'm telling you that you will," growled my father, taking a step towards me. There was an edge in his voice that made me take an instinctive step back. "I've had enough of your rebellious attitude for one day. You've disobeyed us, humiliated us." He lifted his hand, palm up. "And now, you will either take this pill willingly, or I will administer it for you."

My jaw slackened. Was he seriously threatening to force the pill down my throat? "Dad..." I started.

But my father was beyond reasoning. A cold, clear fury burned in the blue embers of his eyes.

I backed away, but he closed the gap between us in several quick strides and grabbed me by the jaw.

Until this time, my mother had sat silent but for her brief interjections, but even the hardest woman's heart can be overpowered by the sharp, instinctual pull of a maternal bond. And for all her considerable flaws, Calista Croft was still my mother. "Titus!" she exclaimed, rising to her feet.

"Sit *down*, Calista!" he ordered, his voice rising in tandem with the color flooding his cheeks.

She wrung her hands in a moment of indecision, and I had the fleeting impression that she might fly to my aid, a mother bear ready to claw the face of the predator that dared attack her cub. But the moment passed, and the invisible strings of my father's hold anchored her to her seat—a marionette in the hands of a master puppeteer. She sank silently back into my chair as I flailed in my father's iron grasp.

He turned back to me, his face now inches from my own. "Open your mouth, Ambrosia."

Clamping my mouth shut, I tried to pry away his hands, but their grip was relentless. He didn't even seem to notice my nails digging into his skin.

"I said, *open your mouth!*" he hissed, his breath on my face a mixture of scotch and cigar smoke.

His firm grip on my jaw began to hurt and I could feel hot tears begin to slide down my cheeks. "Please," I begged, opening my mouth only a fraction of an inch.

But he seized his opportunity. He forced a thumb into my mouth and pried it open, stuffing the pill inside and clamping a hand over my lips.

I screamed, but the sound was muffled by my father's palm. I attempted to spit out the hateful pill, but he pushed me against the wall and used his free hand to pinch my nose shut. I struggled desperately against his hold. But in the end, I had no choice but to swallow.

Once I had gulped down the pill, he released me. I fell to the floor, coughing and spluttering into the Persian rug. I clutched my throat and stared up at my father in horrified disbelief.

My mother had one hand braced against the side of the chair. The other was clamped over her own mouth. She gazed at my father with a mixture of shock and dismay, tears causing her make-up to run in black rivulets down her otherwise perfect face. She didn't utter a word.

Satisfied that his task was completed, Father smoothed his hair and straightened his necktie. "One day you'll realize that I'm doing this for your own good, Ambrosia. Now you will go straight to your room and get dressed," he commanded, his breathing low and ragged. "The Gala starts in half an hour. And if you dare to embarrass us again tonight," he whispered, "you *will* regret it."

I didn't need to be asked to leave twice. I was up off the carpet and scrambling for the door before the last syllable of my father's threat died away. His menacing words hung in the air like a toxic perfume. Barreling through the door, I flew down the stairs.

When I reached the sanctuary of my room, I shut and locked the door behind myself, turning and leaning against it as I fought to catch my breath. Across the room, a rosy monstrosity of a dress was draped over an armchair, wrapped in layers of satin and tulle. It looked obscenely expensive. *And hideous,* I thought.

There was no way I could stomach the Gala after what I had just endured. I was also loathe to give my father the satisfaction of watching me prance into the ballroom dressed up like another one of his Elite marionettes.

The pill that he had shoved down my throat was already taking effect. My mind was blanketed by fog and a wave of exhaustion washed over me like an inbound tide. It beckoned me to rest... to sleep.

To stop fighting...

No! I shook my head in an attempt to rid it of the

encroaching haze. I had experienced this countless times before, and over the years I'd cultivated several tricks for avoiding the worst of the medication's side effects.

The first: *Don't go to sleep.*

Sleep only allowed the medicine an uninhibited entry into my system. And although it seemed near impossible during the first two hours after taking a pill, the best move —both offensive and defensive—against such an attack was to keep moving until the drowsiness passed.

I strode blearily to my closet, ignoring the gown altogether. I yanked open several drawers until I unearthed my favorite pair of running pants and a faded gray T-shirt. I threw them on before grabbing my hoodie from its peg inside the closet and heading for the door.

I poked my head out just enough to catch a glimpse of the empty corridor. Seeing no movement, I crept to the opposite end of the hallway until I reached the old servants' staircase. Few people bothered to use it anymore, so it afforded me a private exit. Slipping down the stairs and past a line of servants carrying last minute decorations, I tiptoed out onto the veranda. I followed the ivy-laden balustrades as they curved down and around to the back lawn, at one point pressing myself into the shadows when one servant called to another about the positioning of the gladiola centerpieces. But the voices soon drifted back indoors. I made one last visual sweep of the area before streaking towards the gate.

Few people knew about the Garden Gate. This was partially because it was located behind a thick curtain of ivy that made it almost impossible to identify if you didn't know where to look in the first place. But the primary reason for its disuse was that it was supposed to be inaccessible. My father had ordered the corroding iron gate to be replaced with one crafted from reinforced titanium alloy. Two imposing padlocks latched the door firmly in place.

Fortunately, during my childhood wanderings throughout the manor house, I had stumbled some years back upon a set of keys tucked away in the lower recesses of my father's desk. I had taken them out of pure curiosity and, for some reason, he never noticed their absence. Finding the purpose of the mysterious keys became a three-year mission. I finally accomplished my grand quest at the age of thirteen when I discovered the hidden Garden Gate.

Slipping beneath its ivy curtain, I drew the keys from the pocket of my hoodie and inserted the biggest into the first lock. It opened with a *click*, but to me it might as well have been a gunshot. I glanced around, but there was no one within earshot. I shook my head at my own paranoia.

The second lock was always trickier. It required both of the smaller keys to be inserted at the same time, but turned in two opposite directions. I jammed them into place and turned them simultaneously—the higher twisting clockwise and the lower twisting counterclockwise. The lock popped free and I slipped through the gate, shutting it behind myself so that it barely made a sound.

Not caring which way I ran, I headed toward Bayswater. A couple miles later, I found myself crossing the road to Hyde Park. It was already twilight and the park had closed for the evening, but I wasn't in the mood to be deterred. I climbed over the wrought-iron fence and dropped to the other side, stumbling due to the haze of the pill yet none the worse for wear.

My feet pounded into the pavement as I sped down the wide lane between identical rows of towering trees. Upon entering Kensington Gardens, I followed the familiar path until I reached the statue at its center.

Peter Pan. The sprightly boy who refused to grow up. I ran a hand over one of the fairies spiraling around the statue's base. If only there were a Telepoint that could take me to Neverland.

Lowering myself onto a stone bench, I pushed back my hood and ran a hand through the blue river of my hair. Running normally helped clear my head, but tonight there were too many thoughts and emotions and drugs clouding my mind to be so easily filtered. I had upset my father more times than I could count, but he rarely lost his temper, and he had *never* physically harmed me before.

My brain sagged under the weight of it all. Leaning forward and cradling my head in my hands, sleep stole over me before I was aware of its creeping presence.

CHAPTER THREE

When I awoke, it was to find that dusk had fallen over the gardens. But no fairies, nor boyish apparitions appeared to enchant me away.

I forced myself to my feet and began the jog back to the entrance. It was only when I reached the locked gate that I remembered the park had closed for the night. I was forced to clamber clumsily over the fence and drop onto the sidewalk along Bayswater Road, staggering in an effort to regain my balance.

Thankfully, there were no Officials in sight. If one run-in with the law had sent my father off the deep end, there was no telling what a second would do. Especially in the same night. It was bad enough that I would have to face my parents again after skipping the Gala. *I'm really doing them a favor*, I thought, pumping my arms. *With me gone, they won't have to worry about their reckless embarrassment of a daughter making a fool of them in front of their important guests.*

Mile after mile I slammed my shoes into the sidewalk, exacting all of my fury and grief on the unsuspecting pavement. As I drew closer to the compound, I could hear the faint wailing of distant sirens echo through the empty street. The strangest part was that I could've sworn I had heard those particular sirens before.

I stopped dead in my tracks. Someone had triggered the manor alarm.

Pulling my hood securely around my face, I began pumping my tired limbs again, quickening my pace until I reached an all-out sprint. I hurtled toward the Garden Gate only to draw to a sharp halt several feet away, my shoes skidding on the wet sidewalk. *The alarm was triggered,* I thought, doubling over, my hands on my knees. *Which means that the gate will be charged with an electric current.* One touch and I would have been zapped with enough power to stop my heart, medicine or no medicine.

But what could have prompted setting off the alarm? Had there been a break in? Only the most deranged variation of idiot would attempt to steal from Titus Croft.

I took a cautious step forward, but didn't dare lay a finger on the iron bars. My eyes strained towards house.

Several appalled guests sought refuge on the outer veranda. I caught momentary glimpses of other frantic figures milling around in the behind the crystal panes of the ballroom, but there was nothing to give me a clue as to what had happened.

I was about to head for the front entrance when I caught a flash of movement out of the corner of my eye. Two figures were darting across the gardens, darker shapes moving against a dark backdrop. They blended into the shadows of the tall boxwoods, flitting from one patch of darkness to the other. Were these two the cause of the alarm? I took a breath to alert the Officials on the veranda, but something held me back. Something that admired the courage it would have taken to break into my home, whatever their reasons.

It took me a moment to realize they were headed straight for the gate where I now stood hidden in the shadows. *The current*, I thought.

Before I could gather my wits enough to shout out a warning, the first of the two figures reached the wrought-iron bars. He was sent flying backward and landed jerking and twitching on the ground. My hand flew to stifle my own cry of alarm.

The second figure rushed to help his fallen companion. He shook him by his jacket until the blond boy stirred weakly. Reassured that his friend wasn't dead, the second boy's eyes darted up to find me watching in astonishment. "Help me," he said in a carrying whisper.

With a start, I realized that I had seen those loose curls and dark eyes only hours before on a figure sprawled across the floor, surrounded by broken hydrangea stems and shards of porcelain.

Henry.

....

By now every light in the house was on. Whatever the two of them had done, it had been enough to cause an uproar throughout the entire compound. The intermittent shouts of guests mixed with the sharp orders of Officials and the deep-throated howls of their dogs. I turned back to meet Henry's dark, pleading eyes, brightened by adrenaline and thinly-veiled panic. "Help me," he spoke again. I looked down at his hands. Though his voice hadn't wavered, I could read his fear in the way his fingers knotted the dark leather of his fallen friend's jacket. "Please," he said, and my eyes snapped back to his. "If they catch us, they'll kill us," he whispered.

My mind spun. Knowing my father—who was the type of man to send a servant packing for setting the table improperly, let alone any offense worthy of the alarm—I suspected Henry wasn't exaggerating. I sent a furtive glance toward his friend. The blond boy groaned and rolled over on his side, curling into a ball as several more twitches racked his prone body.

In the end, my decision was as abrupt as it was final.

Barely knowing why, I found myself wrenching open the heavy lid of the console to the left of the Gate. I stooped down to pick up a rock that fallen from the wall and smashed it into the protective glass casing. It shattered in a hail of shards. I then twisted the top off my water bottle and dumped its contents onto the control panel, stepping back just in time as the power shut down with an explosive *bang* that sent an angry shower of sparks in all directions.

Dragging his dazed friend to his feet, Henry hurried toward the gate. He propped the other boy against the now-harmless wall before digging into the pocket of his jacket. "Stand back," he ordered, pulling out a pencil- shaped device from his jacket. I moved away as he pressed several buttons along its side. He pointed it at the first gigantic padlock and sent a red beam of light searing through the metal. The bottom half of the lock dropped to the ground, completely severed from its handle. He had just sent the red beam slicing through the second as one of the soldiers appeared on the back veranda. "There!" he bellowed. "Three of them! Arak, Kova, mark targets!"

I took a sharp inhale of breath. Did he say *three?*

I stared over Henry's shoulder. Two massive wolves crouched next to their silver-clad masters on the balcony. My father said they were called "watchdogs" by the Officials, whom the cybernetic beasts had been bred to serve. Obedient to a fault, they were genetically and scientifically enhanced with increased strength, speed, and special abilities that allowed them to track their prey. Once they locked onto a target, they operated in much the same way as a guided missile, unable to be thrown off by losing visual contact. The watchdogs' eyes glowed red at the sharp command of their master, registering myself and the two fugitives as targets.

Henry swore under his breath as the watchdogs leapt down from the terrace. He fumbled to remove the second lock. Wrenching it off, he shoved his friend through the gate before slipping through himself and slamming the bars shut behind them. He used the same device to solder the gate shut. "That ought to buy us a few minutes." Henry reached into the pocket of his jacket and produced a thin case. It clicked open to reveal a small syringe filled with a clear liquid. He held it needle-up and flicked the glass.

"What—"

But before I could finish my sentence, Henry spun around. I gave a cry of alarm, but Henry ignored me and plunged the syringe straight into his friend's neck.

The blond boy gasped and slumped against Henry, but appeared to swallow back the pain even as it surfaced. His breathing was still labored, but within seconds he had straightened noticeably.

"What was that?" I asked him.

"Adrenaline shot," Henry said. Giving his friend a reassuring clap on the back, he grabbed my arm. "Come on," he urged.

"But—"

"You've been marked. You want to live? Stay with

46

us," he ordered. Any resemblance to the servant I'd met by the kitchens was gone. This was the voice of a leader, someone accustomed to giving commands and having them obeyed without question. "Now *run!*"

As I allowed myself to be dragged down the dark street, I could hear the screech of metal being torn from its hinges, but I didn't dare look back. The watchdogs would have marked our size, shape, clothes, smell, even the heat signature we emitted, all in the space of a second. There was no way we could simply head for a populated area and blend into a crowd. The wolves could trace their prey behind solid walls.

We raced past mansion after mansion, some with illustrious Corinthian columns standing sentinel in front of their doors, others boasting priceless statues and immaculately-trimmed shrubbery. These barely registered in my mind as I pumped my limbs. Quads, calves, hamstrings, biceps—every inch of muscle screamed in protest. They had already been overworked, and now I was demanding more of them than ever before.

The adrenaline shot must have worked, because Henry's friend was now running even with us. "We have to get to the extraction point!" he shouted.

"And what exactly do you think I'm doing?" Henry gasped, his arms pumping furiously as we flew down the open street. "Shopping for realty?"

"Well, over here we have a lovely Georgian classic—"

"Save your breath and shut up!"

As we ran further south, it was as though we passed some invisible barrier separating the wealthy community of the Elites from the rest of London proper. In place of the opulent mansions of the Heath and its surrounding neighborhoods, rows of ordinary flats began to appear on either side of the road.

Sirens wailed down the road ahead. "Over there!" Henry shouted, ducking sideways into a narrow alleyway between two buildings. We were forced to run single file with Henry at the lead, me sprinting close behind, and Henry's friend bringing up the rear. Every gasp of breath filled my nostrils with the stench of week-old garbage.

From this vantage point, I noticed for the first time the thin bag strapped across Henry's back. Curiosity rose up to grapple with my fear. What had these two stolen from the manor? What could possibly warrant risking the wrath of my father?

A wall loomed at the far end of the alley. "It's a dead end!" I cried.

Henry didn't slow his pace. "Only in that direction!" He jerked his chin upwards.

It was only then that I noticed the fire escape suspended overhead near the alley's end.

Putting on an extra burst of speed, Henry leapt up and sideways, pushing off the brick wall as though it were a continuation of the ground. The momentum propelled him higher than he should have been able to achieve. He reached out and just managed to close his hands around the bottom rung of the fire escape. The iron ladder descended with a clang. It didn't quite reach the ground, but it was now low enough that I could jump to get a foothold on the lowest rung. Henry scampered up as though back-alley parkour were a part of his regular exercise regime. Maybe it was, for all I knew. I would have paused to be properly impressed, but the imminent threat of death by cybernetic dogs sent me scrambling up behind him faster than Gemma at a shoe sale. "Do you do this often?" I yelled up at him.

A maniacal chuckle echoed overhead. "Define *this*."

Reaching the roof, I collapsed to my knees, gasping for air. Why did I have to go for an hour-long joy run right before being forced into a chase scene? I could have kicked myself, but it would have required too much effort. "Thank God," I breathed, reveling in the moment of respite.

But Henry wasn't quite so thrilled. "We're not out of the fire yet," he said, staring down over the edge of the roof.

"What? It's not like those wolves can climb fire escapes, can they?"

"Of course not."

"Then what are you worried about?"

"The stairs," he said. "Look..."

I staggered to where he stood, but it was the view below rather than my exhaustion that almost caused me to faint. Two pairs of green-glowing eyes stared hungrily up at us from the street, prowling along the edge of the building.

"It won't be long before they realize they can break down the doors and use the stairwell," Henry murmured.

49

"You really think they're that smart?"

"Trust me," he grimaced, "I know from experience."

This didn't come as a shock. "So what do you suggest we do now? Fly?" I asked, massaging the stitch in my side.

"If you think you can manage it, then yes, that would be fantastic," he said, matching me sarcasm for sarcasm. "Otherwise, we'll have to settle for getting to another roof. Are you ready?" he asked.

"Is that a joke?"

"Nope," he said, his expression grim. "Follow me." He started running for the nearest rooftop, picking up speed as he went. He leapt over the gap between the two buildings as easily as a child might hop a jumprope. His blond friend followed suit, arching neatly through the air and landing on his feet. They both turned to look at me. "You coming?" Henry called, his voice impatient.

I swallowed. I wasn't overly fond of heights. But the idea of jumping was better than the alternative of being ripped to shreds by watchdogs. Taking a deep breath and backing up, I tried to slow the pounding in my chest. *It's only a few feet. No different than doing the long jump in Physical Training at the Academy.* I started to jog, increasing speed until I knew I wouldn't be able to stop even if I changed my mind.

I leapt onto the short ledge and pushed off with all my might. My legs continued to pump even in mid-air until I landed on the other side. I would have pitched forward to the pavement if Henry hadn't caught me by the shoulders. "Thanks," I panted. The jump left me elated, as though I had leapt the Grand Canyon rather than the short gap between two rooftops.

"Well, I kind of owed you, didn't I?" he grinned, his hands still on my shoulders. "Best keep moving though."

I nodded, suddenly sheepish. I turned slowly, eyes scanning to see which roof would make for the closest jump. "That one," I pointed, starting in the direction of the closest rooftop.

But Henry caught my arm. "We have to get to that one over there," he said, pointing at another roof an unreasonable distance away.

I stared open-mouthed at him. "Are you insane?" I blurted. "That gap is at least eight or nine feet wide! You'd never make it!"

"O ye of little faith."

I narrowed my eyes. "Even if we could make that jump, we'd be trapped. Look," I said, gesturing to the general lack of rooftops beyond the one he seemed to have hand- picked at random. "There's nowhere to go."

"There's an old Telepoint on that rooftop," he explained, still trying to tug me in the direction of the farther roof.

I gawked at him in disbelief. Not only had I run off with a pair of thieves, but it turned out they were clinically insane to boot. "There are only ten Telepoints in *all* of London, remember? There isn't an archway within miles of here!"

"None that *you* would know of," Henry corrected, still

panting from their ascent to the roof. "This one isn't open to the general public."

"Hate to cut this little chat short," interjected his friend tersely, "but seeing as we're being pursued by technologically-enhanced wolves who are hell-bent on stripping the flesh from our bones, perhaps we ought to be mov…" He trailed off, his eyes widening.

"What's wrong?" I spun around to see if a wolf was poised behind me. Nothing there. When I looked back, Blondie seemed to be staring *at* me rather than *past* me.

He reached out a hand toward my hood. It was only then that I noticed several blue strands of hair had escaped their hold and fallen across my face. My scalp prickled as he captured one between his thumb and finger. Releasing it, he threw back my hood. "Oh, for the love of…"

He hadn't known who I was.

Obviously that little shard of information made a difference. He rounded on Henry. "What the hell, mate?" he demanded. "You *knew* it was her and you didn't tell me?"

"She helped us! What was I supposed to do, leave her there?" Henry countered.

"Anything but drag her along!" He swore under his breath, then fixed Henry with a glare. "Deal with this." With no other preamble, he broke into a sudden sprint toward the ledge.

I opened my mouth to shout in protest, but he was already at the roof's edge and catapulting out into empty night.

He hovered there, airborne, my mind slowing down his fall so that for a moment he hung suspended in the in-between. But in the lapse of a blink, he was rolling onto the other rooftop. He picked himself up and dusted off his jacket, none the worse for wear.

I gaped. "How did he..." I trailed off.

The blond boy was now running toward the roof entrance of the other building. But rather than opening the door, he rounded the side and pressed something on the wall. Suddenly the corner of the rooftop began to shimmer. An object appeared where there was once empty space. It was covered by a black tarp, so I had trouble identifying it at first. Whatever it was, it was bulky and towering.

He yanked the tarp from the object to reveal a first generation Telepoint, far less sleek than the newer models and with a much larger console. With the punch of a few buttons, the machine flared to life. How on earth had they known there would be a Telepoint there? Was it even linked to the Globe's Grid?

Henry turned back to me.

"Please, don't leave me here," I whispered.

The words had barely left my mouth before he whirled away and ran for the edge, vaulting across the expanse almost as easily as his friend had done.

My heart plummeted from my ribcage. They were leaving me behind.

I risked my own safety to save their lives, and now they were going to leave me stranded on this rooftop, easy prey for the cybernetic wolves whose howls were drawing closer by the second. In that wild, horrifying moment, I actually sent a silent "thanks" to my father for shoving the lavender pill down my throat. If it hadn't been for the medication, my heart might have exploded then and there.

Coming to his feet on the other rooftop, Henry whirled back to face me. He held out a hand, but to me it was a lifeline. "Jump," he commanded.

Hope and relief blossomed in my chest, then deflated just as fast. "I can't," I called back. "I won't make it!"

"I'll help you," he promised as the door behind me shook on its hinges. Menacing growls made the hair on my neck stand on end. "There's no time. Do it now!" he yelled. "Just reach for my hand..."

In the end, I knew I had no choice. I took a few more steps back and sprinted just as an explosive sound from behind told me the door's hinges had given way. At the edge, I pushed off with my last ounce of energy—every muscle on fire—and leapt into the abyss.

Even in midair, I knew I wasn't going to make it. Reaching out like a flower struggling toward a patch of sunlight, I groped for a handhold in the empty expanse, but I could already feel the weighty tug of gravity from below. The last thing I remembered was Henry's fingers closing around my wrist a split second before my head slammed into the side of the building.

CHAPTER FOUR

Consciousness kept eluding me. I caught flashes of a massive room filled with Telepoints, swarms of people in dark clothing pressing in around me. Angry shouts.

In a longer moment of awareness, I blinked my eyes open to find myself hefted in a pair of strong arms. A heartbeat—presumably belonging to the owner of the strong arms—thumped against my left ear. "…not the end of the world. It's not like we can't destroy a single Telepoint," Henry's voice said from over my head.

"Oh yeah? Really?" demanded a second voice. It's owner sounded livid. "Well what about you dragging her into the central headquarters of the bloomin' Resistance itself——?"

"Will you *shut up!*" hissed a third, deeper voice. "Just get her to Dmitri. It won't do us any good to let her die here."

"Agree to disagree…" snapped the previous voice as my vision faded once more.

....

Opening my eyes, I found myself in a suffocating little room with no windows. It was lit by a single bright light, which stung my eyes. I lay nestled in a narrow bed beneath several heavy, woolen blankets. It had the feel of a hospital room, though without the white sterility I was accustomed to in medical facilities. Gazing around, I saw medical tools laid out on a table nearby. Scalpels, tweezers, a syringe, and others I couldn't name, all neatly arranged on a silver tray. Several were coated in a dark substance that I registered with queasy familiarity.

Blood.

Suddenly the events of the previous night came rushing back in a wave of color and sound. Sprinting to the house as the alarm rang out, standing in the shadows by the garden gate and staring at a boy with dark, pleading eyes. Destroying the console, being chased by the Officials' wolves, jumping the chasm toward Henry's outstretched hand...

As the wave of memories began to subside, I noticed for the first time that I wasn't alone. The servant boy was sprawled awkwardly over a chair across from my bed. Head dipped in sleep, his tumble of loose curls hung over his face like an auburn curtain. So he'd caught my hand after all. Had he really carried me all the way here? *Wherever "here" is*, I thought.

He stirred. The single light on the opposite side of the room cast shadows across his eyes, set deep into a face that was all angles. Sharply-cut jawline, strong cheekbones, straight brows that shot up in surprise. "You're awake," he observed.

I shifted in the bed and a sudden pain jolted through what felt like my entire body. "Don't remind me." I lowered my head back to the pillow, but it continued to throb its own slow, painful pulse.

"I'd keep still if I were you," he said. "So far they've found two cracked ribs and a nasty concussion."

I looked down to find myself wearing an unfamiliar white T-shirt, and though I couldn't see beneath the blue woolen blanket that was pulled up to my waist, the material covering my legs felt decidedly flannel. "These aren't my clothes…"

Henry laughed as the realization hit me. "Don't worry, I wasn't the one who changed them."

I felt the color rise in my cheeks and hoped he couldn't see how relieved that piece of information had made me. "What happened to them?"

"Ripped, covered in blood," he said with a one-shouldered shrug. "We figured you wouldn't be too attached given their condition."

I tried to nod, but it only increased the throbbing in my head. "Where am I?"

"You're in the Atrium." He rose from his chair, arching his back in a wide stretch like a cat waking up from its nap.

"Which is where, exactly?" I asked. "Not important at the moment."

I tried to lift a hand to my pounding temple, but only managed to raise it about a foot before it was met with an unyielding resistance. Metal bit into my wrist as the chain of the handcuffs rattled its displeasure.

"What the—?" I pulled harder against the cuffs. A sudden, sharp pain radiated through my shoulder. I yelped in surprise.

He winced sympathetically. "Oh, and your shoulder was dislocated."

"Do you mind explaining why I'm in *handcuffs*?" I cried. Waking up to injuries was one thing, but finding myself held hostage was quite another. "Because if this is your idea of propositioning a girl…"

"Don't flatter yourself," he said, rolling his eyes. "We had to make sure you wouldn't take off."

"I just saved your life!" I exclaimed. "Is this how you repay people who do you favors? By treating them like prisoners?"

"You're Titus Croft's daughter," Henry said, as though that single fact explained everything. "We have to know we can trust you before you go running back to that cozy little mansion of yours."

"So you distrust anyone with money? Is that it?" I demanded. I would have pointed an accusatory finger if I could have gotten my hand to bend in his direction.

"Well, obscene wealth acquired by questionable means doesn't exactly *inspire* our trust."

I bit back a scathing retort. Forcing down my indignation, I tried to focus on more pressing matters. "And how will you determine if I'm trustworthy?"

"By how well you cooperate," he replied. "If you're cooperative, the restraints will be a temporary annoyance."

"And if I'm not?"

My question produced only a small smirk. "Then you'll stay until you can *learn* to cooperate."

As furious as I felt, I was too exhausted to argue any further, but my eyes hurled daggers as he strolled across the room to a worn-looking armchair. He unzipped a leather bag—which I recognized as the one he'd had slung over his shoulder as the three of us ran—and withdrew a strange metal object. It was silver, made up of a dozen-or- so interlocking pieces that could pivot and twist, like a three-dimensional jigsaw puzzle. "Have you seen this before?"

I *had* seen it before, in a drawer in my father's desk. Once, when I was about ten years old, Prewitt and I had been playing a game of hide-and-seek during which I'd hidden beneath the large oak desk in my father's study. Prewitt had always been woeful at hide-and-seek, so I spent a good amount of time with nothing to do but twiddle my thumbs. Finally, I had decided to have a look around. Imagining myself a great detective, I'd perused the contents of the desk until—to my great delight—I discovered a hidden catch in the bottom left drawer. Pushing it, the wooden panel had sprung back to reveal another compartment. It was there that I'd found the curious object that Henry now held out.

But I had no plans to explain anything to this ungrateful git. "What's your name?" I asked, ignoring his question. "You never did look like a Henry."

He met my icy glare with such steady resolve that *I* wound up being the first to look away. I fidgeted beneath the wool blankets. "It's Rift," he said.

"Rift?" I repeated, not sure I'd heard him right.

He nodded.

"That can't be your real name."

"It's not."

"So what happened to your real name?"

"I lost it."

"Hmm. That was careless of you."

The weight of his stare lifted, but not before I saw a flash of something cross his face. Anger? Sadness? It was so fleeting that I couldn't be sure. He had already turned his attention back to the curious object in his hands. "Can't argue with you there."

My eyes moved back to the odd silver object. I'd never mentioned finding it to my father—doubtless I would have been punished for weeks for sneaking around his private study—so I knew almost as little about it as Rift did. "Why go to the trouble of stealing something if you don't know what it is?"

"I didn't say I didn't know what it was."

"Well, do you or don't you?"

He assessed me for a moment. "It's a small piece to a large puzzle."

"And now you want my help figuring out what it does?"

"Information is always a valuable commodity," he replied. "This device has been hidden in your house for the past six years, ever since your family moved to London. Based on that, I'd assume this isn't the first time it's crossed your path."

"Well, you know what they say about assuming things..."

"Come on, Ambry," he said, the corners of his mouth curving up. "Good little Academy student that you are, you've probably spent hours in that library."

I frowned. "Don't you mean the—" My mouth snapped shut.

"Study?" he finished for me, dark eyes sparking with mirthful curiosity. "So you *have* seen it before."

He'd tricked me. Suddenly, I no longer cared about escaping the room. I would've gladly settled for five minutes of freedom from the cuffs so I could punch him straight in the nose. "Nicely done," I said, hoping it sounded as scathing as I'd intended. "I can see you're quite pleased with yourself."

Rift shrugged and flopped back down into the chair. "I'd be lying if I said I were *displeased*."

"Well I'm glad you enjoyed your little trick, because it won't work again." I wished it were within my power to cross my arms, but the steel of the handcuffs was resolute. I was forced to settle for fixing him with a death glare. "You're not getting anything else out of me."

The interest that had flared in his eyes was gone, replaced now by a look of supreme boredom. "Have it your way. I'll figure it out sooner or later."

"Quite sure of yourself, aren't you?"

"Some call it confidence."

"Some call it arrogance." I twisted my wrists in their bonds as surreptitiously as I dared, still longing for a clear shot at his face.

"If it's unfounded confidence based in pride, then yes, you could call it arrogance. On the other hand, if a talented artist were to tell you their masterpiece was absolute garbage, would you call it humility? No," he said. "It would be a blatant lie. A truly humble person can be honest about their gifts or abilities without seeking to promote himself. Do you think you already know me well enough to distinguish between the two?"

I narrowed my eyes. "I know you're a thief."

Rift returned to his meticulous perusal of the device. "I've been called worse. At least it's accurate."

"You know what else is accurate—"

But any colorful adjectives I wanted to loose at Rift were cut short as the door burst open, revealing a long-legged girl with golden hair cropped so that it just brushed her shoulders. I felt an immediate twinge of jealousy as the girl sized me up with dark, almond-shaped eyes. She looked like a more dangerous, leather-bound version of Orelia. "Get anything out of her yet?" the girl demanded.

"Not much," Rift replied, still looking at the device in his hands rather than me. "She's not exactly being agreeable."

I scowled at him. "So full of gratitude. I'd have thought helping you escape was more than you deserved."

"That might have been true if we hadn't saved you in turn," Rift said without looking up. "Now we're even. In fact, considering the fact that we're now housing and feeding you—not to mention the extensive medical attention—one might even say that you owe us."

"Then let me go if I'm such a burden to you!"

"Enough," spoke a new voice, deep and firm. Its owner entered the room with long, purposeful strides. Like the others, he was clad in dark clothing. His tanned skin was crisscrossed with pale designs, which I thought at first might be the white tattoos that had recently become so popular. But I realized a moment later that they were actually innumerable raised scars. Looking at his face, I guessed he might be in his early thirties, but he carried an authority that surpassed his age. It reverberated in the very air of the room, a commanding presence that made you want to hear what he had to say. Crystal blue eyes, clear and sharp, seemed to take in everything in one penetrative sweep before turning to Rift. "Having trouble, are we?" While the blond girl sounded as though she might be native to Britain, the newcomer's words were laced with a strong hispanic accent.

"You should have known better than to have me do the interrogating, Kade," Rift replied. He was still appraising the metal object, turning it this way and that with deft fingers, clicking slots of metal in and out of place. "It's really Torque's area of expertise."

The one called Kade raised a heavy brow, but said nothing.

"Where is Torque?" asked the girl.

"Don't worry Avienne. I come when I'm called."

To our collective surprise, the voice came from the door directly behind Kade. He strolled inside, sat down, and plopped his heavy boots on the low coffee table. I recognized him as the second intruder, the one who had reached the garden gate first and who had subsequently been thrown backwards by the electric current. His hair was shorter than Rift's and fell in layers to frame a thin nose, full lips, and stormy gray eyes. It was also stripped of all color, white as the cotton sheets I twisted between my manacled hands. He must have dyed it temporarily blond for their little trip to the manor. I took in the piercings on his face and tattoos down his folded arms. "So Sleeping Beauty's finally awake?" he observed.

I had never enjoyed people talking about me as though I weren't in the room. I'd dealt with it often enough from my family. "Yes, she is," I snarled, injecting each word with as much venom as I could muster.

"And in such a good mood too," he said. "Joy. So, what shall we do with her, Kade?"

"*We* won't be doing anything with her," Kade corrected. "I have to run a few errands today, so I won't be able to keep an eye on her myself," he said, casting a quick glance toward me. "Rift, you were the one who dragged her here. She will be your responsibility while in the Atrium."

Rift gaped at him. "But Kade—"

"I'll be more than happy to take responsibility for her, if my friend here is opposed to it," Torque volunteered, giving Rift an understanding pat on the shoulder. "She'll be in good hands with me," he added with a wink.

With the way looked me up and down, I didn't feel as though I were covered by pajamas and a set of sheets. I wriggled further down beneath my blankets.

Kade lifted one eyebrow at Torque. "That is exactly what I aim to avoid."

Torque's mouth fell open. "But—"

"You don't need the added distraction, and she doesn't need a protector from whom she will need protecting," Kade said. "With any luck, she'll be out of here in a day or two."

Now it was my turn to stare at Kade. "A day or two? But my parents... my friends," I said, really thinking more of

Prewitt and Gemma than of my family. "They must be going crazy trying to figure out where I am. I could be dead for all they know!"

"Then won't it make for a spectacular turn of events when you show up in a couple days fit as a fiddle?" Torque said cheerfully. "Who knows? Perhaps you'll even get to read your own eulogy."

I chose to ignore him, turning instead back to Rift and Kade. "They'll be worried."

"They'll be more worried if you show up looking like you do now. No offense, but you're kind of a wreck," Torque informed me.

I didn't see how anyone could not take offense at such a comment, even when delivered in such a weirdly polite tone. But although it pained me to admit that Torque was right, I could tell from my taut, overly-sensitive skin that half my face must still be swollen from my head's meet-and-greet with the brick wall.

"The medications and treatments you've been given take a little time to work their full effect, but you should be out of here in a couple days," Rift explained. "No need to be in a hurry. You've already been asleep for a day and a half."

I blanched. "I slept for over an entire day?"

"Hence our surprise that you finally decided to wake up," said Torque, leaning back and crossing his arms behind his head.

I paused to stare at the four of them. In their dark,

leathery clothes and tattoos they looked like some sort of bizarre underground Dreg rock band. "I don't understand," I said finally. "You drag me here with you, tend to my injuries—whilst I'm *chained* to my hospital bed—start questioning me the minute I wake up, and then what? You'll just send me skipping back home with a lollipop when I'm good and healed?"

It was a moment before Kade replied. "The situation is unique. You see, Miss Croft, this is the first time an outsider has been deliberately brought into the Resistance."

"Well, at least the first to be invited in a non-hostile manner," Torque added as he removed a bit of dirt from beneath one fingernail. He shot a pointed glare at Rift.

I could feel the blood leak from my cheeks. I remembered hearing the word in my brief moment of consciousness, but I hadn't grasped until that moment what it really meant. "The…the what?"

Kade and Rift shared a long, tense look. It was Kade who finally spoke. "The Resistance," he repeated, crossing his arms. "An uprising against the Global Government leaders—to expose them for the tyrants they are and put their power back into the hands of the people."

I stared at him for a long time. When I did open my mouth, it was to release an unsure chuckle. They had to be joking. "You can't be serious. Nobody could stand against the Globe! They have the Officials, the weapons— including the watchdogs—not to mention the world's only supplies of time capsules. You'd have to be insane!" I looked at each of them in turn. Each one's expression was as serious as the next.

I finally turned back to Rift.

He nodded. "You stumbled into a bit more than you realized, Ambry."

This information took several seconds for me to digest. Not only had I assisted the two guys who'd broken into my home and stolen from my father, but somehow I'd managed to get dragged into the center of a supposed global rebellion. I shook my head. "Let me get this straight. You people are planning to overthrow the world's governing system, and you mean to tell me that I'm the only person to come here that's not a part of your little Resistance?"

Torque snorted. "I wouldn't call it 'little,' princess."

Kade nodded, ignoring him. "You can see, therefore, why we need time to decide how best to proceed from here. We will weigh our options during the time it takes you to recover. And speaking of time," he said, rising from the chair he'd so recently occupied, "I should be going. I'm late as it is. Rift, I need to speak with you outside."

Avienne and Torque filed out of the room—the latter shooting me a parting wink—ahead of Kade. Rift was the last to leave. He had closed the door halfway behind him when the word I had been struggling to hold back escaped my dry lips.

"Options?" I said.

Rift paused in the doorway.

"Kade said you're weighing options…"

It was with a certain reluctance that Rift finally turned to look at me, and I could see in his eyes that none of the options would be to my liking. "We are."

My heart sank. When I'd first woken up and discovered the restraints, I had been furious, confused—maybe even curious at certain points. But it wasn't until that moment that fear crept up, stealing into my mind the way Rift and Torque had stolen into the manor. "What will he do with me?" I whispered.

He gave a small shrug. "I guess we'll both have to wait to find out." Without another word, he stepped back through the door, closing it behind himself with a definitive click.

CHAPTER FIVE

The little room was cold without the wool blanket, which had fallen in my attempts to wriggle out of my handcuffs. It now lay on the floor just inches out of reach. I hugged my knees to my chest and scowled. This was something of a feat in and of itself—not the scowling, but the knee-hugging, as my hands were still manacled to the side-rails of the bed. I had been forced to squirm further up to reach a point where the chains would allow my hands to touch. All I could do was sit there and stare at the windowless door.

Waiting.

I was just beginning to nod off when the door flew

open and Rift stepped back inside. My head shot up and a dull throbbing ensued.

Rift shut the door behind himself. "Kade left with several of the others. They have some errands to attend to," he said, strolling across the room and sitting down on the side of the bed.

"Errands?" I tried to force away the image of Kade and a handful of leather-bound Rebels strolling down the aisle of a supermarket, dropping a dozen eggs and some milk into their shopping cart. The image was so ridiculous that it took several attempts to shoo it away.

"I suppose 'diplomatic duties' would be a better term for it," he amended.

I dropped my iron-encased wrists to my sides with a heavy *clank*. "The leaders in this rebellion of yours have diplomatic duties?"

Rift cocked his head to one side. "You didn't think this was the only base of operations in the Resistance, did you?"

In all honesty, I hadn't given it much thought in light of the information I was already struggling to process. It was hard enough to swallow the fact that there was a Resistance in the first place. Against the absolute might of the Global Government, what could they possibly hope to achieve? "So what did Kade say?"

"He's letting you remain on a probationary status while you heal. We can't return you home without knowing we can trust you, but we also have no desire to kill you."

"My, how comforting."

He ignored my sarcastic little quip. "Here, give me your hand."

The shackles clattered angrily as I yanked it away.

Rift sighed. "You do realize it's chained to the bed, right?" His hand shot forward with bewildering speed and grabbed my wrist. To my surprise, he produced a small key from his pocket, inserted it into the cuff, and twisted it. The lock opened with a small click. He moved around to the other side of the bed to free my other hand.

My jaw slackened. "You're letting me go?"

"If by 'letting you go' you mean letting you leave the Atrium, no. Not yet," he added as the second handcuff fell from my wrist. "But I am getting you out of this room. I can think of better ways to spend my afternoon than in a dreary hospital."

I frowned. "But I thought that Kade and Torque said I'm a liability?"

"You are," he said. "But Kade isn't here and Torque isn't in charge of you. I am." He offered me a hand. I almost refused it, but a sudden bout of dizziness made me think better of it. He helped me rise shakily to my feet. "And I decided that if we want to find out whether we can trust you with the secrets you already know about us, we should start by helping you to understand us."

"So where are we going?"

"I thought I'd give you a bit of a tour," Rift replied. He pointed to a small set of drawers. "There should be a change of clothes in there. I'll give you a few minutes."

Rift stepped back outside while I changed. Selecting a pair of dark jeans and a simple black sweater, I shrugged out of the flannel pajamas and pulled the soft, pliable fabric over my head. I closed the set of drawers and glanced up, my eyes grazing the mirror on the wall.

I paused. Gingerly, I reached a hand up to skim the thin line of stitches that came to a halt just before my hairline, surrounded by a truly magnificent bruise. Several dark flecks clung to my scalp, the only remnants of what I guessed to be an impressive amount of blood. It must have been where I connected with the wall. The entire right side of my body ached as though… well, as though it had slammed into a brick wall.

When I went to push up the sleeves of my sweater, I noticed for the first time a small, straight cut along my wrist. I squinted, brushing my thumb over the cut. It twinged in response.

I knocked on the door to indicate that I was finished. Rift ushered me out into the narrow, dimly-lit hallway. "What's this?" I demanded, holding out my wrist for inspection.

"Oh that?" Rift said, glancing at the cut. "I did that."

I blinked. "*You* did?"

"Of course," he said, looking surprised. "I removed your ID chip right after you blacked out, before we brought you with us through the Telepoint."

"You mean you *cut it* out of me?"

"Well what else was I supposed to do?" he demanded. "You don't think I could have dragged you back here with your tracker still in tact, do you? Why not send all twenty-four Timekeepers and their Globe thugs handwritten invitations while I'm at it?"

I crossed my arms but made no reply, although I did glower at him a fair amount as I followed in his wake. We passed a number of people along the hallway, several of whom appeared to be medics. They wore maroon uniforms and white gloves, some carrying clipboards, others pushing patients in wheelchairs.

The end of the corridor opened up into a huge, circular room with a high-arching ceiling. My heart sank. There were *hundreds* of people in this room alone! Until that moment, a part of me had still hoped that Kade and the others might have been exaggerating the scale of the Resistance. Looking around now, that faint hope *poofed* right out of existence. I took a deep breath to steady myself, noting that even in such an expansive space, the air remained stale and metallic. Underground, perhaps? That would explain why the Globe hadn't rooted them out.

Scattered throughout the room were a couple dozen Telepoint gateways. "This is the Arrival and Departure Room," Rift said over his shoulder. "Most people come by Telepoint, although we do have alternate ways of coming and going."

"Such as?" I asked.

"Not important at the moment."

I smirked at the back of his head, making a mental note that there might be other ways to escape their super-secret rebel hive. Besides, I got the distinct impression that the less important Rift made something out to be, the more important it actually was.

Above each Telepoint was a digital screen displaying its corresponding destination. The locations ranged from developed cities such as Rome, Tokyo, and Dublin to more remote areas like Managua, Nairobi, and even one archway labeled "Canopy." I'd seen such Telepoints while visiting my father at the Forum, locked into set destinations that were frequently used.

At the center of the room was a statue of a man in a long coat, tugging a wide-brimmed hat down to obscure his face. The plaque beneath it read, "UNITED FOR JUSTICE, UNITED FOR TRUTH." Behind it stood three Telepoints on a raised dais. "Those look important," I noted, pointing at them.

Rift grunted in response.

"What are they for?"

He turned to me with a raised eyebrow. When I didn't back down, he sighed. "As you said, they're important. Let's leave it at that. And don't get any ideas… those archways are encoded. They can only be accessed by the Commanders and their Seconds-in-Command."

"Who are they?" I asked, quickening my pace so that I fell into step beside him. "I mean, Kade is obviously one of them."

"He's the Commander of the Atrium Sector, yes," Rift said, glancing sideways at me. From the look on his face, I could tell that he didn't intend to divulge any more information on that subject.

"You mean this is just *one* rebel base?" I stared around at the flurry of activity in the vast room. "How many…?"

Rift looked back and raised an eyebrow.

I held my hands up. "Okay, okay. I'm guessing that's not important at the moment either, huh?"

"Um, excuse me?" echoed a disbelieving voice.

Rift and I turned to find Torque and Avienne storming toward us. "What the hell is she doing out of the Hospital Branch? Not that I'm unhappy to see you, darling," he said, inclining his head to me. "But what were you thinking letting her out of that room?" he demanded, rounding on Rift.

"Keeping her locked away isn't going to do anyone any good," Rift answered.

"So you've decided to provide her with *more* information about us? Give her the whole grand tour? We don't even know that we can trust her!"

"I'm right here," I muttered. Neither paid me any attention.

"And why should we expect to be able to trust her if she doesn't trust us?" Rift asked, his dark eyes flashing. "I'm *attempting* to remedy that."

I stared at him in surprise. Why would he be concerned with gaining my trust? Shouldn't it have been the other way around?

It must have made an impact on Torque too. He paused, his open mouth filled with some unspoken retort. Avienne was looking back and forth between the two of them as though unsure of which side to take.

Finally, Torque sighed and ran a hand through his snowy hair. "Just tell me you know what you're doing."

"I do. Trust me," Rift said, clapping a hand on Torque's shoulder. "Look," he added in a whisper so low that I could just barely make it out. "I'm just trying to help her understand, all right? If it doesn't work and we have to go with the second option, more or less information won't make a difference."

I tried not to let my face register that I'd heard this last sentence, even though it produced a chill that ran the full length of my body. I focused instead on the muscle working in Torque's jaw as he considered Rift's argument. finally, he nodded. "Fair enough," he murmured. "But if this goes to hell, I'm not going to be the one explaining it to Kade."

I hadn't realized I'd been holding my breath. Now I let out the stale air that had been trapped in my lungs.

Rift rubbed his hands together. "Well, that's settled then. And so long as you're shifting from 'prisoner' to something more of a 'guest' status, we might as well give some proper introductions. You've already met Avienne Guerrier," he said with a wave of his hand toward Avienne. "And her brother…"

"Thomás Guerrier," said Torque, reaching for my

hand and planting a kiss on my knuckles. *"Enchanté."*

Out of the corner of my eye, I saw Rift roll his eyes. "You're French?" I asked Torque. "I thought you sounded as though you might be from London…"

"I'm British, if you're going by citizenship," Torque replied. "A debt of gratitude owed to our mother. *Mais notre père était français."*

"I'm a little rusty," I said, screwing up my face in concentration. "But did you say your father *was* French?"

Torque's smile faltered. *"Bien fait,"* he murmured in approval.

"Our parents died about five years ago," Avienne said quietly. "I was seventeen, Torque was fourteen."

"Oh." I suddenly wished I had kept my mouth shut. "I'm so sorry…"

"Don't be. You had nothing to do with it," Torque said. "Unless of course you hired the Globe assassin that murdered them."

I swallowed tightly. *Globe* assassin? That didn't add up, but I wasn't about to argue him on it. A moment of awkward silence passed during which I decided to change the subject to something less bleak. "So how did you get the nickname 'Torque?'"

He chuckled. "I'm sure you'll see soon enough."

"Speaking of which," said Rift, turning to Avienne. "I wondered if you might show her the Dining Hall?"

Avienne shot me a wary frown. It was the sort of disgusted grimace that I had often seen Gemma aim at an insect. "Why can't you take her?"

"Torque and I need to pick up a few things," he said.

She tapped her foot, then gave an exaggerated sigh. "If you insist. Come on, Elite." Her hand encircled my upper arm in a tight grip and steered me forward.

I glanced back as Rift and Torque disappeared down a side hallway. "What's so interesting about the Dining Hall?" I wondered, lengthening my strides to keep pace with Avienne's long-legged stride.

"In a few minutes, you can see for yourself," she said.

As we walked on, Avienne pointed out other rooms and branches of the Atrium. "Down there are the sleeping quarters, and over here you have the armory."

"What's that?" I asked, pointing to a long, dark hallway criss-crossed with green beams of light.

She glanced in the direction of my pointed finger. "Commanders Only Sector. No one can get down that corridor without the proper passcodes. Ah, here we are," she said as we emerged out of the corridor and into another expansive room. On the one end, there appeared to be a large dining area. Food was being served in buffet fashion. It was like a Rebel version of Honoratus's cafeteria, minus the waiting staff that came to fill and refill students' drinks. "Let's get something to eat before the match starts."

"The match?" I repeated as the two of us picked up blue trays and filed through the food line.

"Patience, Elite."

Glowering at being addressed as though I were child, I

mechanically selected a grilled cheese sandwich and a steaming bowl of tomato soup before following Avienne to one of the long wooden dining tables. The tray wobbled as I tried to balance it with my left hand. I didn't want to put any strain on my right arm, fearing what it might do to my shoulder. Avienne took a seat next to a dark-skinned Latino boy who she introduced as Mateo. Unlike the majority of the Rebels we had passed—most of whom seemed content to scowl at me from their various positions throughout the room—Mateo proved friendly, albeit not very talkative.

On the other side of the room across from us, I was surprised to see several round arenas, the largest of which offered the best view to those sitting at the tables. "These," said Avienne with a wave of her hand, "are the Sparring Rings. We practice a wide variety of fighting skills from those involving weaponry to hand-to-hand combat. Rift thought you might like to see a fight in action."

"Where is Rift, anyway?" I asked, looking around.

Avienne laughed and pointed. I followed her finger to where two figures were stepping into the largest of the rings. "You won't get a better show than this." Her voice was laced with anticipation.

As I watched Rift and Torque take to opposing sides of the ring and square off, I wondered how Avienne could expect an even fight. Torque was all muscle and energy. He bounced lightly from one foot to the other as though he might explode off the ground at any moment, spinning his staff with expert precision in a series of complex circles that were too rapid for my eyes to follow.

Rift, on the other hand, stood with his feet shoulder-width apart, his hands clasping his staff behind his back. With his head lowered, I couldn't tell whether his eyes were even open.

A computerized voice suddenly echoed across the ring. *"Opponents, acknowledge."*

Rift and Torque bowed simultaneously to each other.

"Take your ready."

The two competitors swung their staffs forward and up so that they held them at arms length, perpendicular to the ground.

"Begin."

Torque sprang into action. He spun the staff so that it became a whirlwind-like blur and leapt toward Rift, who stood unmoving. As Torque brought the staff down on him like a solid whip, I thought the match might end before it really had a chance to begin.

But at the last second, Rift sidestepped the blow and brought his own staff down with a *smack* against Torque's descending back. He sprang nimbly out of reach as Torque turned to retaliate.

"Remember asking how Torque came about his nickname?" Avienne asked, her eyes never breaking away from the match.

"Yeah..."

"Do you know what the word means?"

I screwed up my face in thought, causing my swollen

skin to twinge. "It has to do with rotation, right?"

"Rotation, revolution," Avienne said. "Like a force that causes an object to twist or turn."

"Okay, so how does that explain—" I dropped off mid sentence as Torque jumped into a sudden flip, his body rotating both upward and forward, but also somehow spinning on a vertical axis so that he completed several 360-degree turns in a single move. "Never mind."

Avienne nodded in mute agreement.

As the match progressed, I could tell that Torque held a clear advantage over Rift in terms of both strength and skill. This ought to have left Rift with little to no chance at victory, but I was beginning to see a pattern form. Torque would perform move after mind-numbing move of acrobatic prowess, each of which could have knocked Rift clean off his feet. However, Rift seemed to have an uncanny ability to predict Torque's oncoming attacks, like an odd sort of premonition. "How is he able to know exactly what Torque is about to do?" I asked Avienne as Rift ducked below a flying kick originally aimed at his chest.

"He's quick," Avienne replied, her eyes glued to the match. "He's also good at reading people." Torque had just sliced his staff through the air, but Rift dove over its trajectory, curling neatly into a roll that set him back on his feet before Torque had finished the move's follow through. I suddenly wondered if the idea of Rift reading my face earlier wasn't as irrational as I'd thought. "Especially Torque," Avienne added.

I nodded, still watching the two combatants. Having watched and participated in countless skirmishes during our Physical Training classes throughout my time in Honoratus, I could tell that Rift and Torque had fought one another often enough to be familiar with each other's fighting styles.

Rift darted forward while spinning in a circular motion, jabbing the staff toward Torque. Torque jumped backward onto the outer rail of the ring. He paused for a moment there, poised like an Olympic diver before the plunge. I thought I saw him grin in triumph the instant before he leapt into the most complicated series of rotations I had witnessed yet, and I could tell that the arch of his attack would land him directly on top of Rift.

But as Torque hurtled downward, Rift—who was still on one knee—swung his staff up so that one end rested against the ground. The other end connected sharply with Torque's descending abdomen, knocking him out of the air. He hit the ground clutching his stomach and looking as though he might be sick.

It all happened so fast. I would have missed the whole thing if I had blinked a second sooner. "So he's actually beaten Torque before?" I asked in awe.

"He's one of the *only* people who can beat Torque, primarily because he can stay one step ahead of him," Avienne said. "Torque may be stronger and have a great deal more training, but Rift has learned to anticipate his attacks and use them against him."

A hulking figure suddenly stepped in front of me,

blocking my view of the ring. "So," said a deep voice. "This is the Elite wench."

I looked up to find a tall, muscular Rebel who looked to be around the same age as Kade, possibly mid-twenties. His brown hair was cut short in military fashion and he glared at me as though my very existence was an offense.

"Marius. Always an unpleasant surprise," Avienne said. "Could you possibly scoot just a tad to your left? I'm trying to watch my brother eat turf."

The tall Rebel's boots remained firmly planted. "What's she doing out of her cage, Guerrier?" he asked, jutting his chin out toward me.

Avienne rolled her eyes. "Why don't you ask Rift?" she asked, crossing her arms. "He's the one in charge of her."

"Oh believe me, I plan to. But first..." He snatched my arm, "... allow me to kennel her up for you."

I grunted, trying to wrench out of his grasp, but his hand was a vice. "Let go of me, asshole!" I spat.

"Whoa! Language," he scolded, twisting my wrist up over my head so that I was pulled in close enough to smell his odorous breath. "Maybe you should try some more of those fancy etiquette classes."

"Maybe you should try brushing your teeth," I retorted, wrinkling my nose.

Marius growled under his breath. "You little..." He yanked down on my arm so that my injured shoulder was wrenched out of place once more. Fire erupted from the joint. The burning was so intense that I couldn't even take a breath to cry out in pain.

In a flash, Avienne had leapt to her feet and punched him squarely in the jaw. Not expecting such a swift counter-attack, he released my arm and rounded on her.

Mateo caught me as I staggered backwards. He helped to lower me to a sitting position, my right arm dangling at an awkward angle as I gasped in pain.

"You're out of your league, Guerrier," Marius growled, flexing his enormous arms. His fists hung at his sides like twin sledgehammers. "And I don't see your brother or your boyfriend here to save you this time..."

"Looks like we're missing all the real fun," called a familiar voice. Rift had hopped the side of the ring and was jogging toward us. Torque wasn't far behind. I was surprised to see a bruise beginning to blossom around a cut on Rift's left cheekbone. Blood slid down the side of his face to drip from the edge of his jaw. "Care to explain why you damaged my ward when we just went through all the trouble of fixing her?" he asked. He had assumed a relaxed stance, but there was a murderous edge to his voice that made the skin on my neck crawl.

"Better damaged and under lock and key than healthy and off her leash," Marius snarled. "Maybe *you* ought to be explaining your brilliant idea of giving the prisoner a guided tour of the entire Resistance operation!" he said in a carrying voice, advancing toward Rift. "It might lead others to question your discernment." Every word was pronounced like a challenge.

Rift didn't move, but his fists clenched and unclenched at his sides. "Kade seems to think I can handle it."

"Well, we'll see if he changes his mind when he trots back home to find you giving her sparring tips," said Marius with a glare.

"I'm sure you'll give him a detailed account."

Next to Rift, Torque began cracking his knuckles one by one with delicate, dangerous intent. "As much as I'm enjoying your little welcoming committee, Marius, don't you have patrol duties to be getting back to?"

Marius's eyes darted down to Torque's hands, which were still smeared with blood from the match, before turning to me. "I'm sure we'll be seeing each other again soon, Your Highness," he sneered.

I shivered, pain reverberating down my arm.

Rift's eyes followed Marius and his thugs until they had disappeared down one of the tunnels. As soon as they were gone, he sat swiftly next to me, practically shoving Mateo out of the way. "Let me see," he said, his tone businesslike. He slipped the sleeve of my sweater down so that he had a clear view of my shoulder.

Under normal circumstances, this would have elicited a slap from me, but I was too busy concentrating on not passing out.

"Dislocated again," he diagnosed. "Mateo, hold her still. This may hurt," he warned.

Mateo helped to angle me so that I was supported against the his leather vest. Slim as he was, his arms were surprisingly strong as they held me steady.

"I know this is asking a lot, Ambry," said Rift, "but I need to you to keep that arm relaxed."

I shivered and nodded, letting the arm hang as limp as possible.

Bracing one hand against the front of my shoulder, Rift used his other to create traction. I grimaced, and he looked up. "Doing okay?" he asked.

I bit my lip and nodded.

A few more moments of steady pull on my arm, and I heard a soft popping sound accompanied by fresh pain. I clenched my jaw and hissed.

"Shhh." Rift allowed me to slump forward against him. "It's over."

"He said—he'd be back," I whispered, tremors rolling through my body like waves from the intensity of the pain.

Rift's arm tightened by a fraction around my back. "Don't worry about Marius. I suspect he was born with that unfortunate social deficiency of his."

I made a valiant attempt to laugh, but the slightest movement sparked new waves of agony. I settled for cracking a smile.

Avienne crossed her arms. "Marius isn't my favorite person either—not by a long stretch—but I can understand why he acts the way he does."

"Still, I need to talk with Kade about him," Rift said.

"He's getting out of control."

"I have to agree," I said with a wince.

Avienne shot me a caustic look. "Yeah? Well you might be too if your parents were shot in a raid by the Globe."

My retort died on my lips.

It was Rift who responded. "We've all lost something, Avienne. That's no excuse for taking it out on anyone within arm's reach."

There was a long, awkward pause. "How was the rest of the match?" I managed finally, trying to keep my voice from shaking. "The last thing I saw was you putting Torque on his back." I aimed a feeble smile over Rift's shoulder at Torque, but it wasn't returned.

"I lost," said Rift quietly.

I blinked in surprise. Before Marius and his goons had sauntered up, Rift had appeared to have the upper hand. To make matters even more confusing, Torque was acting oddly sour-faced about his victory. His arms were crossed on the table and he was glowering down at the soup his sister had just pushed in front of him, steam curling around his taut face.

Avienne raised an eyebrow. "That's funny. I've never taken you for a sore winner, little brother. Sore loser perhaps, but—"

With a growl that made the hair on the back of my neck stand on end, Torque shoved himself up and stalked away across the Dining Hall.

Rift sighed. Avienne made to follow him, but Rift shook his head. "Let him walk it off," he said. "I need you to keep an eye on her while I go find Dmitri. He'll want to take a look at this newest injury, and I'm sure he'll be none too pleased." Without any further explanation for Torque's odd behavior, Rift rose from the table and headed off in the direction of the Hospital Branch.

"That's strange," said Avienne. She took a bite of toast and chewed thoughtfully. "Torque usually crows like an over-inflated rooster when he's beaten Rift. It's an obnoxious habit, but I suppose I've grown rather accustomed to it. I can't imagine why he's making such a fuss."

"Didn't you see the end?" asked a willowy Asian woman as she sat down next to Avienne. Her jet black hair was shaved along one side of her head. What hair there was on the other was streaked with violet highlights to match the violet stripes across her black leather vest. "Rift threw the match."

"What?" Avienne's perfect brows shot up. "Ming, are you sure?"

"It looked obvious to me," Ming said. "Torque flipped right over his head, but as usual Rift saw it coming and turned before Torque had even hit the ground. But rather than dodge Torque's next move, he froze... just stared right past him."

"Took a roundhouse kick straight to the head," Matco cut in, thrusting a hand to his cheek. "He got totally blasted."

"Are you serious?" Avienne propped an elbow on the table and rested her chin against her hand.

Mateo nodded. "I'm surprised he's even conscious. Took him a few seconds to get up though."

"Weird," she said, frowning. "Well, first time for everything. I wouldn't worry about it though. Torque will cool down. He may just need an hour or two."

"And possibly a quick dip in the Arctic," laughed Mateo.

She cast him a withering look. "If you like, I can pass that suggestion on to him when he gets back."

Mateo shrank away from her. "*Lo siento...* I didn't mean anything by it."

"Of course you didn't," she scowled. Despite her taunts, Avienne's loyalty to her brother clearly ran deep. "Ah, it looks like your keeper is back," she said.

Rift and a serious-looking man with gray-streaked brown hair were striding toward us. The man wore the maroon tunic of a medic and was carrying a black satchel. When they reached the table, he came immediately to my side and opened his bag, pulling out various medical tools. "All right, let's see what new damage you've gotten yourself into," he said in a thick Russian accent.

My mouth fell open. "Hey, it wasn't my fau—ow!"

"Hmmm." He ran his fingers lightly around the area of my shoulder. His touch was careful, meaning his examination felt only mildly excruciating. "You did a good job getting the shoulder back in place," he said to Rift, wholly ignoring my protests.

"Thanks," Rift said.

"Too bad you couldn't keep an eye on her long enough to spare yourself the trouble," the medic added. He pulled out a pill bottle, opened the lid with a small *pop*, and emptied three white capsules into his palm.

Rift sighed. "I'm sorry for my negligence, Dmitri."

"Spare me the apologies," Dmitri snapped. He turned to hand me the pills and a plastic water bottle. "For the pain," he explained to me. "They'll make you drowsy, but I'm sure you'll find that preferable to your current state."

"Thank you," I replied with only the barest hint of resentment. Looking down at the white pills in my palm, I tried not to think about my last dosage of medication… of my father's fingers prying open my mouth… of my mother looking on, doing nothing to stop him.

I popped the pills into my mouth using my left hand and took a dutiful swig of water.

"From now on, just focus on keeping her in one piece," Dmitri ordered Rift irritably. "I have enough patients to attend to without you sending me repeats."

"Will do," said Rift with a mock salute.

"I certainly hope so." Dmitri stood with his satchel in hand. "Considering the reasons you normally need to call on me, I hope I won't be seeing you anytime soon." Not waiting for a reply, he turned and strode toward the doors.

"You know," Rift said thoughtfully as Dmitri exited

the Dining Hall, "I think that's the nicest thing he's ever said to me."

"Always a ray of sunshine, that one," Avienne agreed.

I started to chuckle, which I realized was a mistake. Pain reverberated through my ribcage and across my shoulders.

"Are you all right?" Rift asked, his eyebrows raised in concern.

"If being all right means having the majority of your body either bruised, broken, or bleeding, then yes, I'm fine," I said, wincing.

"Here, let me help you." Avoiding my injured shoulder, Rift went to my other side and steadied me as a sudden wave of vertigo threatened to topple me to the ground. "I think it's about time we got you back to your room. You've made enough friends for one day."

I nodded. The combination of pain and whatever medication Dmitri had given me was making my head feel as though I'd just swallowed twelve of the lavender pills. "Can I go to sleep now?" I mumbled into Rift's shoulder. The fabric of his shirt stuck between my lips. It tasted like sweat and the coarse fibers tickled my lips, but I couldn't muster the energy to spit it out.

There was a faint rumble as he chuckled. "I think that would be best."

I nodded again, already drifting off. My center of gravity suddenly shifted as he swept me up in his arms, which I might have found gallant if I weren't so confused.

Once I understood why my feet were no longer touching the ground, I was profoundly relieved. Having to stay upright wasn't fun. Too hard. "You'll stay with me, won't you?" I asked. My tongue felt heavy. Maybe that was why my plea had sounded so slurred.

Rift's voice blurred at the edges, like words slowly bleeding out of a waterlogged sheet of paper. But whatever reply he had given was swallowed up in the fuzzy warmth of sleep.

CHAPTER SIX

I awoke to my same little room in the Hospital Branch. This time, however, I was thankful to find that my captors had done away with the restraints. I yawned and stretched. Never before had I been so happy to command a full range of motion.

Well, almost. My right shoulder was still stiff and sore, but I much preferred being injured to being chained up.

At first I thought I might be alone, but a quick perusal of the room told me otherwise.

Rift must have fallen asleep quickly. He hadn't bothered to find himself a more comfortable spot, such as in the plush armchair to the right of my bed. Instead he was propped up in a sitting position with his back leaned against the door, sound asleep. The sight of him stationed between myself and the only entrance for any would-be attackers left me with a profound sense of gratitude.

I eased back against my pillow. It was soft and dense, like the one in my bedroom at home. I'd always preferred it to the overstuffed, fluffy things Orelia tended to favor.

I've already been gone for over two days, I thought. I wondered what Orelia thought of my disappearance. Was she worried for me? I shook my head at the thought. *She's probably celebrating.*

All of a sudden, Rift jerked awake. He bolted up so abruptly that I froze where I lay, like a stray cat petrified by the sound of a car backfiring. Before I could say a word, he was scrambling for his jacket. He grappled with the dark leather until his hand finally emerged from some unseen inner pocket holding a small, beat-up looking notebook. Throwing the jacket aside, he yanked a pen out of his pocket and began to scribble furiously, his brow furrowed, a look of desperate concentration on his face.

I considered coughing or making some movement to let him know I was awake, but curiosity held me back. I continued to watch as he scribbled, his hand now moving more slowly across the paper as though the flow of words were beginning to trickle out. He pressed a hand to his forehead and made a noise of frustration. A few more scribbles. A long pause. Another growl of exasperation.

After two more similar cycles of scribbling, pausing, growling, and raking his hands through his hair, he finally slammed the little notebook shut and hurled his pen across the room, where it hit the opposite wall with a small *thud*.

I jumped in surprise.

Rift's head snapped up.

I rubbed my eyes and tried to look as though I'd only just awoken from a deep slumber, uninterrupted by angry, guttural noises and flying pens. "Morning," I said.

Some of the initial suspicion in his expression shifted to a weary relief. "Good morning." His tone was deceptively calm. "Did you sleep well?"

"Better than I would have thought, all things considered." I rotated my shoulder, trying to ease out some of the stiffness. "Thank you for helping me last night."

Rift shook his head. "I'm not so sure you should be thanking me. It was my job to keep you safe, and I didn't exactly deliver on that."

"You set my shoulder for me," I reminded him.

He waved a dismissive hand. "Dmitri could have done that himself."

"Still, you were the one who took care of it," I pointed out. "And you were also the one who came in time to stop that Marius creep from killing me altogether."

"Well, better late than never, I suppose," he said darkly. I frowned. Why should he be so upset? He wasn't the one who had his shoulder dislocated a second time. Perhaps Kade was a harsher leader than I'd realized and there would be consequences awaiting him when the dark-haired Commander discovered I'd been injured on Rift's watch.

But then I remembered Rift's comment to Torque the day before: *"And why should we expect to be able to trust her if she doesn't trust us?"* Could he really be that concerned about my opinion of the Resistance? And if so, was it for my benefit, or theirs? If they suspected that I had a bitter taste in my mouth toward the lot of them, all they really had to do to protect their secrets was keep me imprisoned here indefinitely. *Well, that or use a less pleasant and more permanent method of shutting me up.* A brief shudder flitted through me. "So, what's on the agenda for today?" I asked, trying to shake off the subject.

Rift stood up. He crossed the floor to where he'd thrown his pen and picked it up, slipping his jacket on as he went. I almost didn't see him slide the notebook back into its hidden pocket. Almost. "I have a few things I have to take care of, which unfortunately means you'll need to tag along," he said.

Unfortunately? I wondered. Did he mean it was unfortunate that I would be obligated to come, or that he'd have to endure my company? "I don't mind. Maybe I can help?"

He considered me with those earthen eyes. "I'm sure we could find something to keep you busy. That is, if you're feeling up to the task," he added. "How's the shoulder?"

I shifted it again and found it considerably less stiff

97

than before. "Much better."

"Good," he said with a nod. "Otherwise Dmitri would probably skin me alive and use me for medical experiments."

I laughed, hoping he was joking.

Rift left the room to give me some privacy. There was a minuscule shower in the adjoining bathroom where I took the opportunity to clean off two days' worth of blood and grime from my sore, bruised body. I'd never been more thankful for something as simple as a shower in all my life. In fact, I realized with a small pang, there were a lot of things I'd taken for granted prior to the past forty-eight-or-so hours.

I took my time, the water caressing my aching muscles and swollen skin. The warmth was so intoxicating that I might have stayed in there for hours, were it not for the possibility that Rift might think I'd drowned and come in to check on me.

Once I had dried off and slipped into another simple outfit—black pants made from some sort of stretchy material and a gray hooded sweater—I knocked twice on the door, which opened immediately. Rift ushered me into the low-lit hall. He started off, with me trotting along behind to keep pace with him.

As we wandered down the corridor, I tried to paint a map in my head of what I knew of the Atrium so far. It probably wouldn't do me a lot of good, what with my mandatory escort, but I concentrated on memorizing it nonetheless on the off-chance that a window opened for me to escape.

We were walking in same direction we'd gone the day before, which meant that this hall would lead to the Arrival Room and, eventually, the Dining Hall, along with a number of smaller rooms and corridors branching out along the way. Rift veered off to the right. "First stop, the Command Center," he said as we approached the first door. His fingers flew across the keypad next to the door, and it unlocked with the groan of slow-moving metal. "After you," he said, ushering me inside.

The room was made up of a vast array of computers, consoles, and security screens featuring what looked like every major part of the Atrium. I recognized the bustling Arrival Room on one of the larger screens, filled with throngs of Rebels coming and going through the myriad of Telepoints. But most of the smaller screens showed rooms I hadn't seen before. Several high-backed chairs were spaced across the room in front of the monitors.

The closest chair swiveled to face us, and I was shocked to see it captained by a slender boy with a small, upturned nose and shaggy blond hair. He couldn't have been more than twelve years old. "About time," he said sternly.

"Sorry to keep you waiting, Cody," Rift said. "I have someone to introduce you to. This," he said, gesturing to me, "is Ambry Croft."

"Croft?" Cody frowned. I could see the wheels in his

head spinning. Then his face began to change, eyes widening and mouth morphing into the shape of an "O." "You're Titus Croft's daughter?"

I sighed. "I prefer 'Ambry,' if it's all the same to you." I extended a hand to him. "Nice to meet you, Cody."

Cody stared at my hand for a moment. He shot Rift a dubious look.

"Don't worry. I can vouch for her," Rift said.

Cody glanced back at me with marginally-less skepticism. finally, he reached up and shook my hand. "Cody Dwyer," he said. "Tech supervisor."

"You mean you're in charge of all this?" I asked, trying to mask my own skepticism.

"Yeah yeah, I get it. How could I be in charge? I'm just a kid," the boy said, rolling his eyes. "In answer to the usual questions I can already see formulating on your face, I'm eleven and a half years old, I am *quite* capable of running this technological playground, and I *do* know what I'm doing."

"Easy, tiger." Rift clapped the boy on the shoulder. "I trained him myself. Well, his mom and I did—hey, Juliet!" he called toward another chair across the room.

A middle-aged woman glanced up from her work, pulling out an earbud. "Rift!" she said when she saw him. She rose gracefully from her chair and walked over to give him a tight hug. "You really should visit us more often, you know," she said fondly. "I hate having to share you with the rest of the sector."

"Duty calls," he said with a shrug. "Ambry, this is Juliet Dwyer. She and Cody head things up here in the Command Center, along with a few others. Her husband John is the head of the Agricultural Branch."

Agricultural Branch? I thought. How many branches of this place were there?

Juliet nodded politely at me. "Kade mentioned something about a… visitor," she said with uncertainty. She appraised me with the same bright green eyes as her son.

"It's all right, Juliet. Ambry actually helped Torque and I escape the Croft compound. We wouldn't have made it back if it weren't for her," Rift said, glancing toward me.

I smiled at Juliet. I couldn't quite put my finger on it, but there was something about her that I instantly liked. Maybe it was her lack of open hostility. "It's a pleasure to meet you," I said.

She shook my hand. "It's nice to meet you too, Ambry. Right, Cody?" she said, nudging her son.

"Oh. Uh… right," Cody mumbled.

I strolled toward the plethora of screens overseeing the various parts of the Atrium, trying to get more of an overview of the place. Unfortunately, most of the corridors looked obnoxiously similar. "This is quite the security system you've got."

"It's a Shieldcorp 2E3," Cody replied. "Newest upgrade. Isn't even available on the market yet."

"Huh. Sounds better than whatever we've got at home."

"It is," Cody said. "I ought to know—I was the one who hacked into it."

I turned to blink at him. "*You* broke through my father's security? That's seriously impressive!"

Cody shrugged, but I could tell he was pleased with himself. He glanced down at his fingernails. "Hacking is my personal specialty. Your system wasn't too much of a challenge."

Rift cleared his throat. "Might've been nice to know about that electric fence though…"

"Hey, how was I supposed to know they went old-school on me?" Cody glared at him. "An electric fence? It's positively primitive! The charge wasn't even linked into the compound's security network—totally offline, off-blueprint, and manually engaged by one of the guards!"

"Whoa, calm down little man. Things happen. We know you know what you're doing," Rift assured him.

"So you've been doing this for a long time?" I asked.

Cody nodded. "I was eight the first time I worked his way past the Globe's firewalls. Remember the media glitch a few years ago?"

My jaw dropped. "*You* were the one who hacked into the G.G.'s evening news program?" I turned to Rift who gave a verifying nod.

"With the animation of the guy popping the inflatable globe?" said Cody. "Yup, that was me. Covering that one up must have taken the Globe a lot of political bullsh—"

"Cody," warned Juliet.

Cody shrugged, but I caught the wince on his face as he looked up at his mother.

I grinned at his smug expression. He might be a genius, but in many ways he was still just a pre-teen boy thrilled to gain the approval of an older girl. "So the Globe *knows* about all of this?" I asked, gesturing around the room.

"They know there's some level of rebellion going on, and that it's organized," said Rift. "They just don't know the scope of it—like how many of us there are or where we're located. And they *definitely* don't want the rest of the Globe citizens finding out."

I nodded. "Knowing that a large group of people were standing up to the Globe would either spread panic or revolution."

"Exactly," said Rift. "Better to let their pride take a hit and claim that one lone hacker broke through their cyber-defense."

"Speaking of which," I said to Cody, "you know they're still looking for you, right?"

"They can look all they want. They won't find me here," he grinned.

Rift chuckled and turned to Juliet. "So you needed me for something?"

"Oh, right," she said. "Can you take a look at this? We've had a few anomalies I wanted to get your opinion on…" The two of them walked over to the computer she had vacated and she began flipping through screens, pointing at various pieces of code.

"So, what do you think of the Atrium?" Cody asked.

"Honestly? I still can't wrap my mind around it," I said, gazing around the room. "I never would have imagined something like this would be possible."

Cody narrowed his eyes as he studied me. "You don't seem like the other Elites I've met," he said.

"How so?"

"I don't know. You seem so... normal," he said. "The others are all like..." He assumed a pompous expression and clasped his hands behind his back, strutting regally around his chair like a starched flamingo.

I stifled a laugh with my hand. "Yeah. That pretty much sums us up."

He giggled and fell back into his slouched stance. Probably from years sitting behind a keyboard. "So what makes you so different?" he wondered.

"Good question. I've been wondering the same thing for years," I murmured. "I guess I've never really felt like I fit into my life back home. I'm always falling short of my parents' expectations. But this," I said, gazing around the room at the screens overlooking the Atrium. "This seems, I don't know...comfortable, somehow."

"Then maybe you should stay."

I opened my mouth, but nothing came out.

Across the room, Rift and Juliet stood back up. "Thanks for the help," she said to him as they approached us.

"No problem," Rift replied. "Any excuse to see you

and the Code-master here is a good one."

"Stop by more often, then," Cody said, pointing at him.

Rift raised his hands. "Okay, okay! Don't shoot!" He grabbed the boy in a playful hold around the neck and ruffled his hair. "Hold down the fort for me, okay?" he said.

"Yes, Sir!" Cody saluted. "Nice to meet you, Ambry," he added.

I smiled. "You too."

Juliet and Cody waved before heading back to their respective chairs.

I slipped out the door in front of Rift. "I like them," I said.

"They seem to like you too."

I raised an eyebrow.

He shrugged. "Well, at least compared to most of the other people you've met so far."

We walked back the way we came and turned to continue down the wide main corridor. I could just see the Arrival Room looming ahead when Rift turned into a door to the left, ushering me inside what turned out to be a narrow stairwell. "Where are we going now?" I wondered.

"Up," he replied.

"My, how ambiguous of you."

Several stairs ahead of me, I thought I heard him chuckle.

We continued up what I guessed to be about three stories, stopping only when we had reached the end of the staircase. "Doing okay?" he asked me as I shuffled up behind him.

"I'm managing," I said with a wince. Half of my body still felt sore.

"Hmm. Perhaps we should have taken the elevator…"

I gawked up at him.

"I'm kidding!" he laughed from overhead. "Come on, we've still got a little ways to go."

I stepped out of the stairwell after him and discovered that rather than a third "floor," Rift was leading me out onto a wide catwalk suspended in open air. Looking down over the railing to my left, I could see the Arrival Room buzzing with activity. Every few seconds, someone would materialize or dematerialize through one of the dozens of Telepoints. Clusters of Rebels talked in groups while others strode purposefully through the room and off into other smaller branches of the Atrium. "We're higher up than I realized…" I said. My voice shook despite all my efforts to sound calm.

"Fun, right?" Rift reached up to grip the upper railings on either side of the platform and hefted himself into a flip, dropping back onto the platform with a light *thunk* that shook the length of the walkway.

I gripped the railing more tightly. "If you want to get yourself killed, that's your business, but *please* leave me out of it."

He raised his eyebrows. "Wait a moment. Are you telling me you're afraid of heights?"

"All normal people are afraid of heights," I said stiffly.

Rift laughed. "Yes, but I could have sworn I saw you jump across several rooftops not two nights ago."

"People are known to do quite a few reckless things under the threat of a messy death," I retorted. "Now where did you say we're headed?"

Rift stepped forward. He gently pried one of my hands from its death-grip on the railing and held it securely in his own. "That way," he said, jerking his head across the room. We were up in the dome of the Arrival Room. The rickety catwalk system appeared to wind its way around its circumference.

To my utter and complete dismay, our destination appeared to be on the exact opposite side. "It's not bad once you get used to it," Rift said as he strode forward, dragging me in his wake.

"Uh-huh." I gripped his hand a little tighter with every jiggle of the suspension cords.

After what felt like years, we finally made it to the other side. "So what is it you have to do up here?" I asked.

"I need to reconfigure the cooling panels," he said, opening a metal compartment to reveal a complicated-looking console. "It's a hydronic system, and we want to avoid any water damage that might result from the condensation. I'm going to give you some credit and assume you've figured out that we're underground?"

I nodded. "I figured it was either that or you all just really have something against windows."

"The former, I'm afraid." Rift leaned down to inspect the screen. "And in order to make sure our location isn't discovered, we need to the outer cooling panels to block out any heat signatures we might be emitting. You know, what with having a few thousand or so people all running around at subterranean levels. The Globe has gadgets to detect stuff like that. Might seem a bit suspicious if someone noticed."

I felt my jaw drop. "There are thousands of people down here?"

"Five thousand eight hundred and sixty-two last I checked," he said.

"Wow," I whispered, looking out over activity below. "So how long have you been a part of all this?"

Rift shot me a cursory glance before turning back to his work. "I don't do backstory."

"Oh, come on," I insisted. "You probably know everything there is to know about me. You could at least tell me something about yourself."

He paused, then shrugged. "There's not really much to tell."

"Hey, Rift!"

I turned. Another rebel was striding towards us. His ebony skin was offset by a number of white tattoos, and he didn't appear bothered by the rickety platforms. The way he leaned on the rails and swung himself from one point to another suggested he was completely at home up here in the rafters.

Rift grinned at the newcomer. "Elijah! Good to see

you." He strode forward and the two clasped forearms in greeting. "Here to help?"

Elijah laughed. "As if you'd need it. Nope, just stopping by. I'm on my way to see Edith about getting these platforms repaired. Been a while, and seeing as I spend a good amount of my life up here, I'm an advocate for routine maintenance."

"Ha. Good luck with that," Rift said. "I'll see you around."

"See ya," Elijah replied. He glanced at me before he turned to go, and I could read the suspicion in his eyes. Not surprising. As a rule, most of the Rebels either viewed me with distrust or all-out hatred.

I sighed, turning back to Rift. "Wait, what's that?" I asked, taking a step closer. Something dark had appeared across Rift's wrist. I could have sworn it wasn't there a minute ago.

Rift followed my gaze. "What, this?" He held out his wrist for inspection. A circular tattoo made of intricate, intersecting whorls of ink was already beginning to fade. "It's called the Circlet. Each of us has one."

"Each of the people in the Resistance?"

He nodded. "It's how we identify one another. Go ahead," he added when he saw me hesitate.

Trying not to appear too eager, I took his wrist and rubbed my thumb over it curiously. "How do you get it to appear and fade like that?"

"Reactive ink," he said. "It only appears when held

over the same type of ink."

"Like when two Rebels clasp forearms," I murmured, continuing to marvel over at the design as it faded. "That's incredible!"

Rift's yanked his wrist out of my grasp as he staggered backwards.

"What?" I asked in alarm.

"It's not possible," he said slowly. "Did… did you just pay me a *compliment*?"

"Compliment?" I wondered. "What are you talking about?"

He continued to grin stupidly at me.

My eyes widened. "You mean *you* came up with this?"

Rift took a small bow. "A few years ago. Took me a long time to perfect it."

I glanced back at his wrist, but the design had now faded entirely. I had to hand it to him, the idea was brilliant. What better way to ensure that fellow rebels could recognize one another without their enemies being able to do the same? And holding Rift's wrist had brought another question to mind…

Looking down at the archways below, I frowned. "Rift, how do you and Torque and the others use the Telepoints that are linked into the Grid? You don't have trackers, do you?"

"Not the same as the ones issued by the Globe, if that's what you mean," Rift replied, not looking up from his work.

"Then how do you get past the scanners and the guards?"

Rift looked up. "Our wrist trackers are programmed to be able to switch identities." Smiling, he tapped his leather watch with the end of his wrench. "Each of us has some sort of watch or jewelry or something of the like. We use them to communicate with one another. There's also a slot in the back where we keep several identity chips. If I need to swap who I am for whatever reason, I can just take one out, hold it over my wrist tracker, and it uploads my new identity."

"But what if someone realizes what you're doing?"

He laughed. "The Globe has enough to keep itself busy without resorting to checking every person's accessories as they go through the Telepoint queues. As long as the scanner beeps and pulls up an identity profile, the Officials tend to be satisfied. Those few of us who go out regularly each keep at least three or four ID chips on hand in case we run into trouble. Now if you'll excuse me, all other questions will have to be put on hold until I can *figure this thing out*," he said, glaring down at the innards of the panel system.

"Have you tried punching it?"

He laughed and pushed his hair out of his face. "Don't tempt me."

A lock of his hair fell back toward his face, and I couldn't help noticing again what a handsome face it was.

The thought unsettled me. It was bad enough that I'd found him attractive when I thought he was just Henry, a server hired for the evening. Knowing that he was a Rebel bent on bringing down the entire Elite society made the realization even more pointless.

I turned away from my unwelcome thoughts and busied myself watching the activity below. The Resistance really was like a hive of bees, each one intent on his or her objective. Everyone seemed to have a job, and even those who were lounging around chatting with one another would eventually say their goodbyes and stride purposefully off to wherever they were needed. How long had all of this existed? Decades? Rift had mentioned that the Atrium wasn't the only base of operations, but it alone was clearly vast. To gain this kind of foothold and secrecy would require incredible resources.

A hand on my shoulder caused me to jump. "Geez, you're on edge!" Rift said.

"If I'm four stories in the air, you can bet I'm *always* on edge," I snapped. "I guess this means you're done with your tinkering?"

"For now, I hope," he replied. "Come on, let's get you back downstairs while you still have control over your bladder."

....

Back in the Dining Hall, I glanced over at Rift. He was leaning against the far wall chatting with Avienne. She'd stopped by to deliver a message from Kade. She laughed at something Rift had just said, laying a hand on his shoulder. It was a move worthy of Orelia's playbook.

My throat tightened. "I didn't realize they were an item," I said to Torque, trying to sound less churlish than I felt. I should have suspected it earlier on. Avienne, like Orelia, boasted that incomparable brand of beauty that all men seemed unable to resist.

"What?" Torque asked. He lowered his sandwich and turned in the direction of my gaze. "You mean Rift and my sister?" He gave a short, derisive laugh. "What would have possessed you to think that?"

I turned to him, equally astonished. "But yesterday when Marius threatened her, he said something about not seeing her brother or her boyfriend around while you two were busy in the Sparring Ring..."

A look of understanding passed over Torque's face. "Ohh. Well, it makes sense why you would've thought that, but it's most definitely not the case." He took an impressive bite of his sandwich and continued, despite the mouthful of food. "Mariuth wavn't talking abou' Rift." He swallowed. "He was talking about Kade."

"Wait a second. Avienne is with *Kade*? As in the leader of the entire Rebellion, Kade?"

"The one and only," said Torque. "They've been together going on two years now. Bit of an age gap, but down here it's not too big a deal in the grand scheme of things."

"Wow." I tried to imagine the stiff, formidable Kade being affectionate, but it wouldn't compute. Saying Avienne was dating him was like saying she'd begun a whirlwind romance with a telephone pole. But then again, I'd only met the guy yesterday. "I guess I just assumed..."

"It's a fair assumption," Torque granted. He glanced toward his sister and best friend. "When we first got here, Avienne developed a bit of a thing for Rift. Not that it got her anywhere," he added. "He's not an easy egg to crack."

"Why's that?" I asked.

Torque looked up from his work. "Has Rift told you anything about himself?"

I shook my head. "I asked, but he said there wasn't anything to tell."

For some reason, Torque found this hilarious. He doubled over his tray, his laughter bouncing out across the room. Several people looked around at us in search of the source of the noise.

"Did I miss something?" I asked irritably.

"I'm sorry," Torque said, wiping a tear from one eye. "It's just that sometimes he really does have a sense of irony." Several more chuckles shook his chest before he continued. "It tends to catch me off guard."

I frowned. "I don't get it."

His laughter having subsided, it was Torque's turn to shake his head, white hair sweeping across his brow. "If Rift wants you to know about himself, he'll tell you, but don't hold out for a monologue. He keeps things closer than most." He swallowed the last bite of his sandwich and wiped his hands on his pants. "I wonder if they've got anything good for dessert…" He pushed himself up from the table and shot me a parting wink before striding across to the serving line. He gave Rift a friendly clap on the shoulder as he passed.

I chuckled to myself as I fished out a steaming spoonful of stew. Torque certainly was a character.

"That looked like a fascinating conversation."

I looked up as Rift slid into the seat Torque had just vacated. "What did you say to send Torque into spasms?"

I shrugged, causing the stew to slip off my spoon. "Honestly, I'm still not sure what it was that set him off."

"What was the topic?" he asked, absently pushing a few loose curls behind one ear.

I felt a blush creep into my cheeks. "You, actually," I replied, not looking up from my studious appraisal of my food.

"Really?" he asked. "Find out anything good?"

I shook my head. "More the opposite."

His eyebrows shot up. "That bad?"

I laughed and shook my head again. "I just meant that I didn't find out anything at all."

"Perfect. I prefer being an enigma," he said, stretching his arms out in front of himself and rhythmically drumming his fingers against the table. "Keeps people guessing."

"Seems a little lonely," I said. "Not letting people in."

Rift's fingers stopped their tapping.

"I'm sorry," I said, worried that I might have overstepped some unspoken boundary. "I have a bad habit of blurting things out before I stop to think."

He paused. "Those are the statements that tend to be the most honest," he said quietly. "The ones we don't bother to censor." His stony expression reminded me of the castles we had studied in our Ancient History course at the Academy—surrounded by impenetrable walls with narrow slivers of windows, encircled by moats, guarded day and night by soldiers.

But with a sigh of resignation, a thin crack appeared in his walls. "You're right I suppose," he admitted. "But loneliness does offer its own form of protection."

"Protection?" I repeated, my brow furrowing. "From what—?"

Rift stood abruptly. His mouth had fallen into a hard line. "I'd better go. I've got a few other stops to make. Torque will keep an eye on you."

He strode away before I could respond, leaving me feeling like a fool for prying.

Torque strolled up with a napkin piled so high with brownies that it looked like a chocolate skyscraper. "Looks like you had quite the fruitful talk there," he said. "Best friends now, are you?"

I rolled my eyes. "You were right. He's about as open as a fifty foot dam."

"Told you talking wouldn't come to much. But it appears you took my advice and turned it into your own personal challenge," he said. "Don't take it personally. He's like that with almost everyone."

"Almost everyone?"

"Well, myself being the obvious exception," he said, flashing a grin.

"You're really close with him, aren't you?"

Torque's grin balanced out—not fading entirely, but instead settling into a smaller, more honest smile. "As far as I'm concerned, he's my brother just as much as if by blood. I'd do anything for him, and I believe he'd do the same for me."

"You're lucky to have such a loyal friend," I said. With a pang, I thought of Prewitt and Gemma. What must they be thinking? For all they knew, I was dead in a ditch somewhere. I immediately tried not to dwell on how plausible that fate might turn out to be, depending on what the Rebel leaders elected to do with me. Rift had mentioned that they would make their decision by the end of the night…

Torque's voice yanked me back to the present. "I am lucky," he agreed. "Even if said friend isn't prone to lengthy, heartfelt conversations." He glanced down at my barely-touched stew. "You're obviously not hungry. Why don't we find something more…*stimulating* to do?"

I narrowed my eyes at the tone in his voice, but it only made him laugh. "Just messing with you, princess. But seriously, it's supposed to be my day off. Let's get out of here. Want to see the gym?"

....

I spent the next two hours watching Torque beat up punching bags and climb rock walls, followed by a visit to the Hospital Branch where Dmitri checked on my progress. I would have expected Rift to return by then, but he was still absent when we headed back to the Dining Hall for dinner.

Even there, Rift was nowhere to be found. I wound up at a table with Torque and Avienne, in addition to the rigid, serious-looking Asian woman called Ming and kind, quiet Mateo from the day before. Ming said little to me, as she was deep in conversation with Avienne when Torque and I arrived, but Mateo opened up the longer we stayed. He wound up telling me a little about how he had joined the Resistance. His mother and sister were killed in the factory where they had worked. According to Mateo, many of the Globe's factories didn't bother trying to meet reasonable safety standards. When the building caught fire, there had been far too many workers and far too few exits. "Some of the women tried to use bolts of fabric to climb down from the upper windows. A few made it, but most of them fell," he whispered.

I could tell from the way his voice died away that telling the story had resurrected a fresh wave of grief. Had his mother and sister fallen from one of the windows? Had they been suffocated by the smoke, or worse, burned to death? Each possibility was more horrific than the last.

"After the accident," Mateo murmured, "I wanted justice. I wanted the Globe to answer for their indifference toward the lower class. They don't see *people* when they look at us. They see tools. But it was at the funeral that a friend told me about a rumor he'd heard...rumor of an uprising."

Later that afternoon as I walked back toward my little room in the Hospital Branch, escorted by Torque and Avienne, I was beginning to worry that I had pushed Rift even farther than I'd thought when he rounded the corner just ahead of us.

"Sorry that took so long," Rift said, more to Torque and Avienne than to me. "R&D can be a nightmare sometimes." He glanced toward me, then back to his friends. "Why don't you two take a break from guard duty? I can take her back from here."

It sounded more like a request than an offer. The Guerriers nodded to him, Torque throwing a curious glance back at us as he and Avienne walked down the hall.

Rift watched until they disappeared down another tunnel. "Come on," he said. "I have something to show you."

CHAPTER SEVEN

"You're quite the multi-talented guy," I noted as we walked. It was my second attempt to break the awkward silence.

Rift didn't say anything, so I continued. "Inventing reactive ink, recalibrating the hydro-whatever cooling thingies, fixing tech-kinks in the Control room, putting out proverbial fires all over the place..." I listed, tallying off the jobs on my fingers.

"I guess it does sound like a lot," he admitted, "but it's all under the banner of the same position."

"And what position is that?"

He was silent for a moment before shooting me a sideways glance. "How about a trade: a question for a question?"

I shrugged. "Fair enough."

"All right." He paused, maybe for effect. "I'm the head of R&D."

"Huh. That's not as dramatic as I expected."

"Well, all of the department heads are also advisors on the Atrium's Council. Oh, and I'm something along the lines of Third-in-Command."

I came to a halt mid-stride, which resulted in a comedic stumble. "*You?* You're not only the head of an entire department, but you're also Third-in-Command for the entire Atrium?"

"Well, head of R&D for now," he amended. "I finally got Kade to let me start training a replacement so I can transition into working as a field agent full-time. It's taken a lot of convincing. I never really wanted to be stuck in research to begin with, but Kade saw I was gifted in that area and wanted to put me to good use."

"And the Third-in-Command thing?"

"It's not an Official title…more honorary than anything. Kade would have made me his Second, but for some reason he's got it in his head that I'm reckless…" Rift said with a smirk.

"But—you can't be more than twenty!"

Rather than confirm or deny my estimate, he gave a one-shouldered shrug. "Okay, you got your question. Now it's my turn."

"What could you possibly want to know about me that you didn't already learn from weeks of spying on my family?"

"Your hair," he said simply.

That took me by surprise. Of all the things he could have asked the daughter of his enemy, he chose my crazy hair? "What about it?" I asked.

"The rumor is that it's naturally that color," he said, pointing to where it cascaded past my shoulders.

"I don't hear a question yet."

He rolled his eyes. "Is it true? That it's naturally blue, I mean."

"Mhmm."

"Wow." He lifted a hand. "May I?" I nodded.

He reached out and took a strand in his hands, leaning in more closely to examine it. I chuckled at his intense expression. "This must have been what I looked like when you showed me the Circlet," I said. His hair was right beneath my nose; it smelled faintly of sandalwood. I had to resist the random urge to reach out and touch one of the soft, loose curls.

"That's amazing," he said, rolling a piece between his thumb and forefinger. He studied it for a long moment. Longer than I'd anticipated. Longer than seemed necessary. Finally, he dropped the strand and cleared his throat, glancing up at me. "And they have no idea why?"

His face was closer to my own than I'd realized. Warmth crept into my cheeks. I swallowed and shook my head. "Nope. If they did, maybe I could have figured out a way to get rid of it."

"Get rid of it?" Rift frowned. "Why would you want to do that?"

"Try to imagine growing up in an Elite family, going to the Academy Honoratus, and being the only one with an unnatural hair color. I can't count the number of times I've been called a—" I broke off, realizing what I'd been about to say.

Rift gave me a wry look. "A Dreg?"

I winced. "I don't like using that term. Unfortunately, most of the people I know don't share the same qualms about it."

"It's not a big deal. At least not to me," Rift said with a small shrug. "So, you wanted to fit in?"

I laughed. "That's an understatement. Once, when I was twelve, I snuck out to a hair salon after school and had them dye my hair a deep, chocolate brown." It had been the same shade as my mother's hair—like rich rivulets of cocoa. I still remembered the strange thrill I felt looking in the wide salon mirror and meeting the gaze of the ordinary girl who stared back at me, my eyes now the only trace of blue to be seen. This was a girl who could go unnoticed, easily lost in a crowd. This plain little girl might manage to fit in, or at the very least *blend* in, among the other Elite children of the Academy. But most of all, this girl looked as though she might actually belong to the illustrious Croft family.

In a world split into High and Low classes, we Crofts occupied the topmost tier of the upper class. While wild and unconventional hair colors were a norm among the lower class, people like my mother labeled such things "outlandish," along with other superficial quirks such as tattoos and piercings.

"What did your parents think?" Rift asked.

"Well, when I skipped home with a toothy grin and my hair dyed to match my mother's, I had expected them to be pleased—possibly even relieved—that I finally fit the part of a Croft." I gave a snort that would have made my etiquette teachers cringe. "Their response was very much the opposite."

"They were upset?"

"They were *furious*. They dragged me back to the same hair salon and demanded that the stylist reverse what she had done. The poor woman hurried to bleach out the brown while Mother and Father watched like impeccably-dressed hawks. I still remember how her hands shook as she went about the process. She was planning to follow up with a blue dye after the bleach had done its work but, somehow, my hair automatically reverted to its original blue."

Rift's eyes widened. "But how is that possible?"

"You tell me. How is it possible for a baby to be born with blue hair in the first place?"

He shrugged, and I could tell from the way he pursed his lips that it was going to nag at him. "I guess your parents were happy with the result?"

"Very. Father even paid some exorbitant amount of money for a new lacquer treatment that would prevent me from attempting to repeat the process—at least until my hair

124

grew out a considerable amount. My hair was blue once more, and blue it would remain." I shook my head, fingering a steely-blue wisp. "I had been so sure that dying my hair would make my parents happy."

"Did they ever explain their response?"

I shook my head. "Not exactly. One day, I actually mustered the courage to broach the subject. My father only said, 'You're an enigma, Ambry. Rarity equates to value.'" That was all he ever seemed to care about: wealth, status, and power. He had collected unique and covetable objects as far back as I could remember, from priceless works of art to ancient scrolls written in long-dead languages that he had no real desire to learn. But it was that day, the day I dyed my hair, that I realized a sobering fact: I was nothing more to my father than another rare specimen to add to his collection. Even my name, *Ambrosia*, the mythological "nectar of the gods," was a testament to my parents' endless quest for power and immortality.

Rift's jaw tightened. "He didn't understand."

"Didn't understand what? That I was trying to make him happy?"

"No, not that," said Rift. "He didn't understand that he already had the most valuable thing he could hope to get."

"What's that?"

"A family," he said. "And a daughter who cared enough about him that she was willing to change who she was to please him." His dark eyes bored holes in the wall ahead.

"Do you have family?"

Rift opened his mouth, but said nothing. I'd clearly caught him off guard. He tried to recover with grin. "You already had your turn."

"Maybe we could make another trade?" I suggested.

"Maybe," he said. Then, as though he'd just realized that we were standing directly in the middle of a corridor, he took my arm and continued in the direction we'd been heading. "Maybe one day, when all this is over, I'll tell you about them."

We snaked our way through several more tunnels before arriving at a heavy, imposing door. It looked thick, like the door of a bank vault. The kind of door that made you want to just keep moving, ominous enough that it seemed to scream *KEEP OUT* all on its own.

Next to the foreboding door was a small keypad. Rift reached up, his fingers flitting across in a way that suggested an acute muscle memory of its combination. When he'd finished, the screen lit to a bright blue. He pushed down on the lever of the door. "After you, Madame," he said, sweeping out his arm.

I stepped in ahead of him into a small room lit with a blue light similar to the one on the keypad outside. It was emanating from a series of cylindrical objects organized along the walls and across several long tables. They ranged in size from the length of my forearm to the length of my fingernail. And there was something oddly familiar about them… "What is this place?" I asked.

"You could say it's an extension of our armory." Rift strode toward one wall. "Actually, I'd have thought you of all people would recognize them."

I picked up one of the smaller objects. "It's funny, they sort of look like…" I clapped a hand over my mouth and stared at Rift, letting the tiny cylinder clatter back onto the table. I swore under my breath. "They're *time capsules*," I whispered. I didn't need Rift to tell me I was right; I recognized their soft, eerie glow. It had been a long time, but I could still remember Father taking me to the Forum when I was a little girl and showing me one of them. I turned to stare around the room. There were *so many* of them. "But where—how—" I stammered. "How did you get them?"

"From some unlucky Officials," he said, lifting a larger cylinder from its metal stand. "The Timekeepers have been issuing these to all of them in exchange for their cooperation on certain political matters."

I snorted at such a ridiculous idea. "You've got it wrong," I said, shaking my head. "Most Officials have never even *seen* one of these, let alone been issued one."

"That may have been the case in the past, but things have changed a lot in the past couple years." Rift carefully laid the cylinder back in place. "And I'm sure the Officials go about their work with much more confidence knowing that should things turn nasty, they could just activate one of these suckers and *presto*…" he waved his arms with dramatic flair.

I raised an eyebrow at him. "The Officials answer to the Globe, not the Forum. The Timekeepers have no say over their assignments."

"Ha!" Rift exclaimed. "Please. They answer first and only to the Timekeepers."

"There's no way the Globe would let the Timekeepers have that kind of power," I insisted. I found myself actually becoming frustrated the more he spoke. "We're talking about the world's military and law enforcement! They answer to the Government, not a random branch of researchers with one limited area of authority."

Rift looked at me with genuine surprise. "Ambry, you know the Global Government is just a front for the Timekeepers themselves."

I blinked at him. Then, I started to laugh. "Wow. That's hilarious, really. And you even managed to look so serious when you said it!"

His returning smile flickered and faltered like a dying candle. "Come on, Ambry. You don't have to pretend here. We've known the truth for a long time." He gestured around him. "That's why we exist. To expose the truth; to put power back in the hands of the people."

I waited for him to put a cap on the joke, but he gave no such indication. "Look Rift, if you want me to play along, you'll be waiting a long time."

Rift's surprise changed to concern. "Wait. You—you really don't know? But…" he stammered. He shook his head and ran a hand through his unkempt hair.. It was the first time I'd seen him at a loss for words. "I guess I just assumed that since your father was one of them, you'd know…"

His worried expression was starting to unnerve me. "Rift, come on. It was funny at first, but now it's getting ridiculous. Everyone knows that the Timekeepers are just appointed to oversee the research and use of the time capsules; they don't have control over what goes on in cities and states and nations. That's what the Globe is for."

"*Just* to oversee use of the time capsules?" Rift asked in disbelief. "Ambry, these capsules are the most powerful weapons on the face of the planet!" he said, gesturing around the blue-lit room. "Do you really think that the people who wield them are subservient to anyone else?"

Some of my mirth began to fade. Did Rift actually believe what he was saying—that the Timekeepers, including my own father, had more power than the Global Government? "It's not possible," I told him. "The original Timekeepers weren't after world domination. They didn't even claim their positions for themselves! They were elected by the governing authorities of more than thirty nations—"

"The Timekeepers were *self*-appointed during a time of worldwide civil unrest," Rift said. "We're too young to remember the chaos brought on by the Global Alliance, but ask anyone old enough and they'll tell you there was panic, hysteria… the whole world on the verge of collapse. The leaders of the fledgling Global Government were in a bind,

and the scientists who had been studying Imhoff's work—
who knew his secrets on how to operate the capsules—
offered them a deal. In exchange for usage of the time
capsules, they would be given the ultimate say in matters of
global importance. They would, in effect, be given twenty-
four thrones from which to rule."

"But the Timekeepers appointed after the first
group… like my father," I began. "They go through an
election process every six years. I know; I've seen the work
my father puts into his campaign!"

"And who counts the tallies?" Rift asked.

I opened and closed my mouth like a fish out of water.
"But…"

He went on. "Even if those elections were open for
every citizen in the world to have a vote—which you know
they aren't—how on earth would ordinary people like us
know the true score of the polls? "

I shook my head as though to dislodge his words. "No,
we learned about the first Timekeeper election when we
studied the Peace Accords…"

"You *studied* them?" Rift laughed scornfully. "Where?
At that Academy of yours? The Brainwashing Factory for
Elite Youngsters?" He began to pace. "Who writes the
history textbooks, Ambry?" he demanded.

I knew the answer to that. It was inside the back cover
of every textbook Honoratus gave us. There would be an
author's name, and then the same words printed after each
one: *Certified Research Specialist, Informational Dept., G.G.* The

Academy had always taught us that the only sources to be trusted were those with the Globe's Official stamp of approval. "I…" I sputtered, feeling off-balance.

To make matters worse, Rift's concern now veered dangerously close to pity. I really hated to be pitied. "Ambry… you've really believed all this time that your dad and the rest of their lot were elected?" He shook his head, auburn curls accosting his face. "That's just what they want us to think. That's what they *have* to make us think in order for things to go on as they are, with the Globe gaining more and more control over our lives with every passing year. For goodness sake, Ambry, even the Globe's initial formation was built on lies!"

"What are you talking about? The Alliance was created because every scientifically-advanced country in the world had nukes trained on at least three others!" I retorted. "It was a last resort to avoid a third World War!"

"Ambry," he said seriously. "The government *lied* to us. There was no nuclear threat."

I gaped at him. "What?"

"That was just the excuse they had the media spew so that the world's citizens would get on board with the creation of one worldwide government," he said.

I bit my lip, trying to come up with a response to what he was saying. I wanted to tell him he was wrong, that there was no way the Forum and the Global Government could have managed to deceive an entire world full of logical, intelligent people.

Then I thought back over the course of my life. Even in the mere six years since we had moved to London, so much had changed. Now there were laws that prevented most open cultural celebrations, even those that pertained to religious groups. The festival in Chiang Mai was one of the few left, and part of the reason I'd gone to such great lengths to attend was because I doubted it would last more than another year or so. If people wanted to celebrate their ancestry or their beliefs, they could do so—but only in the privacy of their own homes. And even that was discouraged. The Globe wanted to unite the world under one banner... one free of differences.

Differences bred hostility. Differences started wars.

I'd heard that many years ago, people were allowed to speak openly about their religious and political beliefs. Prewitt had even heard rumor that it'd been one of America's founding freedoms. Of course, it was hard to prove thanks to the Data Purge that had taken place some time before I was born.

It was hard to wrap my mind around the concept. Voicing one's beliefs was a veiled form of intolerance, which of course was wrong and hurtful...wasn't it? Obviously, anyone could think whatever they wished in their own minds, but there was no reason to push those thoughts on others.

But even as I followed the mental train of these arguments, a word rose in my mind. A simple question that had often bobbed to the surface during dinner conversations with my family or lectures at school, or even talks with Gemma and Prewitt. I knew that questioning one's authority was disrespectful, so I had never allowed it to remain there for long. And yet, here it was again:

Why?

I tasted the question. I let it marinate in my mouth and seep down into my bones. The question burned into my marrow, and the many areas it had begged to address came bubbling up. Why did speaking about beliefs have to be considered intolerant? Sure there were people out there who would persecute others who thought differently than them, but did voicing one's heart and mind always have to be malicious?

And why did differences have to be dangerous? Why couldn't they be beautiful and profound and unique, like the people who held them? And why were the only "accurate" and "trustworthy" sources those stamped with a silver-embossed globe?

Why were lower-level Officials now carrying time capsules and using them to capture teenage runaways?

Who *did* have access to the poll results of each election? What if they could be tampered with? *Or even faked altogether…*

Rift's eyes were sad when I finally lifted mine to meet them. "I'm sorry, Ambry."

I suddenly felt very tired. I leaned back against the wall and sank down until I reached the floor, drawing my knees in close to my chest and hugging them.

Rift slowly stepped toward me. He lowered himself until he was sitting beside me on the floor a hand's breadth away. He didn't say anything. He allowed me to sit quietly, absorbing the horrible truth.

He didn't comfort me. He didn't try to tell me it was going to be okay. That would have been a lie.

He just kept me company as my world fell apart.

I don't know how long we sat there in silence. When I finally spoke, my throat felt dry and my voice weak. "Can you prove all this?" I asked.

He looked at me for a long moment, then nodded. "We have videos… recorded calls… emails. It's hard to keep something this big entirely in the dark—even for the Global Government and the Forum. But more importantly," he added, "we have high-level witnesses who have confessed the truth."

I stared at him. "Who?"

"Several members of the Globe who defected. One was Executive Assistant to the Vice Consulate at the time… quite the scandal for the Globe to cover up. But the most pivotal witness came forward about six years ago," he replied. "His conscience got the better of him, I suppose. And he had hoped that with his testimony, something could be done to stop those at the Forum before they went too far. It's because of him that we have some of those videos and recordings I mentioned earlier."

"Was he a member of the Globe?"

"In a manner of speaking," Rift said. "He was a

Timekeeper."

"A Timekeeper *defected*?" I asked, shocked.

Rift nodded. "Had to fake his own death to get away."

I whistled. "Whatever he did must have been pretty bad to leave the Forum."

"You'd feel guilty too if you'd assassinated Consulate Augustine."

"*What?*" I gasped. Consulate Augustine had been one of the best leaders the Globe had ever had, widely beloved and trusted. "That's not possible! Consulate Augustine died of a stroke! I remember watching it on the news when I was six or seven years old."

"A stroke caused by an untraceable neurotoxin slipped into his afternoon coffee during a visit from this Timekeeper," Rift said quietly. "He came to us soon afterwards… seems his conscience got the better of him." I stared at him for what felt like a long time. Something cool and wet on my cheek startled me. I hadn't realized I was crying. My hands tightened into fists at my sides. "Why?" I asked at last. "Why would they want him killed?"

"Because Augustine had changed his views. He no longer supported one global banner under which everybody thought and acted the same way. He wanted to maintain cultural traditions—even rebuild the ones that had deteriorated under the weight of the Globe. He was even going to promote freedom of speech." I could see Rift's eyes spark at the idea. "Augustine said that under the guise of tolerance, we were being stripped of our identities… that under the guise of freedom, the world was being enslaved. It's all on one of the recordings our informant provided…"

Something in me snapped as I lifted my head to fix Rift with a hard gaze. I was done being lied to. I was done swallowing every story I was fed. "I want to know the truth," I whispered. "About everything."

The corner of Rift's mouth lifted. "Everyone deserves the truth."

CHAPTER EIGHT

I shut my eyes, but sleep fought me off as though I were pitted against it in my own mental sparring ring. I knew that Rift was right outside the door keeping careful watch, but I still felt horribly exposed in the small, sterile room. Just the thought of Marius and his goons still prowling the premises sent a shiver down my spine.

Rift had delivered on my request for the truth. After our conversation, he'd taken me to another corridor of the Atrium, one of those crisscrossed with ominous beams of green light. He'd then entered a long, complicated passcode comprised not only of letters and numbers, but of lines and shapes as well. Immediately, the beams of light evaporated to reveal a solemn black door at the end of the hall.

The Resistance Archives.

We spent the next hours poring over files, phone recordings, videos, emails, and a number of other incriminating pieces of evidence, all of which verified everything Rift had explained. The murder of Consulate Augustine, the rigged elections of the past several decades, the approved time capsule usage in a number of questionable political situations, all splayed out before me proclaiming the crimes of the Global Government—and of the Timekeepers who had given the orders. I even got to read the written testimony of the Timekeeper gone rogue, known throughout the Resistance as "The Informant." Rift was careful not to reveal his true identity. "As I mentioned before, he had to fake his own death. Otherwise he would've been hunted down by Globe Officials and executed for treason," Rift explained.

I scanned the papers. Whoever the brave soul was, he had recounted his own involvement in a number of top secret missions resulting in the death of dozens of high-profile people. A Forum-level assassin. Not only that, but the Archives listed dozens upon dozens of atrocities committed by the Globe. Each one had been carefully covered up, often by framing those who opposed them. More than fifty zealots—probably early members of the Resistance itself—had been charged with the Globe's own crimes by the Globe itself and were subsequently sentenced to a life in the

Catacombs.

A part of me—the girl who had been raised in a privileged Elite family, who went to Florence on summer holiday and spent her winter breaks skiing in the Alps— was devastated. How had I grown up nurtured by such heinous lies? *Well, that's easy*, I thought. *The Academy conditioned us not to ask questions.* It was maddening to think that the system had done everything in its power to brainwash my entire generation. Even in those rare moments when I'd allowed myself to doubt, I would remember the dangers of asking too many questions and revert back to the prescribed answers drilled into us by the Academy.

Now, however, things were suddenly and starkly different. Now I had real, tangible answers. I no longer cared that I didn't fit into the system's mold. I didn't want to fit. If being an outcast meant fighting against the lies that were enslaving my world, then social rejection had just become my highest aspiration.

A voice outside startled me out of my thoughts, deep and commanding. It was Kade. I could only hear bits and pieces of what he was saying, but my throat constricted when I heard my own name.

Slipping my feet down over the side of the bed, I crept toward the door, gently pressing my ear against the cold steel.

"Look, Rift, as much as I dislike it, we really have no choice. Ambry presents a danger to our entire operation."

"But I'm telling you Kade, she's on *our* side," Rift

insisted. "When I showed her the Archives—"

"A move that could have cost us some of our most valuable evidence," Kade interrupted, his voice growing angry.

"—she was shocked," Rift continued. "She had no idea about *any* of this!"

"I know you think she's different, Rift, but can we really risk everything we've fought for on the hope that she switched sides overnight? Her own father is a *Timekeeper*, remember? And family allegiance tends to run deep." There was a pause, and when Kade spoke again, most of the anger had left his voice. "Don't act as though you didn't see this coming. You knew from the beginning that our only options are to keep her here as a constant flight risk, or to send her home with all memory of the last three days Wiped."

I clapped a hand over my mouth. They wanted to Wipe my memory? My breathing came faster as I fought back a rising tide of panic, each breath heating my palm. I had heard of memory wipes being used before, but only on high-level criminals. Well, that or people who knew too much. The machines used to perform the complex procedure could isolate and erase specific events in one's memory, or eradicate larger periods of time altogether.

"Kade, there has to be another way," Rift said, disapproval evident in his voice.

"You know that if there was, I'd be taking it," said Kade. "But my hands are tied, Rift. The safety of everyone in the Atrium takes precedence over the memories of one girl."

There was a pause. I thought I heard Rift sigh. "Fair enough," he agreed. "But at least let me be the one to tell her."

"No one has to tell her," Kade replied. "I'll have a medic back here within the hour to give her a sedative. They can administer the Wipe while she sleeps. Then we'll get her home and it will be as though none of this ever happened."

Kade's words echoed in my mind as though they'd been shouted into an empty auditorium rather than spoken on the opposite side of a door. *They can't do this to me,* I thought wildly.

I couldn't just sit around waiting for them to dig through my brain and steal everything I'd finally learned. I couldn't go back to a life woven out of lies.

Somehow, I had to escape.

"I have to be at a meeting at Gloria's place in twenty minutes," Kade was saying, "but I'll speak with Dmitri on the way out."

"I'll walk with you," Rift said.

Footsteps halted. "Abandoning your guard post?" Kade asked. He sounded surprised.

"There's one more thing I need to talk with you about before you leave," Rift explained. "Besides, I'm sure the door will be able to hold her for at least five minutes."

Kade barked a laugh. "It's reinforced steel. It should be able to hold her for five *years* if necessary," he said, his voice growing fainter.

I listened with one ear pressed to the door as the sound of their footsteps died away. When I was sure they were truly out of earshot, I released the sob I'd been holding back. Leaning against the door, I sank down until I was sitting on cold tile. Go back to my flaccid, mind- numbingly boring life at the manor? Sit through hours, days—*years*—of endless lectures at Honoratus, all the while being pruned and preened by the Elites like my father's overpriced rhododendron bushes?

Just the thought of returning home robbed of the past three days sent my stomach into Torque-worthy flips. How could I keep going about my routine oblivious to the existence of him and Avienne... Kade... Cody and Juliet...

Rift.

No. Losing all of it wasn't an option. But how was I supposed to break out of a tiny room with no windows and only one door, which locked only from the outside? Gritting my teeth, I banged my head back against the door in frustration...

... and all of a sudden found myself falling backward into the hall.

I pushed myself up and looked around, completely at a loss. I turned to stare at the door. My head must have hit the push-handle.

That would mean that Rift had left the door unlocked. How could he have been so careless?

Celebrate your extraordinary luck later, I thought. I

scrambled to my feet and began heading to the right, in the opposite direction from the Arrival Room. *If I steer away from the parts of the Atrium I've already seen in the past two days, maybe I'll run into the exit tunnels Rift mentioned.* At least, that was my off-the-cuff logic.

I walked down the corridor quickly, but not so quickly as to draw attention to myself. I yanked the hood of my sweater up over my hair and stuffed several flyaway strands beneath the fabric as I went.

Most of the hallways I passed through were unoccupied. The few Rebels I did pass were too intent on their own duties to notice the hooded girl who strode purposefully past them, darkly-clad just as they were themselves.

My first few tries were met with several dead ends. Each time, I was forced to backtrack and try a different branch of tunnels, and each time left me more desperate. I finally came to the mouth of a new tunnel where the air felt cooler than it had before. I broke into a wide smile. If there wasn't as much heat in this branch of the underground Rebel system, it suggested that the branch either wasn't used often or it was only passed through briefly.

Both explanations pointed to a possible exit.

With the hope of escape now within reach, I picked up my pace until I was jogging down the narrow tunnel. It snaked its way ahead for several hundred yards before opening into what looked like an abandoned subway station.

Repressing a cry of delight, I saw about a dozen

motorbikes parked on the tracks.

I scrambled down onto them—careful to favor my uninjured arm—and approached the closest bike. Of course, I had no idea how to operate it, but that was the least of my worries. How hard could it be?

I slipped one leg over the bike and settled onto the seat. There was no visible keyhole, which meant the bike must have an alternate method of ignition. I was making a quick study of the commands on the dash when a hand grasped my arm.

Horrified to have come so close only to be caught at the last second, I swiveled in the seat, ready to send a swift punch into my pursuer's face.

"Easy!" Rift cried. He released my arm before I could twist it away.

"Don't touch me!" I snarled.

"Ambry, it's all right, I just—"

"I won't go back!" I whispered. Fury and fear mingled in my voice. "Not so you and your Resistance can erase the last three days of my life! This place, the things I've found out here…" I had no words, only a thousand battling emotions. "I can't just go back to living the same life in the same routine! I can't—" To my dismay, I felt hot tears begin to spill down my cheeks. "I don't want to *forget*."

Rift stared at me with dark, piercing eyes. Slowly, he raised a hand. I'd seen him spar with Torque; there was no way I could overpower him. I flinched and closed my eyes. I waited for his hand to tighten around my arm again, a vice grip I knew I wouldn't have the strength to break. This made it all the more surprising when I felt the pad of a calloused thumb brush my cheek as he captured a stray tear.

My eyes snapped open, and his brown held my blue. "No one should be forced to forget," he said quietly.

"But you followed me—?"

"I'm not here to take you back, Ambry."

"You're... you're not?" I shook my head, trying to dislodge my confusion. Steel-blue strands of hair fell into my face. "But I heard you talking with Kade. You agreed it was the only option."

Rift frowned. "Stealing memories shouldn't be an option to begin with, let alone the only option. I have no desire to adopt Timekeeper practices. But if I hadn't played along with Kade's decision, I never would have been able to get him out of the way."

"Then what are you doing here? And how did you find me?"

He rolled his eyes. It was annoying that he could make even such a sarcastic expression attractive. "I couldn't just let you traipse off on your own. One wrong Telepoint and you could end up smack in the middle of the Baltic Sea. And no, I'm not kidding. As far as finding you goes, I put a tracker in a hidden slot in your boots."

I glanced down at my black leather boots with reproach.

Rift gave my arm a nudge. "Now move over before you get set that thing off and flatten us both."

Still not daring to believe my own luck, it took me a moment to register the command and scoot backwards on the bike to accommodate Rift. He slid a leg over the seat and shifted his weight. There was suddenly very little space between the two of us. I swallowed. "So you're escorting me home?" I asked, not quite sure where I ought to put my hands.

"Someone has to." He rested his left hand palm down over the control panel, and the engine revved to life. "By the way, the ignition on these bikes is specifically engineered to respond only to the Circlet. You couldn't have gone far on your own," he said, shooting me a grin over his shoulder.

"Whose idea was that?"

"Mine," Rift replied. He reached a hand back and took hold of one of mine, pulling it around to rest against his stomach. "You'll need to hang on tight."

The bike growled beneath us as he shifted it into gear. He swung it in a tight semi-circle and I scrambled for a better hold around his midriff. I could feel the muscles ripple beneath his shirt as he laughed. Pointing the bike toward the left-most tunnel, he spurred the machine forward.

As we sped ahead, the air flying past my face smelled musty and metallic, like old iron mingled with damp earth. Rift bypassed the first Telepoint and veered off to the right down a smaller vein of the underground maze. Another portal appeared within seconds, and we shot straight through the arch.

Our surroundings instantly changed. The

subterranean tunnels were gone and we emerged out onto a road lined with tall palm trees. Crystalline ocean waves glittered on either side of the highway as far as I could see, their rolling crests frothy with sea foam. I had to lean forward to catch Rift's voice in the wind as he yelled to me. "This is my favorite segment of the drive!"

"Where are we?" I shouted back. It was always disconcerting to think we could have been transported to anywhere on the planet in a fraction of a second. Judging by the sun's position, it must have been noon-ish in whatever hemisphere we now occupied.

Rift shook his head as the wind whipped through his hair. In the direct sunlight, I could see the red undertones more clearly beneath the loose curls. "Not important!"

I smiled. I suspected that I'd always disagree when he said that.

We followed the roadway for what I judged to be about ten minutes. Once I had gathered the courage, I released my death-grip on Rift's torso. I reached out one arm at a time for the handholds on either side of the bike and leaned back, allowing my pallid skin to soak in the sun's warm rays. The aromas of salt and fish filled my nose, bringing back memories of summer trips to the Mediterranean where Orelia and I would build lopsided sandcastles just out of the sea's reach.

But my mind wrenched back to the present as a tunnel appeared in the distance ahead. "The road goes beneath the water until it connects again with land," Rift shouted.

"And we're following it?"

"Not exactly!" he shouted.

I didn't like the sound of that. "Rift..."

"You'll want to grab hold of me again. We're about to go off-road!"

I blanched. "There *is* no off road!" I yelled, shocked that I should need to state the obvious.

But Rift didn't pay me any mind. I followed the direction of his gaze.

A crane sat above the tunnel's entrance balancing a metal beam high over the ocean's lapping waves. As the tunnel drew closer, I saw a ramp off to one side that appeared to be under construction. A sign guarded the ramp's entrance with a warning: "DO NOT ENTER." The incline continued about fifty yards beyond the sign in an upward slope before cutting off abruptly in mid air.

"Don't worry, I've done this at least a dozen times!"

I realized what he meant to do about two seconds before it happened. "RIFT!" I screamed.

But it was too late. Rift jerked the handle to the right just before the tunnel. We shot straight for the "DO NOT ENTER" sign.

I crushed myself into Rift's back, bracing for the impact. When none came, I opened my eyes just in time to see a shimmer of silver as we passed *through* the sign. *It was a hologram*, I thought as it disappeared behind us like a desert mirage.

Rejoicing at the close call averted, I wrenched my

gaze forward.

It was a mistake.

My stomach collided with my lungs as the bike's tires left the pavement. We careened for the metal beam in front of us. For one harrowing moment, we hung suspended in mid-air. The only wild thought in my head was that we would at least clear the beam, leaving us to crash into the churning waters below.

But once again, I had steeled myself for an impact that didn't come. Instead I felt the tingling sensation of a Telepoint as the brilliant sunlight overhead evaporated. Rift brought the bike to a screeching halt on the dirt path of a densely canopied forest.

He let down the kickstand and allowed the bike to sit idling. He placed his hands gingerly over my own, peeling back the fingers that had clawed into the skin of his abdomen. "Ambry?"

I didn't reply. I was too busy trying to slow down my breathing. With slow, shaky movements, I extricated myself from the strangle-hold I had on Rift. He caught me as I stumbled off of the bike.

Clinging to his proffered arms for support, I managed to stutter, "W—we're alive?"

Rift chuckled. "It appears that way."

Once a wave of vertigo had passed, I was able to let go of him long enough to shove him backwards. "You could have *killed* us!"

Rift yelped, stumbling to regain his balance. "I told

you, I've done it a dozen times!"

I scowled at him.

"You have to admit, it was a rush," he said with a lopsided grin.

I opened my mouth to protest, but paused as I remembered the thrill of hurtling through the open air. He was right—it had been just as exhilarating as it had been terrifying. But all I could say was, "If I weren't up to date on my medication, the shock alone might have done me in."

"Medication?" Rift frowned. "For what?"

"Hypertension."

"So high blood pressure?"

I nodded, sitting down on a nearby log to catch my breath. "I've had it since I was a kid."

His face tightened in scrutiny. "You don't seem like the usual case subject for that."

"And you would know this because...?"

"Well, for one thing, you're in good physical condition," he said. "You got excellent scores in your all of your Physical Education classes, and I know you're an avid runner."

"You do, huh?" I said. "So you all were spying on me?"

Rift strode back toward the bike. I was oddly pleased to see him massage his chest in the spot I'd shoved him. "We had eyes on your house for over a month leading up to the mission itself. I saw you leave several times when things got… heated with your father."

I rubbed my arms, aware suddenly that the climate in the forest was far from the tropical weather we had just left behind. "So that's how you knew about the garden exit?"

He didn't reply, but nodded. "Look, I'm sorry if I frightened you. We have to make at least one segment of each route to the Atrium hidden enough or dangerous enough to discourage unwelcome guests."

"So there was a Telepoint on that metal beam hanging out over the water?"

"Yeah. That was Torque's idea," he added with a grin.

"Why is it that your all's ideas always mean trouble for me?"

"You say trouble." He hopped back onto the bike and patted the seat behind him. "I say 'intrigue.'"

I couldn't help it; I laughed at his mischievous expression in spite of myself. I pushed myself up from the fallen log and ambled back over to where he stood balancing the bike. "Was that the last death-defying segment of the ride?"

"It's smooth sailing from here on out," Rift said. "I promise." He revved the bike once more and set off at a fast but comfortable pace through the trees.

Towering oaks and pines flashed by on either side. It brought back memories of the old black-and-white film reels I'd seen in my eighth year History of the Arts class, the moving pictures flashing in and out multiple times in a single second as they danced across the screen.

As promised, the rest of the ride was straightforward enough. There were no further aerial stunts required—just a brief Telepoint into a crowded Asian marketplace before one final gateway that opened onto a street I recognized as being in Southwark. Even so, I slipped my arms around Rift's torso once more as we flew across the Tower Bridge and allowed myself to lean against him, my cheek resting just above his shoulder blade.

I was so comfortable that by the time we finally wound our way up to Hampstead Heath, my eyelids were becoming heavy. Rift had to say my name at least twice before they fluttered open. "Ambry? We're just down the street from your house," he was saying. "I'm glad we made good time, too. Otherwise you might have slipped right off and into the Thames."

"I didn't realize how tired I was," I murmured, covering a yawn with the back of my hand.

Amusement played across Rift's face. "I can see that," he chuckled.

I suddenly realized that my arms were still wrapped around his waist. I quickly let go and leaned back in the seat. "Thanks for bringing me back."

"It was the least I could do, really," he said, using the toe of one leather boot to draw out the kickstand. "After all, you're the only reason I got out of the Croft compound in the first place. In a weird way it makes sense that I should return the favor by getting you back in."

A sudden fear twisted my stomach. "Won't Kade and

152

Torque be upset with you?"

"Oh, I'm sure they'll have plenty to say when I get back," he said, crossing his arms. "Kade will probably lecture me for an hour or so about the consequences of my rash actions. Torque will inevitably throw things and shout some obscenities, maybe take a swing or two at me. But they'll be all right. They never stay angry with me for long."

"I'm sorry," I said. And I found that I genuinely meant it. "I didn't mean to get you into trouble. Especially with Torque. I know he's like a brother to you."

"I get into trouble with or without assistance. No need for you to feel guilty about it," Rift said. He raised an eyebrow. "Besides, I'd be disappointed if this were last time I did something to send Torque over the edge."

I laughed, but a question arose that had been niggling at the back of my mind since the forest. "Rift," I began. "Why *did* you bring me back? I mean, I know that you didn't think that wiping my memory ought to be an option, but you could have kept me there. Why let me go when I know so much about the Rebellion?"

For a moment, he didn't speak. Perhaps weighing his words. "It was a gamble I was willing to make," he said, a note of finality in his voice. I wondered if he might still be trying to convince himself that he'd made the right decision.

"It's more than a gamble," I pointed out. "If I were to tell my father anything about what I've learned in the past three days—"

"But you won't," he interrupted. There was a surety

in his voice, and something in his expression reminded me of the night I'd helped him and Torque escape. It seemed like an eternity ago, but I could still see the plea in his eyes.

Once again, he was making himself vulnerable to me, allotting me faith that I by no means felt I deserved. "How can you know that?" I asked.

He took a step towards me. "Because I trust you."

I shivered. Somehow those four simple words held more power over me than any amount of threats or demands could have in their place. I knew in that moment that I would rather die than betray Rift's trust. "What should I tell them?" I asked, my breath like a puff of white cloud floating in the air between us. "They'll ask me where I was."

A small smile flitted across Rift's face as he held my eyes. "As little of the truth as possible without getting yourself into any trouble. If you tell them you didn't see who broke into the house, they'll know you're lying." He gave a short, derisive laugh. "I can just see them now, hooking you up to some sort of outdated polygraph test."

I shuddered at the image. "So what do you suggest?"

He rubbed his chin. "You can tell them you saw us escape out the gate and the wolves accidentally marked you as a target—though I'd leave out the bit about you being the one to obliterate the console."

I laughed. "That *might* be wise," I agreed.

"Which explains why you had to run," he continued. "Maintaining a certain amount of truth in your story will help to blur out the fabrications. Open, blatant lies are easy to spot."

It was unsettling to hear Rift talk so casually about weaving together lies with truth. I wondered how practiced he had become in that art. "What about the past three days?"

He shrugged. "You were injured, needed time to recover, scared that the wolves were still targeting you... I'm sure you'll come up with something convincing."

I nodded. The chilly night air had begun to seep through my thin shirt. I folded my arms over my chest.

Rift must have noticed. "I would offer you my jacket, but that might stir up more questions."

"That's all right," I said. "I should head inside anyway before someone sees us talking. They might have people roaming the neighborhood looking for me."

"Right." Rift looked like he wanted to say more, but he snapped his mouth shut as though thinking better of it. "Goodbye then." He turned on his heel to go.

"Wait," I said, letting my arms fall to my sides.

He slowed, pivoting back to face me. "Forget something?"

I hesitated, feeling the blood rush into my cheeks. "What if I need to find you again? I mean, how would I contact you?"

His dark brows rose. "You mean if you decide to leave everything behind and join the Resistance?"

I laughed. "Yeah, sure. Why not?" I tried to make the

words sound as offhand as possible, but the suggestion left me strangely elated.

"Hmm." He reached a hand into the pocket of his jacket. For a moment, I thought he might be searching for the small notebook he'd pulled out that morning. But after digging for a moment, his hand emerged clasping a small, oval-shaped object. "Use this," he said, walking back to me and holding it out.

I took it in my palm. It was a pale, light-weight stone. Scrutinizing it, I could see the Circlet emblazoned in dark whorls on one side.

"There's a club in Soho called The Rebel's Song. If you ever need me, show this to the bouncer named Felix and tell him you want to speak with Curls the Brave."

"Curls the Brave?" I repeated with a snort. "Is that supposed to be you?"

"It's a nickname he's taken to calling me by. He's been using it for so long that I doubt he even remembers my actual name," he explained without a trace of embarrassment. "The Resistance helped out him and his family a few years ago. Show him the stone, and he'll summon me for you."

"I take it you'll use a more direct route to get there than the one we took tonight?"

"Tonight I took special precautions. A quick jaunt to Soho won't arouse any suspicion on the Grid." He was close enough to me that I could smell him—a mixture of leather and salty sea water from the ride. "Don't hesitate to use it if necessary. I'll be there, day or night. Got that?"

It took me a moment to realize that he was expecting some sort of answer. My mind wasn't functioning properly. I had been too busy studying the color of his eyes, which were like rich, fertile soil. I felt drawn into their warmth. It cut through the chilly night air and the exhaustion I'd been fighting to repress. Without thinking, I found myself leaning towards him.

Rift's jaw tightened, spreading his mouth in a thin line. I felt a sudden pressure against my shoulders as he held me at arms length. "Ambry, I—"

An ache filled my stomach. "Don't," I said, flushing as I turned away. *I'm an Elite-class idiot,* I thought, chiding myself for my own stupidity. Was it actually possible to die of embarrassment? If so, I was in mortal danger. "Don't apologize. I'm sorry. I should go—"

At that moment, shouts echoed from the other end of the street. Both of us jerked our heads toward the noise.

"Officials," Rift said.

"Hurry, go!" I whispered, pushing him toward the bike.

Rift hesitated, but the shouts drew nearer, a chorus of howls joining the cacophony. He gave me one last rueful glance before sprinting for the bike. The motor jarred to life and he shot forward into the darkness of the alley.

I stared after him even as the yells drew closer. The gray hood of my shirt was down, and the strength of the full moon's rays lit my hair to a silver-blue sheen. It wouldn't take them long to recognize me.

Sure enough, within seconds I felt the grip of strong hands on my arms, steering me forcibly toward the compound. I hadn't even begun to consider what my parents were going to say when I got inside, but it didn't matter anymore. My thoughts were elsewhere, speeding alongside a motorbike ridden by a wild youth with copper-colored hair and earth-tinted eyes.

CHAPTER NINE

I was trapped in a waking dream.

Or nightmare, perhaps, I thought as I stared unseeing out my bedroom window later that same night.

When I'd arrived back at the compound with an entourage of six armed soldiers, my mother had burst into tears, exclaiming over the state of my injured arm and bruised face and hideous wardrobe choice. While my mother fussed over me and had Charlie call for a medic, my father had assaulted me with a thousand questions. Several were regarding whether I was all right. The rest were tailored to where I had disappeared to for the past three days. "So the thieves ran directly past you, and you can't even describe them?" he asked for the third time.

"It was dark, Dad," I repeated, also for the third time. The family medic, Dr Evans—a thin man with thick glasses atop a thin nose—hovered around me like an anxious butterfly, assessing the damage I'd done to myself. He'd been with us long enough to understand my father's insistence on discretion, so I didn't feel the need to censor my story. "And it's not as though they just strolled past me. They were sprinting, remember?"

Titus slid a hand down over his face. "So you didn't run in the same direction as them?"

"Why would I run *with* them?" I asked, sounding for all the world as though it were the dumbest idea ever conceived rather than precisely what I'd done. "They had just robbed my house!"

He nodded, running a hand absently through his golden hair. Titus Croft was a highly logical man and was therefore ready to accept the most rational explanation. Fortunately for me, my actions Saturday evening had been completely *illogical*. Helping Rift and Torque escape and subsequently running away with them went against every bit of common sense, so in this case, my lies proved far more palatable for him than the truth. "Very well. And how exactly did you escape the watchdogs?" he asked, his blue eyes narrowing.

I swallowed. I had decided early on to follow Rift's advice and insert snippets of truth wherever possible to add

160

credibility to my story. Still, it felt strange to describe Rift's actions to my father, even in anonymity. "One of the thieves used some sort of tool to sear the gate shut, so that held them off for a few minutes while we all ran for it. I ran south, hoping to get to a Telepoint, but I was sprinting so fast that I didn't watch where I was going and ran straight into the road. There was a car coming—it didn't have time to stop," I said, gesturing to the still-slightly- bruised half of my face.

My mother's hands flew to her mouth. "You were hit by a car?" she repeated in shock. One of her bejeweled hands held mine, the other stroking my head. Both were shaking. I met her eyes, so like my own, and suddenly realized how worried she'd been about me. With a pang of sympathy, I found myself wishing that I didn't have to lie, that the wall between my parents and I could somehow be breached.

But the memory of a hand clamped tightly over my mouth as I choked down the lavender pill shouldered aside my compassion. I swallowed and tasted bile. "Honestly, it was luckiest thing that could have happened to me," I said. "It knocked me unconscious, and an ambulance rushed me to the hospital. They used a Telepoint to get me there, which apparently broke the watchdog's tracking signal on me." I glanced down at my wrist, thankful for the miracle of local anesthesia as Dr. Evans used a handheld device to cauterize the skin over my newly-implanted tracker. My father had ordered a new one to be delivered immediately after my return. No doubt he wanted to be sure of my every move from here on out.

Titus was still pacing back and forth next to the bed. "You *were* lucky. That was the only thing that could break their mark once it was set." He sighed again and sat in the chair opposite my bed. "Well then, that explains half your absence. Why didn't you come back home once you regained consciousness in the hospital? And don't tell me it took you thirty-six hours to get to the nearest Telepoint," he added, a dangerous note in his voice.

"Because there were at least two genetically-enhanced monsters on my trail," I replied, narrowing my eyes at him. "And at the time, I had no clue that going through a Telepoint could knock out their tracing signal. Would you really expect me to waltz out into the open when I didn't know whether they were still following me?" I demanded.

My father had no answer for that, but muttered something incoherent about at least letting them know I was alive.

"We're just glad you *are* all right. Aren't we, darling?" said my mother, giving him a sharp, meaningful look.

Titus shifted in his chair. "Yes, of course dear," he echoed.

Dr. Evans tapped his clipboard. "I think it would be best if we could let her rest now," he advised.

Mother nodded to him before he slipped out of the room. She ran a delicate hand through my hair. "Will you be all right on your own?" she asked.

162

"I'll be fine, Mom. Thank you," I said, feeling numb.

Her hand squeezed mine. She stood and moved toward the door, brushing past my father. He looked as though he wasn't through with his questions, but she took his hand and dragged him out behind her before he could continue his interrogation.

Once the door had clicked shut, I fell back against my pillow and sighed heavily. Only an hour back home and I already felt claustrophobic. I wished that Prewitt or Gemma could come by, not because I needed to talk about what had happened—I doubted that I could explain even if I wanted to—but just to have some distraction. *At least I'll see them at school tomorrow*, I thought hopefully.

Although a part of me wanted to stay as far away from Honoratus and any other Globe-affiliate as possible, the draw to see my friends was proving stronger. It had been...

Wait. How many days *had* it been?

I did some quick mental calculations. The Gala had been on Saturday night, so I had been unconscious from then until sometime late Monday morning. I'd spent the rest of Monday and the next day in the Atrium before escaping with Rift, which would make this Tuesday night.

Shivering, I eased myself out of the bed and crossed to the closet to grab a wool sweater. I slipped it on and was headed back to the warmth of my bed when I caught a glimpse of the mirror in passing. I backtracked several steps and paused, my eyes narrowing at my own visage.

The girl staring back at me was barely recognizable.

This girl seemed older... harder. She had the same heart-shaped face and icy-blue eyes, but the leftovers of a black-and-purple bruise blossomed out from the stitches along her temple. At least it was smaller than it had been the day after I woke up in the Atrium.

How could so much change in the span of three days? I felt as though the rug had been pulled out from beneath my feet only to reveal that there had been no floor below it to begin with—just a gaping black hole, no gravity, and now I was expected to maintain my footing in the sudden vacuum of my newfound knowledge.

A sudden knock on the door startled me. "Ambry?" called a familiar voice.

My hand fell away from where it had flown to my chest. "Come on in, Prew."

He opened the door and stepped in cautiously, then blinked in surprise. "You're out of bed already?"

"I'm not dead," I said with a wry smile. "How did you convince my parents to let you in?"

"It wasn't hard. I just explained that I was going to sit there patiently on the front porch and sing some Frank Sinatra classics until they let me talk to you," Prewitt said seriously. "I don't think they believed me at first, but after I got through a few choruses of '*Fly Me to the Moon*,' they welcomed me right in."

I attempted a smile. It made the bruised side of my face ache. "I knew I heard something earlier, but I thought it was just a cat being strangled."

Prewitt assumed an offended expression. "I thought you loved my singing voice!"

This statement alone would normally have sent me spiraling into fits of hysteria—we both knew full well that Prewitt's singing might one day be labeled a military- grade weapon—but I could only force out a half-hearted chuckle that sounded more like a cough. I turned back to the window.

"Hey, what's wrong?" he asked, moving between me and the glass pane. "What happened to you? Come on Ambry, you know you can tell me."

"I... I was pretty sick," I said lamely. "Tried to get up to get some water the other night while I was still feverish and fell down the stairs." Lying to Prewitt was more difficult than lying to my parents.

Sure enough, Prewitt's eyes narrowed. "Liar." He looked from my arm to the bruise blooming along my hairline. "Now if you were to tell me you went back to Chiang Mai and got mugged by a gang of street performers, I might believe you. But sick? Ambry, you haven't been sick since we were twelve!"

"Prew, please," I pleaded. "Just drop it, okay?"

"You disappear for three days without a word, and all I get is some ridiculous excuse that you were suddenly and mysteriously so sick that you couldn't pick up a phone? What really happened to you?"

"I don't want to talk about it, okay?" I snapped, surprising both of us. "Just leave me alone!"

Prewitt looked stunned. His jaw hung slightly open and it was a moment before he could reply. "Whatever you say." He stood and marched to the door, shoving it open. The resulting *slam* echoed into the outer landing. I heard the stairs creak and a moment later the sound of the front door being thrown open.

Glancing down through the window at the front lawn, I saw Prewitt's gangly frame storm across the yard, his hands shoved deep into the pockets of his jacket.

It had to be done, I thought. Even so, my heart sank as I watched him trudge down the street. Prew was the one person I normally told everything, but this was one experience he could never understand.

Prewitt wasn't a rebel. He always followed the rules to the letter—unless, of course, he was tagging along to keep me out of trouble. What was I supposed to tell him? That I'd just spent several days in the central headquarters of a secret rebel group that wanted to take down the Global Government and the Forum itself? That I now felt almost more allied to the Resistance than to my own family? To our own social class? Not only would he be frightened for me, but I would also be giving him information that could put *him* in danger.

Besides... Rift had trusted me.

Better Prewitt just continue to think I was being a royal jerk. After all, one of the many good things about our friendship was that it was impossible for him to stay angry with me for long.

166

....

The next morning, I discovered just how much I had taken Prewitt's patience for granted.

He refused to speak with me for the first half of our classes. Gemma didn't have a clue about what had happened the night before, but only commented with a theatrical roll of her eyes that Prewitt had been in a bad mood all morning and advised me to avoid him until he stopped being such a downer.

By lunchtime, I literally had to drag him out into the courtyard (with my uninjured arm) before he would even look me straight in the face. "Prew, look at me!" I demanded. He kept turning his head to avoid my eyes until I finally grabbed him by the nose. "I'm sorry, okay?"

He glared at me. "Led go ub by dose."

"Only when you finish letting me tell you what a jerk I was to you and how you have every right to be upset with me," I said, not releasing my grip.

My open admission of my jerkiness seemed to placate him. "Fide, otay. Dow will you *please* led go?"

"Sure." I dropped my hand.

Prewitt rubbed his nose, but was now making eye contact with me willingly. "Does this mean you'll tell me where you were for three days?"

I sighed. "It's not that I don't want to tell you, Prew. I just can't. Can you accept that for me?"

He didn't say anything. finally, he raised a hand and

brushed the skin under my bruised eye. "It would be easier if you hadn't shown up looking like someone beat the living tar out of you."

I smiled softly, wincing as the scab on my lip was stretched. "Nothing a couple weeks won't fix."

Prewitt's brow furrowed. "So you're really asking me to pretend nothing ever happened? That I wasn't out of my mind with worry for days wondering if you'd been kidnapped, or worse? That I didn't bike through half of London and traipse in and out of a dozen of the nearest Telepoints trying to figure out where you'd gone? I went to *Mongolia*, for goodness sake!" he said, throwing out his arms. "And now I just have to act like everything's fine when my best friend is standing in front of me, and she's broken?"

His words sliced through me, and I suddenly realized what he'd gone through. How would I feel if the situation were reversed, not knowing for days whether Prewitt were dead or alive? I'd be completely terrified. I would have probably done the same thing he had, running through every Telepoint I could find—despite the fact that most of them constantly change destinations—rummaging through every back alley in the worst parts of every major city hoping not to find a body, and all the while knowing that the world was just too big to have any real hope of finding him. Using my good arm, I pulled Prewitt into a hug. "I'm so sorry, Prew," I whispered.

At first he stiffened, but after several seconds had passed, his arms tightened around my waist. Warm, strong, familiar arms that somehow made me feel safe, even with all I had experienced. All I now knew.

I felt him sigh. "If it's what you really want, I'll let it go," he murmured. "But please Ambry, promise me that you won't pull something like this again?"

I nodded into his shoulder. "Believe me, I didn't have a choice."

"Okay, you *cannot* just go saying things like that and not expect me to ask questions!"

"Sorry!" I said, holding up both hands. "Okay... you don't ask, and I won't blurt out random details to stir up your curiosity. Deal?"

"Deal," he agreed, taking my good arm in his as we strolled back into the cafeteria.

Gemma came prancing up to us. "So, looks like you've managed to cheer up Grumpy Dwarf."

Prewitt glared at her.

"Or perhaps not," Gemma amended, turning instead at me. "Anyway, I never got the chance between classes to ask where you've been! Your parents called mine a couple nights ago in a panic wondering if you were at my house. What happened?"

"I, uh... I got into an accident," I mumbled. "Spent a couple days in the hospital."

Gemma's eyes widened. "Were you in a car crash or something?"

"Sort of. I, um..." I shot Prewitt a pleading look.

"She told me she didn't really want to talk about it,"

169

he said, stepping up and putting an arm around my shoulders.

"Oh, of course. Sorry," said Gemma quickly. "Still, you couldn't let your parents know where you were?" she asked.

"I was unconscious at first, but I called them when I woke up," I lied.

Prewitt glanced down at me, but didn't say anything. Gemma nodded. Her perfectly plucked eyebrows were raised in skepticism, but she said nothing else on the matter. "So, are you two planning to come to Philippe Roche's party on Friday night? It's going to be at his family's lodge at a ski resort in the Swiss Alps," she said, clapping her hands together. "The Telepoint lands you right at the top of the Rinerhorn, so there's no actual hiking involved, thank God."

"That's fortunate," I said, my mouth twitching. The idea of Gemma hiking anywhere was ludicrous. I could almost picture her attempting to scale a snow-capped mountain in a chiffon dress and four-inch pumps.

"I know, right?" she agreed. "And Philippe says they have five private slopes we can use! Not that I plan to ski, of course. I'll probably stick close to the heated pool. But it's still impressive, isn't it?"

"Very," Prewitt said, exchanging an amused look with me when Gemma looked away to wave to someone.

"So, are you guys going to come?" Gemma asked. Her dark eyes widened into sad, pleading saucers.

I hesitated. "Um, I doubt my parents will want me going anywhere for a while." This time, I was one- hundred percent sure that I was stating the truth. "They'll probably keep me on a short leash for the next few weeks."

"Aw," Gemma groaned, looking crestfallen. "What about you, Prew?"

"I'll think about it," he said carefully.

"Fantastic!" she exclaimed, perking up as though he'd promised to attend. "Well, I have to go talk to Samantha Crawford. She mentioned she already knows the big surprise that Philippe has planned for the party and I'm determined to squeeze it out of her!"

As we watched Gemma flounce away toward the corner window table, I had a brief moment of sympathy for Samantha Crawford. That is, before remembering that it was Samantha who had told half the school about our capture in Chiang Mai. I turned back to Prewitt. "Do you really think you'll go?"

He shrugged. "Probably not, but I'll let her think I might until the last second so she doesn't have time to change my mind."

"You're a wise man," I mused.

Prewitt glanced over my shoulder. "Whoa! We've only got five minutes before have to head to Physics. We'd better get something to go." Sitting at the nearest table, Prewitt waved over one of the servers. "Two turkey and provolone sandwiches please," he ordered.

The server nodded and strode toward the kitchens. As

I watched him walk away, I noticed that his dark hair was pulled half-way back, like Rift's had been on the night he helped me escape from the Atrium.

Prewitt spoke up, breaking me from my reverie. "Just one last question, and I swear I'll put the whole thing to rest," he said.

"All right," I agreed, my stomach still fluttering as though I'd swallowed a dozen butterflies.

He ran his fingers through his tawny hair. A nervous habit. "I know you can't right now, but do you think someday…will you ever be able to tell me what happened?" he asked, his brow furrowed.

I paused to consider this. "I can't say for sure," I began, "but there will probably come a time when I *have* to tell you," I said, surprising myself. Ever since that monumental conversation with Rift back in the Atrium, I had known in my heart that life couldn't continue as it had before. I couldn't be the same person. Not after finding out the truth. Now my mind suddenly caught up with what my heart had known all along: I couldn't come back. Not to this life, not to my normal routine. Whether I liked it or not, Prewitt would eventually know what had happened to me because, eventually, I would break out of my gilded cage and stretch my wings.

I would no longer be able to hide who I'd become.

The server returned with our sandwiches. As we gathered our things and headed out of the cafeteria, I glanced up at Prewitt and felt my chest tighten. There were so many things in my life that I would be happy to give up to aid the Resistance: family, school, social standing. But I'd been so focused on what I *was* willing to give up that I hadn't considered what I wasn't.

And walking down the hall next to my best friend, laughing and joking as usual, I began to realize just how much I stood to lose.

....

Thursday passed in much the same way as the rest of Wednesday: in a haze of boredom and culture shock. I took in very little of my lectures. Professors Kim and Ndala were quick to note the change in my classroom diligence and strongly advised me to "pull myself together" to avoid falling further behind. But there was nothing they could say to deter the mental images that arose from the pages of the Archives: photographs of factories set ablaze to burn incriminating evidence, with half-burnt bodies scattered through streets as ash fell like snow; the innocent faces of the men and women sentenced to never again see the sun for crimes they didn't commit; dozens of forensic photographs depicting the victims of Globe assassins, culminating in Consulate Augustine himself.

Professor McCullough, our Ancient Civilizations teacher, cut me some slack. He made no remark whatsoever as I stared unseeing out the window at the drizzling rain that ran in small rivulets down the diamond- patterned panes. If

I unfocused my gaze, I could see my reflection faintly in the leaded glass—that same cold, hardened girl who had stared back at me in the mirror of my room after I'd returned from the Atrium. The girl with the bruised face. The girl with the stormy blue hair and blank, staring eyes.

The girl who knew too much.

When the bell rang, I realized with only mild dismay that I hadn't heard a word of McCullough's lecture, though the screen displays suggested it had something to do with Druid burial sites. I picked up my unopened textbook, shouldered my bag, and trudged toward the door.

"Miss Croft?" called Professor McCullough.

I turned. "Yes, Professor?"

"Are you all right?" he asked. His high forehead was creased, eyebrows knit close together. "You didn't seem quite yourself today."

"Me? Oh, yes, I'm fine," I said, summoning up a smile that felt false on my lips. "Just fell off my horse when my family and I went riding a couple days ago." That was the Official story my father had requested I stick to, and the one I'd already delivered to three other teachers. A neat, tidy accident worthy of a Timekeeper's daughter.

"Oh. Sorry to hear that," he said, his eyes flitting to the bruises along my forehead. "Well, I hope you'll take it easy this week as you heal. If you need an extension on the assignment, don't hesitate to ask."

"Thanks, Professor," I replied, this time with a more true smile. "I think I can manage it though."

McCullough returned the smile and nodded his head before going back to shuffling through the essays we'd just turned in. I shouldered my bag and hurried off to meet the others.

While Gemma and Prewitt were discussing their notes for the upcoming test in Organic Chemistry on our walk home, I spotted a boy who couldn't be more than five years old. He was begging beside a crippled man sprawled out on a dirty mat whose legs were set at an unnatural angle that made my stomach twist. A sign scrawled on a waterlogged piece of cardboard in the cripple's lap read, "*Spare change? Any bit helps.*" Had they normally been there on our walks home? Or was I only now willing to take a good look?

Prewitt and Gemma chattered on without a glance toward the dregs. Slowing my pace, I lagged behind to drop a few coins in his hat. The boy cracked a grin, and I suddenly wished I had more to give. I would've dumped out my entire savings on the spot had it happened to be stashed in my school bag. I dashed back to Prewitt and Gemma before they had time to note my absence.

As we neared our usual Telepoint that would transport us each back home, I noticed two twenty-somethings approaching each other on a street corner. One had long, purple dreadlocks tied at the back of his head and a series of white tattoos lacing the dark skin of his face, the other with short black hair and several lip piercings. Reaching each other, they clasped forearms. I thought I saw the black-haired boy's eyes dart down for a split second, and

I wondered if he caught a glimpse of a Circlet engraved in reactive ink.

By Friday, I was dangling at the end of my fraying rope. My father could barely stand to look at me—whether out of disgust or guilt, I couldn't say. Mother, on the other hand, practically burst into tears whenever she caught sight of my bruised face. Orelia was even less keen to be associated with me than usual, avoiding my eyes in the hallway even when we passed so close that I could have brushed shoulders with her.

In addition to these familial unpleasantries, I had been forced to explain my injuries to several dozen people at the Academy, not to mention having to suffer through a steady stream of creative new insults.

That afternoon, I was standing at my locker with Prewitt when I heard a deep voice thunder through the hall. "Look, Rocco!" a boy from our Trig class called to his brother, pointing at the bruises that still discolored half of my hairline. "Now she's the *black*-and-blue freak!"

Clumsy and unsubtle though his joke was, it proved to be a breaking point.

That's it, I thought, slamming my locker shut. I swiveled around and prepared to drop-kick him so that our faces could match.

But I was spared the trouble.

Prewitt had planted himself firmly between me and my verbal assailant. "Cut it out, Dante," he growled.

"What are you doing?" I whispered. It was one thing

to endanger myself, but the thought of Prewitt getting thrashed on my account was another thing entirely. "Come on Prew, it's not worth it. Let's get out of here," I said, yanking on his sleeve.

"Yeah, Lindstom, you wouldn't want to embarrass yourself in front of your girlfriend," Dante crowed. He flashed a perfect row of white teeth, offsetting his dark Italian skin. "She's got enough to be embarrassed about as it is."

Several of his friends snickered. A small crowd of onlookers had begun to gather around us.

Prewitt shrugged my hand away. "Bruises fade, Dante. At least neither of us will have the lifelong embarrassment of having to buy our way into Honoratus," he said with a meaningful glare.

Satisfying as it was to watch Dante and Rocco's tan faces turn a lovely shade of puce, I found myself shrinking back. The unspoken layers of Prewitt's jibe hung heavy in the air, like the sort of humidity that leaves people practically drinking oxygen: *You may be rich, Dante, but you're still a lower class than us. We are the children of Timekeepers. Your parents had to shell out a substantial fortune to get you two into the Academy.*

I never flouted my Timekeeper parentage, but in his doing so, Prewitt couldn't have picked a more effective way to slap Dante in the face without lifting a finger.

Dante narrowed his eyes. He took two steps closer. "What did you say, Lindstrom?"

"Didn't realize you were deaf as well as dumb," Prewitt said in a low voice.

"Prew, *stop*," I hissed. Dante was one of the strongest fighters in the school, and he didn't bother with fighting clean either. He'd probably sent as many people to the infirmary as Torque had sent to the Atrium's hospital branch.

Dante growled. "You're going to regret that." His fist flew, but Prewitt ducked the punch and swung one leg around, knocking Dante's feet out from under him, sending Dante crashing to the floor. The burly Italian was up again in a flash, twenty times angrier than he'd been before.

But Prewitt's salvation came from the shout of a familiar voice. "What's all this? Get to your classes, all of you!"

The crowd parted as Professor McCullough strode toward us. "You too, Dante," he growled. "And I'll warn you, I don't mean five minutes from now." For a middle-aged man, Professor McCullough was in surprisingly good shape. His biceps caused the silk of his button-down shirt to tighten as he crossed his arms, and he glared at the Montanari brothers from beneath a heavy brow and short military haircut. Our tenth-year class had once watched him spar against our martial arts instructor, Akito, in a kickboxing class. The match had been fairly even, with Akito winning only by a hair.

Dante looked as though he remembered too. He glared momentarily at Prewitt and I before stalking off, followed closely by Rocco and Tate. I had grabbed Prewitt's arm and was about to follow their example, but Professor McCullough blocked our way. "Not so fast, you two," he said. "Although I admire your courage, Mr. Lindstrom, I'd strongly advise you to be a bit more selective with your adversaries," he said sternly. "And next time you pick a fight, make sure it's off of Academy property."

Prewitt lowered his head, his face reddening. "Sorry, Professor."

Professor McCullough gave him a hard look. Suddenly, he reached out and clapped Prewitt on the shoulder. "No apologies necessary. I'll ask you not to repeat this, but I look forward with great enthusiasm to the day when someone succeeds in bringing the Montanari's down a peg or two."

Prewitt nodded. "Right there with you, sir."

"Good lad. And Miss Croft?" he added as they turned to walk away.

"Yes, sir?" I asked, pausing to look back.

"I'm glad to see you're on the mend," he said. "I know you've been met with a good deal of resistance since your return, but it's good to see you acting like yourself again."

"Thanks, Professor," I said as he began walking back down the hall. I wondered whether it was some weird form of withdrawal or merely paranoia that made me think his voice had lingered ever-so-slightly on the word *resistance*. I grabbed Prewitt's arm once more and dragged him outside, eager to get out of the hallway. "What were you doing?" I asked once we reached the marble benches. "Dante and Rocco could have destroyed you!"

Prewitt rolled his eyes. "Nice to know you have such faith in me," he said.

"Well what do you want me to do, tell you that you could have beat them? Prew, you're a decent fighter, but they're the most dangerous guys in the Academy. Not to mention the two-to-one ratio they had in their favor!"

Prewitt didn't say anything, but his expression made me close my mouth. His face was drawn as though I'd just struck him. He shook his head. "I'm going to class. I'll see you there."

I stared after him as the glass doors closed in his wake, a transparent partition that mirrored the separation I felt between us. It was the second argument we'd had that week. I couldn't even remember the last time we'd argued. *Well, he did put up a bit of a fight during our little trip to Thailand,* I thought, running my fingers down the spine of my Quantum Physics textbook. But that hadn't been anything out of the ordinary. This arguing on the other hand, this was different. My stomach twisted at the thought of sidling into my seat next to him in class knowing he was still upset with me.

But what if I didn't go to class? I wondered.
What if, instead, I just left altogether?

There had never been an option before. There had only been my family, Honoratus, Gemma and Prewitt—

180

nothing else. I had never deviated from my socially-approved routine during school hours. But now, well... now I knew more. Now secrets had opened up and swept me away into a cause I believed in, and that cause was directly opposed to everything my family stood for. I felt as though I had walked directly into the spiderweb of my decision. Enmeshed in my hair, tightening around my brain, it demanded an answer.

I couldn't just stroll back into the Atrium. Kade and the other commanders had already decided that I knew too much, and they were prepared to steal those memories away from me at their first opportunity. But what other option was there? The life I once lived in ignorance was over. I knew that. Wringing out a blue strand of hair, I sifted through ideas, desperately searching for a way out until something finally struck a chord.

Rift.

I had almost forgotten his last instructions before he'd sped off. *It would just be him*, I thought. I wouldn't be going back to the Atrium, where they not only wanted to wipe my memory, but where Marius and his thugs would have been happy to chop me up and serve me piece by piece in the Dining Hall. No, I could just meet with Rift. At the very least, I needed to talk to him again. I had to figure out a way to move on and live beyond my old life.

But did I have the guts to leave the Academy and head for Soho on my own, with no Prewitt or Gemma to back me? Just the idea of going alone caused my foot to take an automatic step closer to the double glass doors, which suddenly seemed so inviting…

No. I couldn't do it. If I had to sit through one more lecture taught by another Elite marionette, I would probably start ripping out every blue strand of hair on my head, one by one. Before I could talk myself out of it, I spun on my heels and marched across the courtyard.

I reached the front gates, where one of the guardsmen stopped me with an unsure wave. "Where are you off to, Miss Croft?" he asked. Suspicion weighed down his normally-cheerful greeting.

Giving myself a mental kick, I floundered for a decent excuse. "I, um…" I hesitated. "I have to meet my father for an appointment."

"An appointment?" Toby repeated.

"Yes, he… er… wanted to introduce me to some of his new colleagues at the Forum." I said it with as much confidence as I could muster at a moment's notice. I'd decided to play the power card, using my father's reputation as a distraction.

Sure enough, the very mention of both Titus Croft and the Forum in the same sentence was enough for Toby. He bobbed his head. "Of course, Miss Croft, I won't keep you. You're obviously in a hurry." He signaled for Sam to open the gate.

I flashed him a grateful smile. "Thanks." Not waiting for a reply, I dashed through the widening gap between the iron bars.

CHAPTER TEN

Nervous energy tingled up and down my arms as I exited the school compound. I'd actually done it! I spun in an elated circle as I made my way down the sidewalk. I'd left Honoratus in the middle of the day, and had even come up with a halfway decent excuse!

I was so busy congratulating myself on my quickly-constructed escape that I almost forgot which way I was supposed to be heading. Pulling my hood up to cover my hair, I stopped at the corner of Prospect and Edwards to get my bearings. The closest Telepoint would have been the one just down the street from the Academy's entrance, but I didn't want to chance passing by the guardsmen again. It would also be better to use a random archway so that I wouldn't be easily traced.

The next closest Telepoint would be the one at the visitor's entrance of the Yale-New Haven Children's Hospital. I had only used that gateway once before, so it ought to give me a quick, inconspicuous exit.

Nobody appeared to be following me, but the uncomfortable weight of eyes on my back didn't lift. I quickened my pace to a jog as I turned left onto Park Street. When I had finally reached the Children's Hospital, I stood in line for one of the twin Visitor Telepoints outside its entrance. The left gateway was for Arrivals. Every ten seconds or so, another person or set of people would materialize and stride quickly out of the arch, most carrying balloons and stuffed animals for ill loved ones. On its right, the Telepoint marked for "Departures" was zapping others off to their various return destinations.

When my turn finally came, I punched in my terminus and stepped into the portal. I felt the familiar tingling sensation of the teleportation process—as though my skin were receiving tiny electric shock waves—a flash of speed and color, and a moment later I was stepping out of the crisp autumn air of Connecticut and into the twilight of Piccadilly Circus.

The past couple decades had seen Soho and its surrounding vicinity degrade into the worst area of London. Once a cultural highlight where visitors and locals alike would flock for its entertainment venues, great food, and quirky shops, it was now a cesspool of dive bars and dodgy nightclubs. Its nightlife was the only attribute to live on after the War, but without its former diversity of draw. It was now infamously known as a Dreg hotspot, and most Elites gave it a wide berth. I doubted whether any of my classmates would be caught dead in a place like this. *Well, I considered, they might be caught dead if they ended up here, but certainly never alive.*

Even during the day it wasn't the sort of place you wanted to go for a stroll, and I felt highly out of place in the gathering dusk. It had been mid afternoon in Connecticut, but that was about five time zones back. I yanked down on my jacket so as to hide as much of my white Academy uniform as possible, but I was sure I still stuck out like a sore thumb among all the other darkly- clad pedestrians. I also didn't have a clue where I could find the club Rift had mentioned—had he called it the Rebel's Song?

"Um, excuse me?" I said to a random woman walking past.

The woman turned to me. She had choppy purple hair, thigh-length leather boots, and a glittering gold septum piercing that made her look like a thin, glamorous bull. "What do you want?" she asked. Her tone suggested it had better be good.

"Sorry," I said, wishing I'd waited for a less hostile passerby, "but could you tell me where I can find the Rebel's Song?"

At the mention of the club, the woman's face changed. She stared at me as though seeing me for the first time. Her gold-contact-covered eyes took in my gray hoodie pulled low over my Honoratus skirt, finally honing in on the loose strands of my hair where they fell from beneath my hood. The pierced corner of her mouth quirked up. "Take Shaftesbury Ave up to Wardour, then hang a right onto Old Compton. It's the old Prince Edward's Theatre," she added. "They revamped it after the War."

"Thanks," I said, still surprised at the abrupt change in the woman's countenance. The bull-ring lady walked on and I shook my head. A wisp of hair caught in my eyelashes and I reached up to push the blue tendril behind my ear.

Suddenly, a lightbulb went on in my head. *My hair*, I thought. I had forgotten that it might actually be an asset on this end of town rather than a detriment. Nobody around here was likely to recognize me, and weird appeared to be the norm. I pushed my hood back and let the soft fabric fall onto my shoulders as I headed north up Shaftesbury Avenue.

Sure enough, I found myself drawing less attention from passersby now than before I had lowered my hood. It brought a small smile to my lips and a skip to my step. For once, my freakish hair was proving useful.

Turning onto Old Compton, I could have guessed that I was drawing closer to my destination even without having been given directions. Several teenagers stood beneath an old lamppost that flickered feebly, throwing random spurts of light over their game of *Rogue*. Any one of them would have fit in perfectly in the Atrium. I stared, hoping to catch a glimpse of their faces, but when one of them—a boy with a red mohawk who looked to be about nineteen—looked up at me with a dangerous leer in his eyes, I abandoned my attempts. "See something you like, babe?" he called out.

I ducked my head and picked up my pace. The laughter of he and his friends reverberated off the graffitied walls behind me as I approached the old theater building. The ancient brick facade was crumbling slightly, but I could see that certain parts of its outer walls had been restored where they must have fallen down completely. The faded *PRINCE EDWARD* sign that must have once resided over the entryway now lay discarded by the dumpsters, replaced now by a sign reading *"THE REBEL'S SONG"* alongside the outline of a singer with spiked hair yelling into a microphone. A small group of people stood in line outside to pay.

I fell in at the back of the queue, hoping I didn't have to produce some kind of ID. It didn't seem like the sort of place that cared whether its customers were underage, but one could never tell. From up ahead, I could hear one girl trying to talk up the bouncer. Probably trying to flirt her way out of the cover charge.

But the bouncer wasn't buying it. Straightening up so that all six-and-a-half feet of him towered over the her, he fixed the minx with a glare that could wilt a cactus. He held up one beefy hand. A fat silver ring encircled the smallest finger. "Save your charms, sweetheart. My wife's way hotter than you," he rumbled in a thick Cockney accent. "Now cough it up."

The girl tried to appear crestfallen, but quickly realized her sullen pouts would do her no good. She wrestled in the pocket of her jeans—no small feat, since they were practically painted onto her body—and produced several wadded up bills. She slapped the money into his awaiting hand before flouncing off through the doors. I could hear the music pulsing behind them as they opened and closed.

When I turned back, I found myself directly in front of the massive bouncer. "Cover charge," he said flatly. His thick arms were crossed so that his already huge muscles seemed doubly out of proportion, the veins standing out on his biceps like yarn taped across the outside of two flesh-colored balloons.

"Oh, right." I dug around the inner pocket of my jacket and produced what money I had, hoping it would be enough. As I pressed the bills into his hand, I added, "Do you know where I could find Felix?"

The bouncer fixed me with beady eyes too small for the rest of him. "Depends on what you want with him."

"I, uh, need to talk to him," I said weakly. I searched my other pocket for the pale stone Rift had given me, fishing it out and flashing its Circlet pattern to the bouncer. "I was told he could help me get in touch with... Curls the Brave?"

He squinted first at the stone, then at me, and I wondered for one horrifying moment if Rift had made up the entire nickname and its backstory just to humiliate me. But the bouncer's large face broke into an even larger grin. "You know Curls?" he asked, lighting up. "Man, I haven't seen that kid in ages! How's he doin'?"

"Pretty good," I said, relief washing over me. "Are you Felix?"

"I am indeed," he said, nodding to me so that for a moment it was impossible to distinguish between his head and his neck. "And any friend of Curls is a friend of mine. Thrash, take over for a minute, would ya? I got somefin to take care of."

Another beefy guy dressed all in black stepped in to take Felix's place as he grabbed my forearm and dragged me into the club.

The music inside was deafening. Everywhere I looked, people in dark or neon clothes were jumping and writhing on the dance floor, their movements mirroring the beat of the song. Colored lights roved through the room, flooding it in fluid sweeps of purples and yellows and greens. "What?" I yelled as Felix tried to shout something to me over the din.

"I said, I gotta send a message to 'im! You can wait upstairs," he added, gesturing to a black spiral staircase that wound its way up to a third floor balcony. "I'll send 'im straight up when he gets here."

I wanted to ask how long he thought that would take, but Felix was already moving back through the crowd and off into a side room, the crowd parting before him like minnows dodging a barracuda.

I turned back to the spiraling stairs and began to climb. I wasn't a big fan of heights to begin with, and it didn't help that the entire staircase shook precariously with every *thrum* of the bass. This produced a smaller version of what I had experienced when flying through the air behind Rift on the motorbike—terror mixed with exhilaration. Yet even though I didn't like the feeling of the steps rocking beneath my feet, I felt like the very structure of the building was pulsing along with the music, like a physical reflection of its tempos and harmonies. The singer screamed into his mic as the band moved back into the chorus:

> *Say I'm insane, or say I'm a dead man*
> *But never say I went down without a fight.*
> *There's not much left in this world to live for,*
> *But I'll gladly die if the cause is right.*

Reaching the top of the stairs, I wondered how long I would have to wait for him to show up. It wasn't as though I'd given him much of a heads up, and who knew how many Telepoints he would have to take to get here? I sat down at a small table next to the banister overlooking the club, which gave me a perfect aerial view over the kaleidoscope of motion below.

I was so caught up in watching the dancers and musicians that I didn't notice I had attracted company. "Hey, babe," said a deep voice.

My head bolted up from my arms. Standing next to

my table were two guys who looked to be in their late teens. One was decidedly shorter than the other, but both looked as though they could pummel the Montanari brothers into last Tuesday. The taller one with what looked like a dragon's claws tattooed around his throat slid into the chair next to me. "Never seen you here before. Want to dance?" he asked in a thick Aussie accent. He leaned in close enough that I could smell the heavy aroma of vodka on his breath.

"I'm actually waiting for some friends." I said, leaning back until I was pressed against the banister. Every self-defense move I'd ever learned at the Academy flashed in a sequence of motion through my memory.

"Aw, don't break my heart, love," he teased, his mirth dissipating into displeasure. His hand lurched out for mine, strong fingers closing around my wrist. "You can make new friends too, can't you?"

"She's not accepting friendship applications at this time," growled a familiar voice. I swiveled my head just as Rift strolled up to the table, Torque following in his wake. For some reason, both were sopping wet, their dark clothes plastered to their skin and their hair dripping small puddles on the floor.

Rift placed a wet hand on the claw-tattooed boy's shoulder. His knuckles went white as he tightened his grasp. The boy grimaced in pain. "Alright! Relax, mate!" he said, releasing his grip on my wrist. "I was only asking her to dance!"

"Then perhaps you should try for a girl who's more

plastered than you are," Torque suggested, giving both him and his friend a shove toward the staircase. "You might have more luck."

The two sent fiery glares at Rift and Torque. But they must have mulled over Torque's advice because they turned to slink back down the stairs, presumably in search of more willing prey. "Thanks," I breathed as Rift took Drunk Guy's place. Torque pulled up a chair opposite me, his clothes making squishing noises as he sat down.

"Sorry we took so long," said Rift. "We would have gotten here sooner if Torque hadn't insisted we take a detour..."

"I thought it would be safer to change Telepoints in Manhattan!" Torque retorted, throwing up his hands. "How was I supposed to know they had a system glitch?"

Rift rolled his eyes.

"Hey, I was just as displeased as you were at the alternate route, alright?" he snapped, water trickling over his furrowed brow. "We were supposed to be making a simple stopover in New York, not training for a bloody triathlon."

"Anyway," Rift said, shaking his drenched head. "What happened? Why did you send for me?"

At this, I felt my face flush. I'd been so focused on getting to the club in one piece that I hadn't even figured out what I was going to say when he arrived. And now here he was, looking at me expectantly and probably assuming I had a better reason for summoning him than having suffered through a few rough days at school. "I just," I started, not knowing where to begin. "I tried, okay? I really did, but I can't just go back into my old life knowing the truth. It's driving me crazy," I said helplessly, wishing he could see into my memories of the past few days. I felt like one more week would see me locked away in a psych ward.

Rift stared at me. "What are you saying? That you want to come back to the Atrium?" He gave a disbelieving laugh, but his eyes hardened when I didn't respond. "You can't be serious!" he said, his voice rising.

I was shocked to see color spill into his cheeks. I had been prepared for him to laugh at me, to think I was just an ignorant rich girl who was ridiculous to complain about what a horribly cozy life she was stuck with. But what I hadn't expected was the anger that flared into his voice. "I smuggle you out, and now you want to go waltzing right back in like you're part of the club? Kade was ready to have you *Wiped*, Ambry!" he practically yelled over the din of the music, dark eyes flashing.

"Well, I'm *sorry*!" I snapped, my temper rising to meet his. When Rift had first appeared, I had wanted to rush to him, to hug him and let him make me feel safe again, like I finally belonged somewhere. Now I wanted nothing more than to put a dent in his stupid glare. "I'm sorry if I don't like being trapped in the dead center of the Elite society, knowing that I'm just another stupid pawn in their plans! I'm sorry I'm so discontent being part of a family where my father is partially responsible for half the world's problems and having to go along with it like the fool I've been my whole life!"

By the time I had finished my tirade, Rift had forced himself into a semblance of calm. He opened his mouth to say more, but paused. Instead, he rose slowly from the table, motioning for Torque to follow. "Wait here," he whispered with a look that said our conversation wasn't over.

He and Torque crossed the room as though they were heading for the staircase. Suddenly, they leapt toward the shadowy corner booth. Each grabbed at something.

Or, as it turned out, someone.

Angry snatches of "*Ow, what the*—!" and "*Get off me, you stupid Dreg!*" could be heard in between the notes of the newest song. Rift and Torque emerged out of the shadows, each holding a struggling figure who had been hiding behind the booth. Torque had Gemma by the arm; Rift was grasping Prewitt by the collar of his school uniform.

"Wait!" I shouted. "I know them!"

"Oh, joy," said Torque in disgust, shoving Gemma toward the table.

She stumbled, but quickly caught her balance and whirled around to face him in a flurry of satin and red nail polish. The infuriated bouncing of her long, dark curls made the comparison between her and Torque all the more ludicrous. It was like a poodle squaring off against a wolf. "Touch me again, Dreg, and I swear I'll have you sent to the deepest cell of the Catacombs before you have time to wipe that stupid smirk off your face," she snarled.

"Touchy," said Torque, raising his hands in mock defeat. The mention of the Globe's most heavily fortified jail didn't appear to phase him in the slightest.

"Prew, Gemma, what are you two doing here?" I asked, horrorstruck. I would have been frightened for them, sneaking into a place like this, but anger displaced my concern.

Prewitt jerked out of Rift's grasp. "I came back to get you back in the courtyard at Honoratus, but I saw you heading toward the gate. So yeah, I grabbed Gemma and we followed you."

"You mean you ditched the rest of your classes and trailed me to Soho?" I asked, raising my eyebrows. Prewitt had never skipped a class in his life. "I have to say I'm impressed, Prew."

"You would have done the same if you saw me taking off like that," he pointed out. "Especially if I'd been acting the way *you* have for the past week."

"And how have I been acting?" I challenged.

"Oh, I don't know," he mocked. "Depressed, distracted, looking as though you might jump out a window any moment..." He tallied off adjectives on his fingers.

I clenched my fists at my sides. As much as I hated to admit it, he was right. I wouldn't have stood by and watched him leave the Academy without finding out where he was going.

"This is all very touching," said Torque. "But there's the small matter of what we're to do with you now that we've caught you spying in on our little chat," he said in that oddly polite tone of his that simultaneously spoke of untold horrors were they to cross him.

Gemma took a menacing step forward so that she was inches from his unyielding frame. Her head barely grazed his broad, well-muscled shoulders, but that didn't seem to intimidate her. "Are you the ones who did this to her?" she asked, gesturing toward me and my innumerable bruises.

At this, Torque appeared genuinely taken aback. "You think that *we* did that?"

"Well, from the sound of it, she was obviously with you two Dregs when she disappeared," said Gemma.

Clearly affronted, Torque's hooded eyes narrowed at her. "Do you really think I'm the sort of person to hurt a girl?" he demanded.

This made for an interesting question considering the fact that Torque looked as though he'd very much like to hurt Gemma at that moment. "I don't know what sort you are, but if your morals rate anywhere within range of your hygiene," said Gemma with a sniff, "then I'd assume you could be capable of just about anything."

"Look, *princess*," growled Torque, his fists taut. "I'm not in the mood. You have no idea what I went through to get here tonight. Let me give you a hint: it involved a quick dip in the East River—and not the pleasant end."

"They didn't hurt me, Gem," I cut in, tugging Gemma's arm to pull her away from Torque, who was looking madder by the second. "They actually *helped* me."

"These guys?" asked Prewitt. He raised an eyebrow as he looked Rift and Torque up and down, taking in the dark clothes, tattoos, and Torque's various facial piercings.

"I was in trouble and they got me out of it," I said, trying to avoid as many details as possible. "They were the ones who got me to a medic."

Prewitt looked somewhat mollified, albeit skeptical, but he still shook his head. "Either way, we're getting you out of here. Come on..."

He took my hand, but I didn't budge. "I need to talk with them," I said.

Prewitt's hand fell away, his face abashed. "Ambry," he whispered, moving in close so that he stood directly between me and Rift. "These guys are bad news. Besides, we have to get back before they send people looking for us."

"Prew, do you think I would have come all the way here if I didn't have a good reason? Just give me a minute, okay?" I tried to convey with my eyes how important this was without actually voicing my desperation in front of Rift.

But the look on Prewitt's face told me that he hadn't received my telepathic transmission.

I took his hands and gave them a reassuring squeeze. "Wait downstairs and I'll be right there."

"I'll escort them out," Torque volunteered cheerfully. He took Prewitt by one arm and Gemma by the other. Before either one could protest, he was steering them back to the head of the staircase.

"Let go of me, you scum-soaked piece of—!" Gemma

was shouting, but her voice was drowned out by the blaring music and cheering crowd.

Rift watched Gemma's exit in mild fascination. "With a nose stuck up that high, it's a wonder she doesn't drown when it rains."

My mouth twitched. "She carries an umbrella."

Rift raised his eyebrows, and I thought I saw the faintest trace of a grin skirt across his lips, but it vanished just as quickly as he resumed our conversation. "I can't take you to the Atrium, Ambry. They'll send you right back where you came from, the only difference being that you'll remember none of it. I mean it—Kade and the others are already considering ways of recapturing you." There was less anger in his voice now; I thought I even detected a hint of compassion.

"But there has to be some way of proving to them that I can be trusted!" I raced through the recesses of my mind sifting through ideas, grasping for anything that might give me a foothold. "Oh! What about that thing you stole, the... what did you call it?"

"The Anagram?" he ventured.

"Yeah, that," I said, not bothering to hide my eagerness. "What if I could find out what it does and how it works? Would that be enough evidence for them to know I'm serious, that I want to be a part of what you're doing?"

"It's possible," he admitted, crossing an arm and pressing his knuckles to his chin. "They definitely want answers."

"Great!" I exclaimed. "I'll do it."

"But would you be able to handle it?" he asked.

"Of course I can handle it," I insisted. "I could trail my father, eavesdrop on conversations—"

Rift shook his head. "I'm not talking about whether you could *accomplish* it, Ambry. I'm asking whether you could handle going behind your parents' backs. You would be betraying them to the people who want to destroy everything they've been working toward their entire lives." His voice was so cold that I was surprised the words didn't come out in a puff of fog. "Could you follow through with this plan and live with yourself knowing you were the one to obliterate all their dreams? Even the society they embody?" he asked.

That made me pause. After finding out the truth about the Forum's power, I'd been too angry with my parents to consider that *they too* had grown up deceived.

"I'll make you a deal," Rift said. "You take some time to consider my question, and I'll talk with Kade. That way if the time comes... *when* the time comes," he amended, "you will be able to make your choice knowing that you took the time to think it through."

"I don't think time will make much of a difference," I said, feeling deflated. "Even if I spend weeks weighing out the options, and even knowing what I could lose... *who* I could lose," I added, my voice breaking. I had to take a deep breath before I could continue. "I can't stand by while the world crumbles around me. Not if I have any power to help stop it."

Rift fixed me with that all-knowing gaze of his. It made me feel like he was peeling back the layers of my mind like an onion. "Time always makes a difference," he said in a quiet voice. But even though his earthen eyes were looking into my own, I had the strangest feeling that he wasn't speaking to me at all. "If only so that you can look back later and know you didn't rush into the decision."

I blinked, breaking the visual connection. "Fine," I murmured. "I promise I'll think about it."

"Good," he replied. Wringing out the hem of his shirt —which I almost found comical, as there was now probably more water on the floor than on his clothes—he turned to the stairs. "Better get you back to your friends."

The way he said "friends" suggested he didn't think much of my taste in company, but I kept my mouth shut and followed him mutely down the spiral staircase. I needed his help. No need to provoke him into recanting his offer to talk with Kade.

Torque had corralled Prewitt and Gemma over to the bar, where the two of them watched in unabashed disgust as he kicked back a vial of green liquid. Two similar vials sat empty on the bar next to him.

"Lovely," said Rift, his voice thick with sarcasm. Torque had just called for another shot, but Rift stepped between him and the barmaid. "Never mind that. We're leaving," he told her.

Her ruby-red lips sank into a pout. She glanced from

Rift's loose, auburn curls to his river-soaked shirt, which highlighted the lean muscles in his chest and arms. "Shame," she purred, but she quickly turned her attention to a pair of new clients who had just arrived at the bar.

Gemma and Prewitt slid down from their barstools and strode quickly toward me. They were obviously eager to put some distance between themselves and the snowy-haired Rebel.

"What? I figured if I'm gonna get stuck playing nanny, I might as well have a little fun," Torque said, hopping down from the barstool. There was a slight slur to his speech.

Rift looked at the vials and glanced sideways at me, rolling his eyes.

Torque shoved open the doors and strolled into the night air, the rest of our oddly-assorted group plodding along behind him. Rift sighed. "I'd best get him home while he's still in a good mood."

I wouldn't have described Torque's mood as being in any way "good." He had just knocked over a trashcan and was now exchanging threats with a rough-looking gang of teens. But I decided to take Rift's word for it. "How will I be able to get back in touch with you?"

He shook his head. "Don't worry about that. I'll send word when Kade gives me an answer," he said in a way that discouraged further questions.

"All right," I replied. "Well, goodbye."

"Goodb—oh you've got to be kidding me…"

He was staring up at Torque, who had scaled the side of a billboard across the street. He had just reached the platform at the base of the sign and was eyeing several motorbikes parked directly below him. "Check it out, Rift! I can totally land this..."

"Hold off, Torque," Rift called, jogging over. "Those aren't ours, remember? We came on foot... and partially by river."

Torque scowled down at him. "You're an inexcusable drag, you know that?"

"So I've been told," Rift said, folding his arms.

Prewitt had finally had enough. He took advantage of Rift's distraction, crossing over to me and grabbing me by the arm. "Let's get out of here before *that* one," he said, pointing at Torque, "does something to make the Officials show up."

"Bye—" I called as Gemma and Prewitt dragged me off down the street.

Prewitt hailed the first cab he saw. He yanked open the door and allowed Gemma and I to slide into the seat first before cramming himself in next to us. "Piccadilly Circus," he said. "The faster, the better."

CHAPTER ELEVEN

The lecture I had been dreading didn't come until we had safely reached Prewitt's home in Chelsea. The Lindstroms' valet ushered us inside, taking our school bags and coats as we passed.

I decided to call home to let my parents know I was spending the night with Gemma and Prewitt so they could help me catch up on all the school work I'd missed. This sort of request wasn't anything out of the ordinary; the Lindstroms actually had a guest room specifically devoted to Gemma and I from all the times we stayed the night, complete with two double beds and our own cappuccino machine. They'd also given Prewitt a lengthy talk around age thirteen detailing exactly what would befall him were he to be caught straying into our room at night. I could still remember how furiously he'd blushed.

Even so, my father was skeptical. He reluctantly agreed that I could stay over, but insisted on speaking personally with Maurice and Evelyn to ensure that I was being truthful as to my whereabouts. The Lindstroms graciously obliged, assuring him that I was well in hand.

Once we had concluded our teleconference in Maurice's office, I accepted a steaming mug of cider from Evelyn's maid and followed a disgruntled Prewitt into the den. He turned on me the moment the maid was out of earshot. "What were you thinking, Ambry?" he demanded. "Going alone into a place like that? You could have gotten yourself killed!"

"Or worse, I'm sure," Gemma added, sinking into a plush armchair near the fireplace and crossing her legs. "The whole place was teeming with Dregs."

I glared at her. "You know I hate that term, Gem."

"That doesn't change the fact that it's applicable," she said with a practiced shrug. "How on earth did you wind up needing help from those two anyway?" she asked, obviously referring to our less-than-pleasant encounter with Rift and Torque.

"It's a long story," I said wearily. I crossed to the fireplace and sank onto the floor by Gemma's chair.

"We've got time," said Prewitt. He crossed his arms, a shrewd look on his lean face. The glow of the fire highlighted his straight nose and high cheekbones. "You can't weasel your way out of this one, Croft."

"Wait a minute," I said slowly. "How did *you two* sneak out of Honoratus without getting caught?"

"I called the Academy on the way and asked to speak with Professor McCullough," said Prewitt. "I told him that we'd forgotten to mention it, but your dad had asked Gemma and I to accompany you to your follow-up appointment with the medic since both he and your mum couldn't get off from work."

My mouth dropped open. "That's brilliant!"

"Every now and then I do come up with a good plan," he said. "You don't have to seem so surprised about it."

"But back to the topic at hand," said Gemma. "How did you wind up with those two?"

I sighed. "Did you two actually hear anything about the night of the Gala?"

"Not much," she said, lifting her mug and taking a long sip of cider. "My dad told me that there had been a burglary, but he didn't know what had been stolen. He *did* mention that he'd never seen your dad so angry—which I know is saying something—so obviously whatever-it-was must have been important."

"Or at the very least, valuable," Prewitt added.

I nodded. Prewitt had known my father long enough to understand his priorities. "Well," I said. "I sort of ran into the two burglars as they were leaving."

"You *ran into them?*" Prewitt asked, his golden eyebrows raised. "Honestly, Ambry, you have the worst luck of anyone I've ever met."

"I was coming back in through the Garden Gate, which just happened to be their exit route," I explained, my agitation thinly-veiled at this point. "Anyway, the Officials showed up with those monstrosities of theirs—"

Gemma gave a little gasp. "*Watchdogs?*"

"—and the geniuses had them target all *three* intruders," I finished, shivering at the memory of the wolves' cruel eyes glowing as they marked us.

"But didn't you just say there were two burglars?" asked Gemma.

I nodded grimly. "The third being myself, apparently."

"Are you telling me you were chased by *werehounds?*" Prewitt went several shades paler and stared at me as though I were a corpse that had magically sat up and begun breathing again. "I take it back, what I said earlier. You're the luckiest person alive."

I proceeded to fill Prewitt and Gemma in on the night of the Gala, giving them the abridged version. I recounted our close brush with the watchdogs, being chased through back alleys and up the fire escape. When I got to the part about having to jump across rooftops, both Prewitt and Gemma gaped at me. "You really did that?" Gemma asked, her almond-shaped eyes wide with wonder.

I snorted. "I'm pretty sure that with enough adrenaline and a couple of manic wolves to add extra motivation, a person can do just about anything," I assured her. "Plus, I didn't exactly land the last jump."

Prewitt inhaled sharply, which was a mistake as he'd just taken a sip of his cider. It took several seconds of coughing and spluttering before he was able to speak. "*What?*" he finally managed, dragging his sleeve across his mouth.

"I fell short of the other roof by about a foot," I said, recounting the sensation of catapulting into the black void, grasping desperately for a handhold. "Thankfully, Rift caught me."

"Rift?" Prewitt repeated. He stood up, oblivious to the mug still grasped in one hand. Cider rained like a mini monsoon over the carpet at his feet. "You mean that Dreg you stayed behind to talk with? *He* was one of the thieves?" he demanded. "So what, you just thought it'd be nice to meet up with him for a cozy little chat, did you?"

I massaged my forehead. How had I forgotten they now knew Rift and Torque's names?.

Gemma's jaw had come unhinged. "You mean to tell me that those two ingrates were the ones who broke into your parents house, and *you ran off with them?*" she asked in disbelief.

"Um, I was *chased* off, remember?" I said, scowling. "Being hunted down by wolves wasn't exactly what I had in mind for my Saturday night."

"They could have been serial killers!" Prewitt exclaimed. He was gesturing so wildly that he could have been directing air traffic. "They could have dragged you through a Telepoint to some godforsaken third-world country and put a knife in you, and nobody would have ever known!"

"Well, as you can see by my obvious lack of stab wounds, that didn't happen," I said, holding out my arms. "Besides, they could have murdered me just as easily here as they could have in Tibet or Namibia."

My calm demeanor was having an opposite effect on Prewitt. "But it *could* have happened!" he retorted, his voice rising until he was practically shouting.

"Alright, that's enough!" Gemma said. She slammed down her mug of tea so hard that it sloshed its contents all over the glass end table. "Sit down, Prew, before your parents come in wondering why you've suddenly lost your mind!" she scolded.

Prewitt kept his narrowed eyes fixed on me, but said nothing more as he lowered himself back into the armchair.

"That's better," Gemma said in a tone of matronly approval. "Maybe *now* we can actually get somewhere with Ambry's story. So," she continued, turning back to me. "You said that one Dreg—Rift, was it?" I nodded.

"He caught you?" I nodded again.

Gemma screwed up her face. "Which one was he again? The cute one with the tattoos, or the cute one with the curls?"

"Oh, please," Prewitt said darkly, crossing his arms.

I couldn't help it. I cracked the barest hint of a smile. "The one with the curls."

"Ah." Gemma snuggled back into her chair. "So what happened then?"

"Well, then I blacked out when I hit my head against the building—"

At this, Prewitt emitted a faint growling noise. It sounded as though he'd swallowed an angry kitten.

"—so they brought me back with them."

"Back?" Gemma asked. She leaned forward with interest. "To where?"

I ran a finger absently around the top of my mug. "I— can't really say."

"Can't, or won't?" asked Prewitt.

I made an exasperated sound and set the mug down on the stone hearth with a *thunk.*

"All right, fine, you *can't* say where," Prewitt sighed. "But do you mean to tell me that you were with those two Dre—" He broke off as I narrowed my eyes. "—those two *guys* for three days?" He looked thoroughly displeased at the idea.

"If it helps, I was only conscious for half that time," I said, shooting him what I hoped was a maddening smile.

"What could have possibly been so important as to delay your homecoming for an entire day and a half?" he asked. "And no, it doesn't help!"

"Oh, I don't know, maybe the fact that I had a concussion, several broken ribs, and bruises that would put a professional wrestler to shame?" I retorted, biting back a few other choice words. "And I don't really care if it helps or not!"

"Can't you two hold off bickering for five minutes?" demanded Gemma.

"You forgot to mention the shoulder," Prewitt muttered.

I grinned with malicious triumph. "True. I guess I also neglected to mention that it was reset and thereafter dislocated a *second* time."

Prewitt gaped at me. "Ambry!"

"Both of you, just STOP!" Gemma shouted, stamping her foot. Her fuzzy-slippered feet made the effect more amusing than menacing. Nonetheless, Prewitt and I turned from our shouting match to stare at her.

"Honestly, could you two be more like an old married couple? Ambry, stop trying to give Prewitt an aneurism. *We're* the ones who spent days in a panic, wondering whether you were dead or alive. And within a week of your return, you're traipsing off again without a word! He's only upset because he cares about you, so don't be such a prat."

Immediately, the truth of Gemma's words sliced through my frustration. I rubbed at my arm, regretting my outburst. Gemma was right; I had been so busy trying to defend myself that I'd forgotten why Prewitt was mad in the first place.

"And you," Gemma continued, pivoting in her slippers to face Prewitt. "What's done is done. You can't change what happened to Ambry. But if you would stop freaking out about her injuries for more than two minutes, maybe we could figure out how to help her."

Gemma's reasoning seemed to short-circuit Prewitt's wrath. Reddening, he mumbled something vaguely apologetic.

"Good. Now," said Gemma, turning back to me. "You obviously aren't going to tell us where you were or exactly who you were with, other than the two we met in that ridiculous club, but what I *would* like to know is how you got back home after whatever happened to you. Does that sound reasonable?"

"Sure," I replied meekly. "And Prew, I'm sorry. I was a jerk. Again."

Prewitt heaved a deep sigh. "Indeed, you were."

I opened my mouth to make some sort of indignant reply, but Prewitt held up a hand. "But no more than I was," he finished. "I think we were neck-and-neck."

"I might have led by a nose," I said with a small smile. "I'm a Croft. I've been trained by the best in the subtle arts of stubbornness and righteous indignation."

Prewitt managed a half-hearted laugh. "So how did you get back?"

I bit my lip. "Well," I began, measuring my words. "There's not too much to explain. I took a couple days to rest and heal, then Rift drove me home."

Gemma and Prewitt sat in silence for a moment, allowing me time to continue. When I didn't, Prewitt leaned forward. "That's it?"

"That's it," I said.

"My. That was anticlimactic," said Gemma.

Prewitt wasn't so easily convinced. "In that case, why the jaunt over to Soho tonight?" he asked, his voice unnaturally breezy. I could tell he was putting a great deal of effort into keeping his tone light.

"I had to take care of something…"

"Had to? As in, past tense?" he asked, looking hopeful. "So whatever-it-was is taken care of now? You're not planning on staying in touch?"

"How exactly would I be able to keep in touch?" I asked, hoping to evade the question with one of my own. "Today was a fluke, Prew. There's no way I could pull another grand escape from Honoratus."

Prewitt considered me for a long moment before leaning back, apparently satisfied that I would have no means of contacting my unsavory new acquaintances. I made a valiant attempt not to frown at him, forcing my mouth to remain even-keel as Gemma quickly turned the conversation back to the upcoming party at Philippe Roche's. She was wondering whether the rumors of life-sized ice sculptures and horse-drawn sleigh rides were true.

Meanwhile, I mulled over my own words. Without intending to, I had made a fair point: how could I hope to receive contact from either Rift or Torque now that I was back within my Elite society bubble? Between the manor and the Academy, I would be unreachable. Every moment of every day was mapped out for me. Not only that, I now had Prewitt and Gemma on high alert. I wouldn't be able to slip away again without drawing their attention.

All my hope of a reply from Kade dissipated as swiftly as the ribbons of smoke curling their way up the chimney.

....

"Shove over," ordered Gemma, effectively terrifying the first-year student who had dared to occupy her usual seat. The pale boy turned three shades of red as he snatched up his backpack and tray and scampered away, presumably to find a more welcoming table.

Gemma slid into the now-unoccupied chair next to Prewitt. "Ninth-years," she tutted.

"Lunch hour is halfway through, Gem," I pointed out. "You can't blame him for assuming the seat was open."

"And yet I blame him nonetheless," Gemma replied. She slipped a dainty forkful of Alaskan salmon between her lips, which were magenta. It appeared to be the color of the day, as they matched both her shoes and her eyelashes.

Shocking as it was, I found myself *grateful* to be back in school. The weekend had dragged on relentlessly as I waited for a response from Kade. Maybe having something else to focus on would help time pass. "So Gemma, anything on the social agenda this week?" I asked, more out of boredom than interest.

"Well, Ursula Petrick is having some sort of soiree on Wednesday night, but you couldn't drag me there for all the gold in her family's Swiss bank account. Honestly, she's the most insufferable girl," Gemma said with a roll of her eyes. "And then Roderick and Yvaine's parents are holding a gala on Friday. I haven't been to the Allard estate in years. Did you know it's set next to their vineyards in the Loire Valley? Gorgeous landscape. Oh, which reminds me…" Without warning, she turned, stood up, and hoisted an unwitting Prewitt to his feet. "I need your help to secure an invitation."

"What?" asked Prewitt. He yanked his arm away, looking startled. "Why do you need my help with that?"

"Well, I *may* have mentioned to a couple people that Yvaine's sudden improvement in Trigonometry might have had less to do with study and more to do with a certain handsome professor who's taken a liking to her," Gemma said, assuming her best expression of innocence.

"Gemma!" Prewitt exclaimed. Half the girls in the school were in love with young Professor Esparza, so this didn't come as a total shock. Still, if rumor got out about a professor-student indiscretion, it would likely mean that professor's head on a chopping block. "How on earth do you expect *me* to convince Yvaine overlook that?" he asked.

"Well, I've noticed over the past few months that she stares at *you* a great deal in the classes you share—though perhaps not in Trig," she added with a wink.

"I don't—" Prewitt began, but Gemma was already hauling him away toward the Allards' table.

I watched them go, wishing my own problems were as simple as a belated party invitation. How long did Rift expect me to wait for an answer before I went insane? I picked absently at my food, sulking in a stew of self-pity.

I was so wrapped up in my thoughts that I was startled when a server behind me suddenly asked, "More tea, Miss?"

"No, thank you, I'm fine…" My sentence fell short when I met the waiter's laughing brown eyes. Standing before me in full serving attire, extending a steaming pot of tea, was Rift.

He looked utterly pleased with himself.

It took me a moment to recover from my initial shock. "What the hell are you doing here?" I whispered, rising from my seat.

"Oh please, don't get up," he said, holding up a hand. "Might draw more attention. Are you sure you wouldn't like to try some of the Black Oolong? Delightfully earthy aroma," he said, sniffing the pot.

"Are you insane?" I hissed. "If you're caught here…"

"Who would catch me? It's not as though I run in these particular circles." He winked. "I'm Dreg scum, remember?"

"Prewitt and Gemma know who you are," I reminded him, glancing around to see if either of them was headed back to the table. "And trust me, Prew hasn't exactly warmed up to you guys. He'd be more than happy to alert security. In fact, he'd probably pay decent money to escort you out the door himself."

Rift assumed a hurt expression. "And I thought we'd gotten on so well…"

How could he stand there joking? Prewitt and Gemma could be back any minute and his cover would be blown. "Can't you take anything seriously?" I asked.

"Only serious things," he replied, a mocking grin plastered across his face.

I glared at him. "Get out of here *right now* before someone—"

"Wait, hold on," he interrupted. Shaking back his sleeve, he made a great show of studying his leather-banded wristwatch. "Give him a minute."

"Give *who* a—?"

But my question was cut short by an explosive *bang* echoing from the hallway. It sounded as though someone had detonated a small bomb on the other side of the building.

Every head in the dining hall swiveled to face the double-doors, some with their forks frozen halfway to their gaping mouths. There were several moments of terrified whispers mingled with loud exclamations before a voice reverberated through the speaker system. All fell silent to listen. *"Attention all students and staff: there has been a technical malfunction in the Biological Research Facility..."*

I turned back to Rift. He looked almost comical holding the tea kettle as he shrugged. I imagined him bursting into a solo performance of "I'm a Little Teapot" right there in the middle of the Academy's cafeteria. "Little known fact: Torque is a strong animal rights advocate," he informed me.

The unmistakable roar of a tiger echoed in the distance.

I tried to focus on what Provost Bridgeport was now saying, but my mind was struggling to keep up. "—*already working to address the issue, so please remain calm and proceed to the nearest exit in an orderly fashion.*"

Mass chaos ensued. The dining hall erupted as every student fled toward the courtyard, some knocking slower-moving classmates out of the way in the process, all screaming in a multilingual chorus of terror.

"Watch it," Rift said, grabbing my arm to steady me as two of the rugby players shoved past, shrieking in decidedly un-masculine tones. Rift shook his head. "Privileged children never are good at following directions," he lamented. "Come on, this way."

Still holding my arm, Rift angled the two of us upstream and pushed through the onrushing tide of students, all of whom were streaking toward the doors. I thought I heard Prewitt and Gemma call my name at one point, but it was lost in the cacophony.

Reaching the doors to the kitchen, Rift pulled me inside and out of dodge. "Well, this seems familiar," he said, gesturing first to the kitchen doors and then to his server's uniform.

I had to agree. It was all giving me a strong sense of *deja vu*, save for the fact that the hydrangeas had been substituted for uncaged wild animals. "Did Torque really release all of the specimens in the research lab?" I asked, feeling vaguely stupefied.

Rift nodded gleefully. "Excellent distraction, right?"

"There was a tiger in there," I stated.

He nodded again. "And several falcons. They should be fun to catch. I think there may have even been a komodo dragon…"

I stared at him. "All this just to talk to me?"

"Well that, and we figured why waste an opportunity to liven up the dreary day-to-day lives of the Academy students?" He picked up a steak knife from the stainless steel counter and twirled it deftly between his fingers. "It must get so monotonous here—classes and lectures and all."

"Well, I think you've just succeeded in creating the most cumulative excitement Honoratus has ever had, all in a single day."

Rift beamed. "What can I say? We shoot for the stars."

"So what did you go to all this trouble to tell me?" I wondered, suddenly aware of how alone the two of us were in the abandoned kitchen.

"Ah, that." He rummaged around in the pocket of his uniform, producing a letter. It was sealed with a wax imprint of the Circlet. "I have your answer from Kade and the other leaders."

I reached out for the folded paper, my hand shaking slightly. This piece of paper could determine the course of my life. If Kade accepted my proposal, I would have a way to help the Rebel cause, to fight the unseen injustices of the

Global Government. If he rejected it…

My fingers brushed Rift's. I wished there were a way to divert the blood rushing to my cheeks. Keeping my face downcast, I slipped a finger between the folded creases and broke the seal. I unfolded the letter and silently read the brief note enclosed:

Permission granted.
We know the purpose, we need locations.
—K.

"He's never been particularly chatty," said Rift.

"You don't say?" I mumbled. I read the message once more before folding it back up and stuffing it in the pocket of my uniform. I tried to force down my elation, not wanting to seem pathetic, but my lips curved in and of their own accord. I felt like someone had finally unlatched the door of my cage and offered me a chance of escape. I could *contribute* something, help right some of the wrongs committed by my own family. "So now what?" I asked, excitement bubbling over my skin.

"What do you mean?"

"Well," I said, "you've sent my school into lockdown mode and we're probably the only two people in the building."

Rift raised his eyebrows. "You want to go outside with the others?" he asked.

I hesitated. "Won't it look a little suspicious if we

wander outside now?"

"Probably," he agreed. "We can wait here until the Animal Control squadrons round up all the furry friends Torque unleashed. Besides, there was one more thing I wanted to mention..."

"Really?" I'd thought Rift had merely been sent here as a messenger for Kade. What else could he want to talk with me about?

He hesitated, balancing slightly on one foot. "I wanted to offer my help."

"Help?" I repeated.

"In finding more information about the Anagram," he explained. "I doubt your father will have made it an easy task."

Some of my excitement evaporated. "So Kade doesn't think I can do this on my own?" I asked.

"Kade doesn't exactly know I'm offering," he said carefully. "And I'd prefer we keep it that way."

"But isn't that cheating?" I asked. "I thought he was letting me take on this mission so I can prove myself?"

"The point of all this is to prove that you're trustworthy, not that you're some master spy," Rift reminded me. "The real test is in you offering the information you find to Kade, and thereby proving your loyalty with the Resistance. If you get a little help *acquiring* that information, well..." He shrugged. "The more the merrier, right?"

"You're forgetting one thing," I said. "In order to help

me, you'd have to find a way into the manor. No offense, but you're not exactly inconspicuous."

"You mean I'm not the poster-boy image of an Elite?" he asked, feigning shock. "Dear me, how could I have overlooked something so pivotal?"

A strange snuffling noise caused both of our heads to swivel toward the doors. A black bear had just meandered into the kitchen and was now sniffing at a bag of potatoes.

We both froze. "Don't panic," Rift whispered. "Move slowly so we're less likely to startle him." He reached out a hand and took me by the arm, carefully leading me into a door marked "STORAGE CLOSET." He yanked the door shut behind us, slowing it at the last second to avoid making any extra noise. We could hear the bear lumbering through the kitchen. There were odd thumps and clatters as it knocked over whatever kitchen utensils it was perusing.

Now that we were out of immediate danger, I took a look around the storage closet. It was filled with brooms, buckets, mops, and an assortment of rags and cleaning solutions. The scent of bleach and chlorine made me feel as though I'd just stepped inside our pool house.

Rift took a glance around and chuckled. "Don't worry about me getting into the manor," he said. "I'm obviously good at sneaking in and out of places."

"As evidenced by the night we met," I said dryly. "I seem to remember you needing a bit of assistance when Torque fricasseed himself. You two literally would have been dog food without me."

"Well then, it's lucky I'll have you with me again," he said, his voice deepening. He was several inches away from me in the narrow breadth of the closet, but in the low lighting we might as well have been pressed together like leaves between the pages of a book.

I found my throat tightening. I swallowed and raised a hand to brush a blue strand of hair behind my ears, bumping my elbow against several mops in the process. I scrambled to catch them before they could crash to the floor, thankful to have a reason to look away from him. I was fairly certain that my face must have been on fire. When I managed to get the mops back into an upright position, I turned back to find Rift grinning unabashedly at me.

I glowered at him. "What?"

"Nothing," he said with a smirk that spoke the opposite.

I narrowed my eyes.

"It's just, your hair never looks so blue as it does when offset by such lovely coloring in your cheeks," he mused.

I flushed a deeper shade of crimson and scowled. It was one thing having to struggle with unrequited feelings, but to have my nose rubbed in it? I hadn't known Rift for long, but it seemed out of character for him to be so insensitive. "No thank you."

Confusion chased away his amusement. "What?"

"I said, no, thank you," my voice cold as the metal of the shelf pressing into my shoulder blade. "I don't want or need your help. Kade assigned this mission to me, so I'll do it on my own, in my own way."

His smile fell away entirely. "Ambry, hold on. Just think about it…"

"I *have* thought about it," I said. "If I get caught, I can make up some excuse. If you're caught with me…" I shook my head. "It would be both our necks on the chopping block."

Rift spluttered something incoherent, but I was past the point of caring. The thuds and thumps of the bear's investigative meander through the kitchen had faded away, so I decided it must be safe to exit the storage closet, which I did with as much flounce as I could muster. I had actually been on the verge of taking Rift up on his offer to help, but after his little comment, I decided I would rather spend a few extra hours skulking around my father's study than sacrifice what little pride I yet retained.

"Don't you think this might go more smoothly if you had some help?" he asked, picking up his pace to match my angry stride.

"If you thought I was so inept, you shouldn't have passed on my message to Kade," I snapped.

"Ambry, I don't think you're inept at all," he insisted. He took several quick strides so that he was now walking backwards, directly in front of me. "I just happen to believe—quite logically, I might add—that two people can cover more ground than one."

"Oh, don't spare my feelings now," I said, marching

purposefully toward the courtyard. "I know how invested you are in finding the information you need about the Anagram, but I'll do my best not to screw it up."

"Come on, Ambry, you don't really—"

Rift was interrupted by the loud, buzzing tone of the intercom. *"Attention, students and staff: all biological specimens have been successfully returned to the Research Facility. You may now re-enter the building and return to your classrooms. Lectures will resume immediately."*

We swiveled toward the courtyard doors. Students were already beginning to file back into the building. They were in far less of a hurry now than they'd been during their departure. Some were complaining loudly that school ought to be canceled for the day and the hallways sterilized while others walked by in nervous clusters, hypothesizing as to how the specimens managed to escape in the first place.

Through the wide glass windows I could see Prewitt, a head taller than the majority of our classmates. He caught sight of me and began pushing his way forward with renewed vigor.

"Looks like your time's up," I said flatly, turning back to Rift. "Say hi to Torque for me."

Rift looked as though he was going to argue, but Prewitt had just elbowed his way through the glass doors. "Ambry!" he called.

"Over here, Prew," I called back.

I turned to give Rift one final warning, but he had disappeared. I did notice, however, that the kitchen doors were swinging.

"Where have you *been*?" Prewitt demanded. "Gemma and I were looking everywhere for you! We were starting to think one of the tigers had gotten to you."

"Well, here I am," I said, spreading out my arms. "All in one piece."

He frowned. "But you weren't outside?"

I shook my head. "I heard the announcement and… uh…panicked a bit, I guess. I wound up hiding in the storage closet in the kitchens."

Prewitt rubbed his forehead. "I stand by my original statement. You have the worst luck of anyone I know."

"I know, I know," I said. I looped an arm through his. "But enough about my terrible luck. Let's get to class before they find one last wildebeest roaming the halls."

As we walked, I slipped a hand into the pocket of my jacket, reveling at the touch of cool, crumpled paper between my fingers.

CHAPTER TWELVE

Now I had a mission, and I decided not to waste time in my search for any information about the Anagram.

I arrived home from Honoratus in record time and—after a quick ocular exchange with Meredith—practically sprinted for the front door. School always ended at three o'clock EST, which meant it was already eight in London. Titus might already be back. And even if he wasn't, I doubted I had more than an hour to go poking around uninterrupted. "Ah, good evening Miss Ambrosia!" said Charlie with a bob of his gray head. "You're in quite a hurry!"

"Hey Charlie," I greeted. "Do you happen to know if my father is home yet?"

"Not that I'm aware," Charlie replied. "He left for the Forum early this morning and hasn't been back since."

I tried to look crestfallen. "Oh. Okay. I'll have to ask him later," I said vague wave of my hand. "Just some school stuff."

Charlie smiled sadly and nodded. "If there's anything I can do to assist you in the meantime, Miss Ambry, please let me know."

"Thanks," I said. I was about to hurry for the stairs when a thought occurred to me. "Actually Charlie, there is one thing that would really help me out…"

"And what might that be, my dear?"

"Well, I have to write a paper on Imhoff for school, and nobody has better sources on him than my dad. The problem is, I kind of put this off until the last minute," I admitted, shuffling my feet.

"When is your paper due?" he asked.

"Tomorrow," I said, trying to sound dejected.

"Hmm." Charlie frowned. "You know how your father feels about anyone going into his study unaccompanied."

"I do, but I'd only need like ten minutes to look through some of his books," I pleaded. "And with everything that happened last week, I already feel behind…"

Charlie's frown softened, but lines of worry remained

etched in his forehead. He glanced around to be sure no one else was within earshot. "You understand, Miss Ambry, that I'm the only other person with access to that room, and even that is for dire emergencies. If anything were to be left out of place…"

"I'll put everything back exactly as I found it. He'd never even know I was there," I assured him.

Charlie said nothing at first. I was bracing myself for a "no" when he finally shook his head and sighed. "Let's be quick about it then."

We took the servants' staircase up, bypassing the second landing and reaching the third floor. It was, as usual, bereft of people. My father and mother were the only two people to frequent this part of the house, and Mother was at some sort of Global Art Convention in Florence for the next two days.

Charlie walked to the study door and laid his thumb on the keypad. The lock disengaged with a neat little *click*. He stepped back to let me pass. "It will look suspicious if I don't return downstairs," he said.

"I understand," I replied. "Ten minutes and I'll be out, I promise."

He nodded, then walked briskly back toward the servants' staircase.

With one last glance around to be sure I wasn't seen, I pushed through the door.

Stepping inside my father's office was like stepping back in time. Ornate frames preserved and displayed a number of artistic masterpieces—including two Da Vinci's, a Van Gogh, and several Picasso's. A scattering of protective glass cases held an assortment of historical artifacts spanning every known era of human history. I suspected the Smithsonian would dish out a large fortune for even a handful of my father's collection.

The bookshelves were all carved from rich mahogany and laden with hundreds of thick volumes and odd-looking objects. I glanced through the litany of titles:

Grappling with Time: A Detailed Look into the Mystery of Imhoff's Harness
Modern Theories in Quantum Physics
Bastian Imhoff: Brilliant or Bedlam?
The Life and Works of Bastian Imhoff

Being my father's own private study, it was the only room in the house that the servants didn't clean on a routine basis. Too many valuables. If they did venture in to tidy things up, it was only under Titus's direct supervision and constant scrutiny. Already a thin layer of dust had begun to settle over the shelves and across the many bindings, adding an air of antiquity and mystery to the room.

It also added an advantage to my search.

I scoured the room methodically, looking for any place lacking the telltale dust. There were several points along the bookshelves where my father appeared to have picked up a volume, but there were no hidden compartments in their pages nor any signs that he'd done anything more exciting than sit down to read them. Slamming the last one shut with a scowl, I turned my attention his desk.

This was a different story. The whole thing was practically shining with use. His teleconference screen was still up, displaying an image of the Forum in all its pomp and majesty. I wrinkled my nose and reached for the keypad, clicking the silver hourglass icon. I immediately sighed.

It was, of course, locked. Titus might have an outdated security system for entrance to the room, but he wasn't a fool. And unfortunately, his computer was programmed to open only to his private password spoken in his own voice.

Since the computer was out, I decided to try the desk drawers. Almost all of them lacked any detectable dust, so I started by filtering through their contents. Most of it was nothing of consequence…

The sound of footsteps at the door caused me to jerk up so fast that I nearly hit my head on the top of the desk. They were too heavy to be Charlie's.

I dropped the papers I'd been holding and tried not to slam the drawer in my haste to get it shut. Then, trying not to make a sound, I dashed for the only hiding spot in sight— the leather armchair in my father's reading corner. I practically dove behind it seconds before I heard the door slide open.

Crouched next to the chair, I leaned forward on my hands to maintain my balance. I could hear my father walk around the back of his desk and slump into his straight-backed office chair. He began to type.

Within minutes, my legs were beginning to ache and my feet tingled with the early stages of numbness. How long could I remain poised there before I lost my balance and toppled into plain view? Even if I could manage to hold out in my precarious position, it was only a matter of time before Titus decided to study one of the plethora of books behind me.

The typing came to an abrupt stop. I chanced a quick glance around the back of the chair to see Titus pull out his phone. "Call Number Four," he growled. If the phone could have registered the venom in his voice, I was sure it would have self-destructed in an act of self-preservation. He leaned back and held the device to his ear. I ducked behind the chair once more as he began to swivel in his seat.

"*Now* you answer," he growled. There was a pause as the person on the other end spoke. "Oh, you were busy, were you? No, you see, *I've* been busy," Titus hissed. "In and out of private meetings with practically every member of the Forum, trying to quell their well-warranted panic! And where were you in the midst of all this chaos?" he asked, his voice acidic. "Leave it to you not to be bothered to show up, even in the midst of a true crisis."

There was a pause as he listened to the other line. "I don't give a damn if you had lunch plans with the

Consulate! Forum business always takes priority, a fact you ought to be well aware of by now!" Another pause. "Yes. At least there's that. Although why the two of you are the only ones not to have been attacked, I'll never understand. Your security is as lax as they come." The person on the other end spoke again, and Titus laughed darkly. "I think that might be the first intelligent idea you've had in all the years we've worked together."

There was another short pause, but whatever was said must have been poignant indeed because my Father suddenly hushed the person on the other line. "Idiot…" he said, his voice dropping to the low, dangerous decibel that made the hair at the back of my neck bristle. "Do you really think it wise, discussing this over the phone?" he growled. "*Of course* the line is supposed to be secure, but I'm not leaving anything to chance. That rebel band of Dregs is becoming more and more bold, and we don't know what resources…"

A sudden knock on the door startled me, nearly causing me to topple from my precarious stance behind the armchair.

"Wait!" Titus barked. Then, returning to his conversation, "We'll discuss this in person. Meet me in ten minutes. You know where. And this time, I would advise you to be prompt." I heard the *thunk* of the phone being set on the desk as another knock sounded. "What is it?" Titus snapped in a loud voice.

The door creaked open and I heard Charlie's familiar

voice. "Good evening, Master Croft."

"I'm rather busy at the moment, Charles." My father sounded irritable as the clicking of computer keys resumed.

I could imagine Charlie's short, polite bow. "I apologize sir, but Suarez had a few questions about the menu, and as Mrs. Croft is away…"

"She has a phone with her, doesn't she?"

"Oh. Yes, of course, sir." The door began to creak shut.

"Wait," Titus said.

The creaking stopped.

I heard the gentle *thrum thrum* of Titus' fingers drumming the top of his desk, then the sound of my father's chair being pushed back. "I'm going out anyway, and I need to speak with you on the way down regarding the stricter screening process we've implemented for new employees. That disaster at the Gala will *not* be repeated."

His muffled footsteps crossed the carpet, and I let my breath out in a slow exhale as the door finally clicked shut. I gave it a moment to make sure he was really gone before emerging from my hiding spot, wincing at the cramp in my knees. I wasn't sure if anything I'd overheard might be relevant, but one thing was certain: I *had* to find out who my father was meeting.

But how was I going to get out of the house?

I hurried to the door and cracked it open, peering out cautiously, but no one appeared to be nearby. I eased the door shut behind me and began cantering toward the servants' stairs with the awkward stride of one attempting to balance speed and stealth.

As I reached the first floor, a plan had started to coalesce in my mind. I slipped into the servant's hall after waiting for one of the maids to enter the kitchen, then ducked into the storage closet where they kept spare uniforms. *Rift must be rubbing off on me,* I thought.

I grabbed a black shirt and white apron from the rack, then rummaged through a box of odds and ends until I found a badly-creased wool hat. It would have to do.

I yanked on my disguise as quickly as possible— making sure no blue flyaways escaped the wide-brimmed hat— and hurried back out toward the servants' exit, ducking my head when I passed one of the kitchen staff. I doubted he'd even notice me; staff were always being fired and hired at the manor so unfamiliar faces were well within the norm.

Pushing through the exit doors, I scuttled across the parking lot toward the gate. I'd almost made it when a hand caught my arm.

I whirled around to find myself face-to-face with Charlie. "Miss Ambry, what on earth do you think you're doing?" he demanded. I didn't think I'd ever seen his face so red. "Is nearly getting caught in your father's study not close-call enough for one night?" he spluttered.

"Charlie, even if I could explain, it would take too long," I said in a hushed voice. "But I *have* to find out where he's going!"

Charlie's wizened hand tightened around my arm. "Ambry, listen. I know you've been through an ordeal recently, and I'm trying to take that into consideration, but all of us are under strict orders to make sure you stay in the house!"

I could have easily twisted out of his grip, but the idea of having to use even a small amount of force against him was more than I could handle. "Please, Charlie. You know how much I care about you, and I hope you know I wouldn't be asking you to put your job on the line twice in one day for me without good reason."

"But—I…" Charlie didn't release my arm, but his hand trembled. He rubbed the other hand over his eyes. Watching him fumble for a reply made my heart ache, but this went far beyond either of us.

"Charlie, *please* trust me," I whispered. "I just need a couple hours at most."

Charlie looked utterly torn. finally, with a sigh that spoke volumes of regret, he released his meager grip on me. "Two-four-nine-five," he mumbled.

I shook my head. "What?"

"Twenty-four ninety-five," he repeated. "The passcode to the gate. You'll need it to get out."

I smiled. "Thank you, Charlie. I—"

"One hour," he interrupted, not meeting my eyes. His voice was tired. "If you're not back by then, I'll have no choice but to call your father myself and admit that I've failed you both." Without another word, he turned and trudged back into the manor.

I wrenched my eyes away from his slump-shouldered form and made for the gate, punching in the code Charlie had given me. *If he knew, he'd understand,* I told myself. *He'll forgive me.*

. . . .

The gate swung open and I hurried around to the front of the compound in time to see my father stalking across the darkened street. Was he planning to go on foot the whole way to this meeting place? What if he got in a cab? Or worse, a Telepoint...

But there was nothing I could do to control that. All I could do was follow as close as I dared, making sure to keep a good twenty or thirty feet between us. At first, I tried to stay out of the direct patches of light from the streetlamps overhead. In the end, however, I realized that I was far *more* conspicuous in my lopsided wool hat, darting from shadow to shadow like some mad private investigator.

My father continued down the street until he reached an intersection, where he crossed the street to his right.

I hurried to the end of the gaggle of people crossing with him, dodging an impatient car that nearly hit me as I scuttled onto the sidewalk. It took some maneuvering to make my way through the sidewalk traffic, but I managed to escape the crowd in time to see Titus stroll through the entrance to a park.

He meandered down the lamplit path toward a large

pond at the park center. Now that we were out in the open, I was forced to shove my way through a large circle of bushes to avoid being spotted.

I peeked over the top of one of the shrubs.

Titus sat down at an empty bench facing the lake. His mystery colleague must still be en route. Unfortunately, there were no trees or shrubs near enough to offer a hiding spot where I might be able to overhear—making it the perfect spot for a private conversation.

Something *tap tap tap*'ed my shoulder. "Miss me, princess?"

I nearly screamed with shock, but a rough hand covered my mouth. It was only after a moment of struggle that I realized I recognized those deep blue eyes. The black hair had thrown me off. "Torque! What are you trying to do, scare me to death?" I demanded.

"Wouldn't that be a waste," Torque chuckled, kneeling down next to me sliding the straps of his backpack off. "Like the wig?" he asked, indicating his messy mop of black hair.

"Love it," I snapped. "How did you even know I was here?"

He held up what looked like some sort of portable tracking device, then pointed at my feet.

I glanced down at my boots. "Right. I totally forgot about the tracker Rift put in there."

"Rift has Juliet keeping tabs on you. She alerted him when you left the manor outside school hours," Torque said.

"Lucky you left it in there. Otherwise you'd be stuck here with no accomplice."

"I don't *need* an accomplice," I retorted. "I told Rift I can do this on my own!"

"Well, you'll learn quickly dearie that being in the Resistance isn't about being on one's own. We help one another. That's all there is to it," he said, pulling out a pair of binoculars. "This isn't about you and your pride. It's about all of us."

Darn it. I didn't have a good response to that one. "Speaking of help, where's Rift?" I asked.

"Tied up at the moment. Metaphorically, not literally," he added as he aimed the binocular through a sparse section of bush. "So, why are you trailing your dad?"

"He's meeting someone from the Forum, and it sounds like it might have something to do with the Anagram. My dad wouldn't talk about it over the phone... he wanted to meet in person."

"Perfect," said Torque. "Must be good if he's being that paranoid."

"But how are we supposed to hear what's going on?" I wondered.

Torque grinned, then fished a piece of gum out of his pocket and popped it in his mouth. "Leave that to me, sweetheart." He grabbed the backpack, got to his feet, and wedged his way out the opposite side of our bush formation, leaving me alone with the binoculars.

I trained them back on my father. Still no sign of the

person he was supposed to be meeting. I almost pitied the poor guy who'd dare make my father wait.

A moment later, Torque strolled into my field of vision. He'd put on some sunglasses and a pair of headphones and was bouncing his head to whatever music he had playing. When he reached the bench, he plopped down next to my father, seemingly oblivious to the scowl Titus shot him.

Still chomping his gum and bobbing to his music, Torque unzipped his bag and pulled out a soda. He then spit his gum into his hand and stuck it to the side of the bench before taking a swig from his drink.

My father watched with thinly-veiled contempt. finally, he leaned over and prodded Torque on the shoulder.

Torque gave him a wide, dorky grin and pulled out one of the headphones, but he allowed the grin to fade more and more as Titus spoke. finally, he rose with a shaky nod and what looked like some sort of scrambling apology and hurried back down the path.

I waited another minute before the sound of shuffling leaves behind me announced Torque's return. "What was all that about?" I asked.

Shhh!" Torque motioned for me to look through the binoculars.

I slid over and aimed them at the bench. A large, beefy man with balding brown hair had wandered up the path, looking slightly winded. He sat down on the bench next to my father. "Who is that?" I wondered.

"I'm not sure. Rift would probably know," Torque said.

"Too bad he's not here."

"Doesn't matter." Torque handed me one ear of the headphones. "I stuck a recorder chip to the gum. Should have a pretty good sound range."

My eyes widened. "That's brilliant!"

Torque gave a self-satisfied shrug as he inserted one of the earbuds, offering me the other. Even expecting it, it was still a shock to hear my father's voice in my ear.

"...*was about to leave*," my father was saying.

"*Come on, Titus,* said the pudgy man. His accent sounded native to the northern part of England. "*Fifteen minutes isn't a lot of time to cross the whole blasted world!*"

"*Our world's technology doesn't leave room for excuses,*" my father countered.

The man waved his words off. "*Let's just cut to the chase then. I believe you left off with my overly-lax security. On that note, I've doubled my guards and will soon be installing a surprise or two, just in case.*

"*Wise thinking, if you value your skin. They'll probably be coming for you next. For all we know, they may be on their way even as we speak,*" said my father.

Through the binoculars, I could see the large man shudder. "*What happens if they manage to acquire them all?*"

"*If the worst were to happen and they did manage to apprehend all of the components, they would still have to figure out how to use the key.*"

240

My heart skipped a beat.

"And if you had actually attended *today's gathering,"* my father continued, *"you would know that we've reached a decision regarding that possibility. The instructions would have to be destroyed."*

There was an angry exclamation from his colleague.

"What other choice would we have, Bellanger?" demanded Titus.

My ears perked up. Bellanger? "I know that name…" I whispered to Torque.

Titus continued. *"So long as even one of us survives, the knowledge survives as well. Instructions can be re-written. And even if the Quartermasters were to fall, the key is better rendered useless than lost to a worthless band of Dregs."*

"I suppose I can't disagree with the logic." Bellanger shook his head. *"To think that they've managed to get this far…"*

My father nodded curtly. *"Zhou was right. We're fighting something larger than we care to admit. But better acknowledge that our enemy is formidable than delude ourselves into thinking these attacks aren't linked."*

"Mhmm," Bellanger agreed. *"Well Titus, any other horrible news to report while you've got me here?"*

Through the binoculars, I could see Titus purse his lips. *"Nothing comes to mind. Then again, I do have one more less-than-pleasant stop to make, so one never knows."*

Bellanger gave a satisfied humph and began the arduous process of heaving himself up from the bench. He tottered to his feet and began to walk in the direction he'd come from.

"And Bellanger?"

Bellanger turned.

I could see every detail of my father's smirk through the binoculars. *"Watch your back."*

After my father and Bellanger had parted ways, Torque immediately called to update Rift. "Hey mate. Follow Ambry's boot tracker and meet up with us at the nearest public Telepoints—and bring a location drive, all right?"

He listened for a moment, then handed me the phone. "Why me?" I asked.

"Your mission, your update. Besides, he wants to make sure you're okay."

I rolled my eyes and held the phone up to my ear, exclaiming when Torque suddenly hoisted me to my feet.

"Walk and talk," Torque said. "I want to see where Bellanger's headed."

"What just happened?" demanded Rift's voice on the other end.

"Torque happened," I grumbled. "Nothing to worry about."

"Oh, good," he said, sounding relieved. "Where are we in the search?"

"*We* aren't anywhere," I corrected, following Torque's lead as he battled his way out of the shrubs. "Torque and I, however, were just privy to an interesting conversation." I proceeded to tell him about discussion between him and Bellanger.

When I got to the part about the Quartermasters, Rift groaned. "We had hoped there would only be one more to find," he said. "But still, two isn't horrible. We managed to procure the first two in less than a week once our plans were fully laid."

I raised my eyebrows. "How do you know there are only two left?" I asked, lengthening my strides to keep up with Torque.

"*Quarter*masters," Rift said, enunciating the first two syllables. "Quarter meaning one-fourth, which suggests that there are four of them total, each with one piece of the Anagram."

"Still an assumption," I pointed out. "But what are Quartermasters anyway?" I asked.

He sighed. "We've suspected for some time that there's a smaller contingency within the Timekeepers that holds more authority than the rest. An upper tier, you might say. Apparently, it must contain four select members: the Quartermasters. The most powerful people in the world."

I rubbed the goosebumps that rose on my arms. "And my father is one of them."

"He is."

I glanced ahead to where Bellanger was getting into a cab and thought over his conversation with Titus. I'd always known my father commanded a great deal of power and respect, even among his colleagues at the Forum. But to know that the man who raised me was one of the four most powerful people in the world? It was more than unnerving.

Somehow being one of twenty-four had made him just one of many, lost in a sea of dark blue robes. But one of four… "Do you know who the others are?" I asked.

"We found out the identity of one other some time ago," he said. "Jun Zhou, the Timekeeper representative from China."

Torque hailed us a cab and I slid in next to him on the weathered seat cushion. "My dad just mentioned him." I vaguely remembered Timekeeper Zhou. I had been eight years old when my father brought Orelia and I with him to the Forum and introduced us to the rest of his associates. Zhou had seemed at first like a friendly old tortoise, completely bald with a thin, wispy beard. He bobbed in a comedic little bow when we met. However, when his nervous-looking assistant had hurried up to whisper something in his ear, his entire countenance transformed.

A rage had burned in the dark embers of his eyes that had his assistant veritably cowering in terror as Zhou ordered him to wait in an adjoining room. I wouldn't envy the person who crossed him. "So he's the one you robbed before my father?"

"Mm-hmm." There was a pause before Rift spoke again. "Kade and Avienne led a small group that broke into Zhou's compound in the Jiangsu Province three days before Torque and I snuck into your place. It wasn't an easy task, mind you. They managed to get Zhou's piece of the Anagram, but we lost five Rebels in the process." His voice was grave.

"I'm sorry," I said softly. "Did you know any of them?"

"All of them," he said. "Good people."

I gave a somber nod, though I knew he couldn't see it. "I'm sure they didn't deserve to die."

"No, they didn't," he agreed. "But they understood that some things are worth dying for."

I didn't know what to say to that. I looked down at Torque's muscled forearm, thinking of the Circlet lying hidden on his skin. I'd only known about the Resistance for a few days; these two had been working at the center of it for who knew how many years. How many of their friends had fallen in pursuit of their cause? I couldn't understand that kind of loss.

Rift broke the silence with a sigh. "Well, thanks to you, we have some intel to go on. I'll have to get off of here in a sec. I'm heading to the archway." I could almost see the mischievous gleam in his eyes when he spoke again. "What do you say we pay old Bellanger a visit?"

CHAPTER THIRTEEN

"But what if Bellanger decides to go somewhere else?" I asked as we strode toward the Telepoint line. Rift had met up with us just down the street from an Italian restaurant where Bellanger had taken a detour for a cup of gelato. Now the three of us wove along behind the portly man like watchdogs stalking a marked target. I pulled my moth-eaten wool hat down more closely around my ears, shoving a few loose strands of hair out of sight. If Bellanger recognized me, we'd all be in trouble.

Next to me, Rift chuckled. His hair was still pulled back in a low tail with several escaping curls. I resisted the odd urge to reach out and tuck them behind his ear. "Humphrey Bellanger is the laziest Timekeeper the Forum has ever had the misfortune to employ. He has workers to do everything for him. And this," Rift pointed at Bellanger's back, "is probably the only physical activity he does on a daily basis. If he goes anywhere other than straight back to his top-secret hideout, I'll eat my boot.

An odd sparkle lit Torque's eyes. "You may have just given me an idea…"

Since he didn't finish the thought, I elected to ignore it. "So how are we supposed to follow him there?" I asked.

"We're not trailing him all the way there right now," Rift said. "Even if we knew where it was he was going, it would look too suspicious for the three of us to enter the exact same coordinates immediately after a prominent Timekeeper. Those are the sorts of anomalies the Officials watch for while on duty. For now, we just need the coordinates."

"Which is where I come in," Torque said, pulling a silver flask from inside his jacket. He winked at me as he slipped a dark pill between his teeth. "Bottom's up, love." He cocked his head back and took a swig from the flask.

"What was that?" I asked him.

"A way to ensure that the guard is occupied while Rift gets the coordinates to Humphrey's jump," Torque replied.

"Oh, and I'll warn you," Rift added. "This won't be pretty."

We fell silent as we stepped into the back of the line

directly behind Bellanger. As we waited, Rift and Torque would make the odd bit of conversation here and there so as not to appear suspicious. I stared at the back of Bellanger's head. He was balding, and only the hint of gray at his roots suggested that his hair might be dyed that shade of brown.

We had almost reached the Archway when I turned back to find that Torque had adopted an uncharacteristically worried expression. He was muttering under his breath. "I don't think I can do this…"

"You'll be fine," Rift said, clapping his shoulder. "Less than a second and we're there!"

"No, no no no, I can't, I don't want to…" Torque said, shaking his black mop of a head. I was impressed that the wig didn't budge.

Ahead of us, Humphrey had just entered his coordinates and the dark folds of his cloak were disappearing through the Archway.

Rift gave Torque a little nudge forward. "We'll be right behind you, mate!"

Torque faltered. He shook his head again, looking a little green. "I don't feel so good…" A shudder racked his body, and before the Official on guard could make a move, Torque proceeded to puke all over the ground directly in front of the Telepoint. This patch of ground also happened to include the Official's silver boots. Now I knew what idea Rift must have given him.

The blond Official jumped back, exclaiming loudly in a language that might have been Swedish.

"Sorry mate, I'm so sorry," Torque was saying, holding his hands out apologetically. Behind him, I thought I saw Rift slip something from his pocket and insert it into the console in the time it would have taken me to blink.

The Official scowled at poor Torque as he shook vomit from his boot. "Get him out of here!" he ordered, reverting to English.

Whatever Rift had inserted into the console was already back in his pocket. He took Torque by the arm. "We're so sorry," he repeated as we dragged a white-faced Torque out of the line.

We half-walked, half-carried him over to one of the tables at an outdoor cafe across the street. He slumped into the mesh-wire seat, wiping a bit of vomit from the corner of his mouth with a look of extreme distaste. "I didn't care for that."

"Your sacrifice was not in vain, my friend," Rift assured him. "We have what we came for. Now let's get out of here."

"What was that you took while we were getting in line?" I asked Torque as Rift offered him a hand and pulled him up. We began walking up the street the way we came.

Torque cast me a sideways glance, still looking a little queasy. "A handy little pill that makes one briefly and violently ill. As you might imagine, we use it only in dire circumstances."

"Inspired performance, by the way," said Rift, patting Torque on the back.

Torque glowered at him.

"If this whole Resistance thing falls through, you two could have impressive acting careers in your futures," I added.

"If this whole Resistance thing falls through, we won't have a future," Rift said. "Which is why it's so important that we get our hands on the last two pieces of the Anagram."

Something stirred in my memory at his mention of the mysterious puzzle. "My father referred to it as a key. Do you know what it opens?"

"We know the door," said Rift. "We're just not positive about the contents behind it."

"Don't let him fool you," Torque butted in. "We're *next* to positive… we just need the proof."

We paused at a street corner. Rift pulled out the small device he'd inserted into the Telepoint. It was a miniature thumb-drive, no bigger than the nail on my pointer finger. He plugged it into his wristwatch and stared at the tiny numbers that flashed across the screen. "Looks like Bellanger is holed up on an island somewhere in the South Pacific," he said.

"So what now?" I asked.

"Now, we call Kade. I know it may seem like I do whatever I like, but I do still answer to him," Rift said, cocking a smile. He pulled a cell phone from his jacket, punched in a number manually, and held it briefly to his ear. "Kade, we've got it," he said. "Coordinates are fifteen degrees south, one hundred forty-eight degrees west."

I made a point of filing away the coordinates—force of habit probably. My mother once said that people tend to memorize coordinates now the way they used to memorize telephone numbers back when her grandmother was a little girl.

"Everything went perfectly." he said after a pause. "So when do you want us to follow?" He listened for a moment and then turned to Torque. "You, Ming, and I will Telepoint there in the morning after Bellanger has left for London."

"Wait, just the three of you?" I asked.

Rift held up a finger. "Uh huh. And what about Ambry?" There was a longer pause. He began tapping his finger against the phone, looking agitated. "Kade, I really think…" he broke off, interrupted by the voice on the other line. He glanced at me and shook his head.

Frowning, I snatched the phone from him. "Kade, please listen. I want to help!"

Kade sighed on the other end of the phone. "No, *you* listen, Miss Croft. You did well getting the information we needed, but Rift and Torque have been doing this for years. You, on the other hand, aren't trained for this sort of mission. You'd only be a liability."

"I've taken self-defense and martial arts courses since I was five!" I argued. "I can do this! Besides, if they were to get caught, you could pretend I'm your hostage to stall for time." I looked up to find Rift smiling at me. Well, smiling

251

in his own way. I'd noticed that he tended to smile with his eyes when it would be inappropriate to smile the conventional way.

"I don't think any story would be sufficient to explain you showing up on Bellanger's private, *secret* property," Kade argued.

"But I—"

"It's a *no*, Ambry," Kade said, his voice now stern. "You may be used to getting whatever you want back at home, but if you want to be a part of what we're doing, you need to learn to follow orders. Am I clear?"

His words stung. Not just because of their insinuations —that I was just another spoiled Elite brat whining to get her way—but because of how wrong he was. If he only knew how trapped I'd always been in my home, at my school, in my family, he'd never think I was accustomed to doing just as I pleased. Money didn't equate to freedom.

I closed my eyes and sighed. "Yeah. Got it." I shoved the phone back at Rift and stalked away to sit on the curb while he got his final instructions.

Torque plopped down next to me. "Don't worry your pretty blue head, princess," he said. "Besides, this probably isn't the sort of thing you'd enjoy. Odds are there will be a lot of guards to deal with and a lot of guns by association."

I said nothing, but continued to glower down at the flecks in the sidewalk while Rift continued his conversation with Kade.

Footsteps from behind told me Rift was approaching.

"Ambry, Kade wants to speak with you."

My head jerked up. "What?"

"He wants to talk to you again," Rift said, offering me the phone.

Perplexed, I raised it to my ear. "Hello?"

Kade's voice sounded irritated. "I spoke again with Rift. He went out of his way to assure me that you would be a valuable addition to the team on this task."

I almost pulled the phone away from my ear to stare at it in amazement, but Kade was still talking. "Rift has also given me his word that you will follow all of his orders, and that in turn, he will take full responsibility for you. But there is a caveat to all of this; if you decide to participate in this mission, there's no going back. I mean that literally: you won't be able to return to your family's home or to your school again. There's too great a risk that your allegiance will be discovered."

My excitement dimmed.

One day.

That was all I had left of my normal life. I thought of Prewitt and Gemma; the three of us had grown up together. We'd spent most of our lives in each other's company. Leaving them behind would be like leaving a huge piece of myself that I could never hope to get back. More so than my parents and sister, those two *were* my family. How could I say goodbye to them on such short notice? *No,* I thought, my heart lurching with a sudden realization. *I won't even be able to say goodbye. They'd never let me go.*

But this was what I'd signed up for in the first place, wasn't it? Wasn't this what I'd been hoping for?

Kade continued. "Naturally, your family and friends will search for you, so you'll have to go dark for a while after this mission. You'll stay in the Atrium, training with the other new recruits and assisting where able. You'll be one of us," he said, his voice far less stern than it had been before. "Can you agree to that?"

I opened my mouth, but guilt choked out my reply. Prewitt's face floated into my mind—his golden hair disheveled as usual, his smile sad. I remembered what he'd asked as we stood in the school courtyard after I'd apologized for my first disappearance. *"Please Ambry, promise me that you won't pull something like this again?"*

I can't, Prew, I thought, looking into his pleading eyes. Eyes that I knew so well. Eyes that I might never see again. *I can't promise you that. I have to let you go.*

I forced the image of his pain-ridden face out of my mind and focused back on the phone pressed against my ear. "Yes," I said firmly. "I can handle that."

"Then welcome to the Resistance," Kade said. "Good luck."

The call disconnected.

"What was all that about?" Torque wondered, frowning.

"I'm going with you tomorrow," I said, hardly daring to believe my luck.

Torque's eyes widened. "Kade's seriously letting you

come along? Wow. Seems like the ice-man is thawing out."

"Maybe by a fraction," Rift said. "Although he did also say he wants you back at headquarters in the next ten minutes, Torque."

"And with that, I recant my previous statement," Torque said, bouncing to his feet. "I'd best be off. What about you?" he asked Rift.

"I'll stay and make sure Ambry gets back safely. She has some packing to do tonight."

"She does indeed." Torque reached for my hand and planted a kiss on my knuckles. "Glad to have you aboard, m'lady." And with that, he turned and vaulted off down the street, weaving easily through passersby.

I handed the phone back to Rift. "What did you say to convince him to let me come along?"

"I just told him the truth," Rift said. "That you'd be an asset to the team, being one of the only people in the know about the Anagram—not to mention those fighting skills you picked up at that snooty Academy of yours. I've seen some of the videos taken for your exams... you're not half-bad, Croft."

I rubbed my neck as though I could stop the blush from creeping up it. "Thanks."

He continued. "I also explained that you weren't arguing with him because you were used to getting your way, but because you really believe in what we stand for and want to help in any way you can."

Tears began to well in my eyes. It was strange having

someone other than Prewitt and Gemma to stand up for me. I was all the more grateful for it knowing that after tomorrow, I wouldn't have the two of them anymore. I stared up at him. "You really said that?"

He nodded, offering a hand and pulling me to my feet. His mouth tipped in a grin. "I also told him that you're stubborn and that if he didn't give in, you'd probably show up anyway and compromise the whole thing."

I rolled my eyes and returned the grin. "Well, I have to admit it's true. I'd already memorized the coordinates." A tear escaped and slid down my cheek. I turned my head and tried to brush it away discreetly.

"Hey," Rift said. He caught my chin and turned it so I was facing him. "That was really brave of you. I know it won't be easy, letting go of your friends and family."

"My family won't be the hard part," I admitted.

He smiled. "Well, I think you'll find that the Resistance is a sort of family too. And we look out for our own," he said softly, brushing away another tear from my cheek with his thumb.

I met his gaze, and the look in his eyes caught me off-guard. It was that look that had frightened me when I woke up for the first time in the Atrium, like he was opening a door to see straight into my soul. Only this time, it felt like that door was swinging open both ways. Maybe it was because I'd made my decision to commit fully to the Resistance. Maybe that sacrifice had sparked a new level of trust. Whatever the reason, there was a rawness—a vulnerability—in the way Rift smiled at me now, and I caught a glimpse of him. Not the exterior façade he liked to put up, but who he really was. The person whose true name I had yet to learn.

There was a long pause. Longer than a normal break in conversation. By the time I'd gathered my wits enough to say something, it felt too late. There was a part of me that wanted to lean toward him again. I glanced at his lips, slightly parted only inches away. What would it be like to close the gap? The pull toward him was almost magnetic…

But then I remembered what had happened the last time I had tried something like that. *He's not interested*, I reminded myself. *No need to make a fool of myself and be rejected again*. I broke my eyes away, folding my arms and glancing sheepishly down at them. "I'd better get home and pack," I said. "Besides, Charlie said if I didn't get back within an hour, he'd call my father himself."

"When did you leave?" he asked.

"8:18," I replied. "He seemed pretty serious, so I made note of the exact time."

Rift glanced down at his watch. "It's 9:02. So we've got exactly sixteen minutes before that butler of yours rats you out."

I thought of Charlie's crestfallen face when I'd insisted on leaving. "If he did, I'd deserve it," I murmured.

Rift frowned. "Don't talk like that. You helped to accomplish a lot today, Ambry. If you deserve anything, it's a medal," he said, putting a comforting arm around my shoulders. "Come on. Let's get you home."

CHAPTER FOURTEEN

While Rift hailed a cab, I managed to get hold of Charlie on the manor's phone line, pretending to be a potential maid candidate. Charlie said very little, but agreed to meet me at the gate.

With a little monetary encouragement, we convinced our driver to pick up the pace and wound up making it back with time to spare.

"Did you get what you needed?" he asked without looking at me.

"I did," I replied. "Thanks for letting me go."

"Well, I'm glad to see you heeded my advice and

made it back by the agreed-upon time," he said, a tremble in his voice. "You should know that your father returned about ten minutes ago. He didn't ask, but I believe he thinks you to be studying in your room."

Not knowing what to say, I nodded mutely.

Charlie nodded back, his eyes grazing mine, then he turned and walked away.

I reached the maid's closet without incident, but with more than a moderate amount of guilt. Within minutes I'd returned my stolen clothes and was headed upstairs.

It wasn't until I reached the second landing that I crossed paths with my father. "Ambrosia," he said, cocking his head. His profile was hard and angular; Orelia had inherited those sharp features and sharper personality. Other than my eyes, I couldn't see myself in any part of him. "I thought you were upstairs studying?"

"I was," I replied smoothly. "I just ran down to the kitchen to get a quick snack." *It's unnerving how fast my lies are improving,* I thought with a pang.

Titus nodded. "You seem to be adjusting well considering your recent… incident." He seemed to hesitate a moment. "I'm glad. If not in behavior outside the classroom, you've always been an impressive student when it comes to your school work."

I glanced at him, surprised. "Oh. Um, thanks." I shouldered my bag, not quite sure what else to say. What *did* you say to your estranged father when you knew you were about to run away to join his enemies and might never see him again? I didn't exactly harbor a deep and binding love for the man, but despite all the ways I'd felt betrayed by him, I did care about him. "I hope you have a good night…Dad."

Titus turned to me. I hardly ever called him "Dad" anymore. These days it was usually "Father" or "Sir." The lines in his face softened. He set a hand on my shoulder. It was the most affection I could remember receiving from him in years. "Goodnight, Ambry."

....

Once in my room, I closed and locked the door before pulling my backpack down from where it hung on my door and tossing it onto the bed. I set my hands on my hips and stared at it for a moment. The Resistance could provide me with clothes and food and other basics, so Rift had advised me on our taxi ride back to bring only what could fit in a backpack.

I gazed around the room. There were very few things that held any attachment for me. After some thought, I crossed to my dresser and picked up a framed photo of our family on vacation in Tuscany. I was probably about eight years old—the year before my father became a Timekeeper. That had been the most peaceful, relaxing week I could remember. I looked at my parents, tanned from the warm Italian sun, and Orelia in her favorite white sundress. We might have actually been happy together that day.

I stashed the photo in the backpack before gathering a few other necessities: a few favorite clothing items; a necklace from my grandparents, both of whom had died when I was young; a wad of several hundred merits I'd kept stashed in case of emergency. And last but not least, I pulled down a photo album filled with pictures of Gemma, Prewitt, and I. The two of them had given it to me for my seventeenth birthday—the last birthday I'd ever share with them, if all went according to plan. It spanned most of our lives: from playing on the elaborate playground in Gemma's backyard together when we were five to photos of Honoratus field trips in Prague, Cairo, and a dozen other foreign cities. There had been cotillions, movie premieres, vacations, and other less-than-sanctioned adventures, all of them filled with tight hugs and perfectly-preserved laughter.

I lay on my bed flipping through the pages until I fell asleep, my pillow damp with quiet tears.

....

Titus was already gone when I went downstairs for breakfast the next morning. "Good morning, sweetheart," said my mom. She was sitting at her usual spot at the head of our unnecessarily-long mahogany dining table. "Lanette made us French toast this morning."

I moved to sit down, but then thought better of it. I crossed over to where she sat sipping her coffee and gave her a quick kiss on the cheek. "Shouldn't we start calling it 'eggy-toast,' or something more culturally ambiguous?" I asked with a roll of my eyes, taking the seat across from Orelia.

"My my, someone is feeling affectionate this morning," said my mother, raising her eyebrows. "Could it be because of a certain young man who came calling last night?"

Orelia's fork froze, her piece of toast suspended above a puddle of golden syrup. "A certain who-now?" She turned to me in obvious disbelief. "You had a *young man* over last night? And I'm just now hearing about it?"

I was just as surprised as she was. "What are you talking about, Mom?" I asked, pouring myself a glass of orange juice.

"I'm talking about our lovely centerpiece this morning," she said, gesturing to the vase of blue roses on the table. "They were left at the gate with a note saying they were for Ambry."

Frowning, I grabbed the small card tucked amidst the flowers. Who would have left me roses in the middle of the night?

Orelia was quite possibly more curious than I was. "Well *who was it then*?" She narrowed her eyes. "If you're letting me get worked up about this only to say it's Prewitt..."

My mother's only reply was a conspiratorial grin.

I scanned the note, but it merely said, *"For Ambry."* I shook my head, setting it next to my plate. "There's no name."

Orelia set her fork down with gusto. "Let me get this straight: you finally have a secret worth telling, and you aren't going to share?"

"I'm serious! There's no name! And it's a good thing knowing you... the rumors would escalate to a secret engagement by the end of the day."

"But you must have *some* idea of who sent them!"

Rather than argue with her—which I knew to be pointless—I began shoveling French toast into my mouth. However, I couldn't help but turn over the possibilities in my mind. If the flowers *had* come from Prewitt—or anyone at the Academy for that matter—it wouldn't make a difference. Odds were I wouldn't lay eyes on them again after today.

The reality of that thought almost made me physically ill. Unable to keep up the pretense of being hungry, I set down my fork and reached for one of the roses instead. It's comforting scent helped the sudden nausea subside.

My sister crossed her arms, sinking into one of her familiar sulks.

"Oh, come now, Orelia," said my mother. "It's all right for Ambry to have her secrets." Mom turned to wink at me.

My stomach twisted. *You have no idea.*

Orelia made a faint growling noise and glared at me as though I had denied her a fundamental birthright.

"Well, I'm afraid I have to be off," my mother said,

264

rising gracefully to her feet. "The Global Arts Festival in Beijing starts in half an hour. You girls have a nice day at the Academy."

She started to leave, and I found myself standing up so fast that I bumped the table, knocking over the remnants of my orange juice. While Orelia exclaimed about my supernatural klutz powers, I ran around the table and threw my arms around my mother. It took her a moment to react, but then I felt her slender arms envelope me. My head was tucked just under her chin. I took a deep breath, wanting to remember her—how she smelled, how her arms felt around me.

Sure, Calista Croft had made her share of mistakes over the years. There were countless times that she had chosen to side with my father even when she *knew* he was out of line. But she was still my mom. And just the fact that I'd seen the resentment there in her eyes when he mistreated me proved her love, even if she hadn't been brave enough to act on it. "Have a good time at the festival, Mom. I... I love you."

She laughed. "I love you too, sweetheart." She pulled away, holding me at arms length. "I could get used to the effect this mystery boy and his flowers seem to be having!" I rolled my eyes, and she smiled. "I'll see you this evening," she said as she turned to go.

I watched her walk away, and a tear finally managed to escape my eye. She was already in the hall, so I let it run down my cheek unhindered. "Goodbye, Mom."

....

It was strange, walking through the Academy gates knowing that it would probably be my last time entering the school grounds. I yanked on the hem of my skirt. *Last time having to wear this ridiculous uniform too*, I thought with grim satisfaction.

Rift's instructions had been very specific: I was to arrive at school early and hand-deliver a note to Provost Bridgeport "from my mother" detailing my excused absence for the remainder of the day. It explained her last-minute decision to invite me along for the Global Arts Festival in Beijing, and welcomed the Academy to contact her to verify this information—if they felt it really necessary—though she might be difficult to reach during the keynote speaker's presentation. That ought to buy me at least enough time to vacate the premises without interference.

Next, I needed to remove my tracker; the last thing Rift and the others needed was to have a thousand Officials descend upon the Atrium in pursuit of me. The removal itself should be easy, aside from my longstanding prejudice against being cut by knives. Thankfully, Rift had a contact within Honoratus that could do the job for me as I had no real desire to slit open my own skin. I was also more than a little curious to see who the Resistance had planted within the Academy. After removing the tracker, the Resistance mole would destroy it.

Seemed straightforward enough.

I made it to Bridgeport's office about twenty minutes before the first bell. "Good morning, Miss Croft," he said, leaning forward in his chair. "To what do I owe the pleasure?"

"Good morning, sir," I said, giving him my most innocent smile. "I just came by to drop off a note from my mother." I held out the note and prayed that Mateo was as good at forging signatures as he claimed.

Bridgeport leaned forward on his desk to accept the paper. He spent several moments perusing its contents. "Hmm. Beijing, you say?"

I nodded.

"I've been there several times," he said, adjusting his glasses. "Never for the Arts Festival, I'm afraid."

"It will be my first time attending," I said brightly. "My mother thought it would be an advantageous experience."

"I couldn't agree more," said Bridgeport. "It's just a shame that it takes you away from your classes."

I bit my lip and tried to stay calm as Bridgeport began to fold the note back up.

Finally, he handed it back to me. "But so long as you touch base with your professors regarding any work you might have to make up, I don't see it being a problem."

I smiled, allowing the tension that had been building in my shoulders to ebb away. "Thank you, Provost."

"You're most welcome, Ambrosia. I'll see you

tomorrow then."

"See you tomorrow," I said, dipping my head in respect. I closed the door to his office and exhaled.

One job down: one to go.

Rift had said that his contact would meet me in the chem lab at fifteen minutes before the bell—the first lab didn't start for several hours. When I reached the door, it was to find it slightly ajar. I stepped inside and glanced around. Lots of Bunsen burners and beakers. No people.

I waited for a couple more minutes before glancing down at my phone. Only ten minutes until the bell. If whoever-it-was didn't show up soon, I'd run the risk of bumping into Prewitt or Gemma on the way out, and I doubted I'd be able to hold myself together without them noticing something was off.

I was about to leave when the door opened.

It was Professor McCullough. "Surprised to see me?" he asked when he saw my stunned expression.

I gaped at him. "It's you? *You're* the mole in Honoratus?"

"What were you expecting? A janitor?" he asked, chuckling.

I shook my head. "I can't believe that all this time, you were working for them! How did you get involved—"

"I'll tell you all about it sometime," he said with a grin. "But for now, how about we get that pesky tracker out of you before first bell?"

I clamped my mouth shut and nodded mutely.

Offering him my wrist, I pulled up the sleeve of my sweater. "Thanks for doing this."

"Well, I figured a girl like you wouldn't be used to this sort of thing," he said. He pulled a switchblade from his pocket and flicked it open.

I tried not to flinch at the sight of the blade. "Yeah. I guess I'll have to start getting used to it though."

He paused from lowering the knife to glance up at me. "It's not the easiest life, I'll admit. But it's worth it, I assure you." He turned back to my wrist and pressed the blade to my skin, making a small incision over the faint scar from where Rift had removed my previous tracker. I winced at the sharp, biting pain, but I managed to refrain from embarrassing myself by yelping.

It was over quickly. McCullough used the point of the knife to lift out the small tracking device. "With this little bugger gone, I'm sure you'll have a much more pleasant trip back to the Atrium." He wrapped the tracker in a small piece of gauze before pocketing it. "I'll give you an hour's head start before I destroy it. To anybody watching, Ambrosia Croft will still be safely within the walls of Honoratus."

"Thank you," I said as he pressed some more gauze over the incision and pulled out a vial. "I really appreciate this."

"Happy to help," he said. He unscrewed the vial and swabbed some of the liquid over my cut. The bleeding immediately subsided. "And I want you to know that I really admire what you're doing, Ambry. It takes a lot to switch sides, especially if you've been raised in Elite society."

I pulled down my sleeve to cover the tape. "Like you said, it's worth it."

McCullough smiled. "We should stagger our exit. Why don't you go on ahead? You're on a tighter deadline than I am. I can wait a few more minutes."

I nodded and hurried for the door. "I guess I'll see you in the Atrium," I said, still marveling at the surreal thought.

McCullough held up a hand in farewell.

I slipped out the door and into the hall. Several students were already milling through the corridor with bleary morning looks plastered across their faces. I'd need to move fast if I wanted to avoid running into anyone I knew. I shouldered my bag and hurried down the hall.

I was almost to the doors when the sound of a familiar voice made my heart sink. "Ambry, wait up!"

It was Prewitt.

"Hey Prew," I said. My stomach dropped even as my mouth lifted in a forced smile.

"I was hoping to catch you before the bell," he said. "Do you want to study this afternoon for that linguistics test in Ndala's class? I have a terrible feeling he's going to make us write our answers using IPA."

"Uhh…Yeah, that sounds great," I said.

Prewitt frowned. "Ambry, what's wrong?"

I tried to look perplexed by his concern. "What do you mean?"

"Don't lie to me, Ambry. I can tell something's off. What's going on?" he asked, putting a hand on my shoulder.

I looked him squarely in the eyes. "I'm fine, Prew. Really," I said. "I just have to go to this Art Festival thing with my mom, so I won't be in class."

His eyes narrowed. He didn't believe me.

I shrugged off his hand and tried to move past him, but he darted back in front of me. This time he grabbed me by both shoulders. "Something's wrong, isn't it?" he asked. "Something big, otherwise you'd tell me."

"Prew, I—"

"No, let me finish," he said tightly. His expression became serious, almost desperate. "I've felt you slipping away, Ambry. And don't bother trying to convince me that I'm imagining things. I *know* you. We've been friends since we were five, remember? I can tell when you're hiding something from me. And I don't know if you're worried about putting me in danger with whatever-it-is you're up to, or if you just don't trust me anymore," he said, his voice catching. "But you have to know that *I'm on your side*. No matter what."

I bit back tears, fighting for a response. *This* was why I'd tried to avoid Prewitt. I would never be able to fool him…

So my only choice was to hurt him.

"You may be on my side, Prew," I said, unable to help the tears that spilled down my cheek. "But that doesn't mean I can trust you."

Prewitt looked stricken. I couldn't have hurt him more if I'd sent a swift punch to his gut.

I had to get away. It was too much, knowing I'd been the one to put that look on his face. So I turned and forced myself to walk away from my best friend, leaving him standing alone in the hallway.

It's for the best, I thought as I walked. *I can't let him get involved with this.* Salty tears wetted my lips. I licked them away and focused on regaining my composure. Falling apart wasn't an option. I wasn't out of the school yet and I only had ten minutes before I was supposed to meet up with Rift.

I had just opened the front doors when I heard my name again. "Ambry!"

I spun around to see Prewitt sprinting towards me. Before I could say a word, he threw his arms around me in a crushing embrace.

It caught me completely off-guard. At first I let my arms hang limp at my sides. But when he didn't let go, I wrapped them around him, taking in the smell of his clothes and the rapid beat of his heart against my cheek.

"Remember what I said," he murmured in my ear. "I'm on your side. No matter what."

"I know," I whispered. I released my hold on him and pulled away. "See you later, Prew."

He nodded, a tear slipping from his eye. "Bye, Ambry."

CHAPTER FIFTEEN

Rift was waiting for me on a bench two streets over from the Academy. "How did it go?" he asked as I approached.

"Fine," I muttered.

His brow furrowed. "What happened?"

I sighed and sat down next to him, exhausted from crying. I'd sobbed so hard after leaving the school that it had taken the entire walk over to calm myself down. "Ran into Prewitt," I said, staring down at my hands in my lap. My sleeves were still wet with tears. A residual shudder ran through me.

Rift's expression was unreadable. "I'm sorry, Ambry."

"Hey, this is what I signed up for, right?" I asked. "Can't leave with strings attached."

He nodded, but didn't say anything. After a long pause, he asked, "By the way, how did you like our contact?"

"McCullough? That was a surprise. I mean, he's always been one of the nicer professors, but he acted like such a staunch advocate for the Globe! He was always going on little tirades about the importance of the Global Alliance in between lessons."

"Makes for the perfect cover," Rift replied. "And he's been playing the part for over a decade, so it probably comes second nature by now."

I shook my head. "I still can't believe how far-reaching all of this is."

"The Resistance?"

I nodded. "You all have been operating for so long, and I've only known about it for a little over a week now."

"That's a high compliment. To be as effective and widespread as we are and still maintain our secrecy requires an incredible amount of effort. One false move and it could all be over. Oh, speaking of which," He fished in his jacket and pulled something from his pocket. "I hold in my hands a brand new identity for you," he said, grinning.

He handed me a black leather-banded wristwatch. The band was etched with interconnecting swirls, much like an elongated version of the Circlet. "It's beautiful," I said as I fingered the leather.

Rift seemed pleased with my reaction. "The new tracker with your updated information has been made to look like the battery of the watch, just in case someone gets the bright idea to look inside."

"Clever," I said. "So who am I?"

Rift pursed his lips. "That's quite the profound question, Miss Croft. However, the answer on paper would be Amber Reynolds—a seventeen year-old girl from Illinois with decent grades and a penchant for martial arts."

I smiled and stroked the smooth surface of the watch. "So I can still go by Ambry?"

"Of course," he said. "We wouldn't want you to lose your name."

"Like you did?"

Rift's smile faltered. "Right. Like I did." He shivered and stood, zipping up the front of his leather jacket. "We'd better get going."

"Oh. Right." I grimaced, wishing I could install a filter over my mouth.

We stopped in a restaurant along to way to grab some food and give me a chance to change out of my school uniform. Slipping into jeans and a T-shirt did wonders for my mood; it was liberating to think I'd never have to wear the white Academy skirt-blouse-cardigan-combo again. From the restaurant, Rift opted to follow my example from the Rebel's Song outing and take the Telepoint at the Yale-New Haven Children's Hospital where the guards there were less likely to recognize me. Sure enough, the guards barely cast me a glance as Rift and I filed through the queue. "Jakarta," Rift said. The guard punched in the coordinates, and Rift motioned for me to go first.

I stepped forward and slid my wrist over the Informational Reading Pad. Even though Rift had explained my new name, it was startling to see "Amber Reynolds" flash across the screen beneath a picture of my face framed by chocolate-brown hair.

The young Official glanced at the screen, then back at me. "Dye your hair?" he asked.

"Just last week," I said, twisting a blue strand around my finger. "Like it?"

He cocked his head. "It's not bad," he said flashing me a handsome smile. "Looks natural on you, somehow."

"Thanks," I said as I stepped through the portal...

...and suddenly found myself on a busy metropolitan street.

It was early evening in Indonesia. The road bustled with thick throngs of people. Jakarta *was* supposed to be one of the largest cities on the planet. "Good place to get lost, huh?" asked Rift from behind.

"It really is," I replied. I turned to him and smiled. "You remembered."

"Remembered what?"

"My hair," I said. "I told you I dyed it a chocolate-brown when I was younger."

Rift smiled. "I thought you'd like that touch. Now you can pretend that it was that color all along, until you *voluntarily* decided to take a fancy to that shade of blue. And speaking of which," he added, raising an eyebrow. "I think that Official back there took a fancy to it as well."

I laughed. "You're not serious."

"What?" he asked.

"He wasn't interested in me."

"Um, he most definitely was," Rift argued. "He couldn't keep his eyes off you." His tone was disapproving. In fact, it verged on annoyance.

Was he... no.

Then again... I glanced over at Rift as we walked. A muscle ticked in his jaw.

Was Rift *jealous*?

"I doubt he even remembers my face by now," I said finally. "And even if he did, Officials aren't my type."

"Oh really?" he said, raising his eyebrows. "And what pray-tell is your type?"

"I don't know," I said with a shrug. "Someone not decked out in Globe garb, for starters."

"Someone more like... Prewitt, perhaps?" Rift asked with a practiced nonchalance.

I stopped. "Prewitt?" I laughed, more shocked than amused. "You think I'm interested in *Prewitt*?"

"Well, would that be so hard to believe? He's obviously interested in you."

"That's ridiculous!" I said. "Prewitt's my best friend! He's like a brother to me."

His eyebrows rose. "I've seen him look at you, and I

doubt his feelings could be classified as fraternal."

"Fine," I said, dodging a few Indonesian kids who flew by on their bikes. "Think what you want. It doesn't matter either way since I won't be seeing him again anytime soon." Even the thought of it was enough to summon a fresh batch of tears, but I clenched my fists in an effort to repress them.

Rift must have noted my change of tone. "I'm sorry, Ambry," he said. All traces of mirth vanished from his face. "I know you care about him. It must have been hard to say goodbye."

"I'll be fine," I said without looking at him.

Rift hailed us a cab, which turned out to be a three-wheeled contraption he referred to as a "bajaj." The blue auto-rickshaw was captained by a bent-backed little man with sparse white hair. Rift gave him an address and a handful of merits, and his face broke into a smile that crinkled his eyes. We clambered in, and the bajaj slipped into the thick stream of traffic.

I wasn't in the mood to chat anymore, so we rode the rest of the way in silence. Traffic was terrible, but we eeked our way through until our driver turned off onto a side street. He brought us to a halt outside a crumbling tenement building.

"Thanks," Rift said with a small bow.

"No, sanks to *you!*" said the man with an enthusiastic wave.

Rift grinned as the bajaj sped away. "I probably paid him five times what he's used to getting," he explained.

"Nice fellow."

I nodded in agreement. "Where are we anyway?"

"This is one of the direct Telepoint routes to the Atrium," said Rift as we walked up the cement steps. They had once been a bright turquoise, but most of the paint was now chipped and faded.

"So there's a Telepoint in there that's not linked into the Grid, like the ones we used when you helped me break out?"

"Of course." Rift pulled out a key and inserted it in the lock. "The Resistance commandeered a number of the older models around the time of its conception—the leaders knew they'd need a discreet method of transportation that wouldn't be able to be monitored by the Globe. You could say we have a Grid of our own."

He turned the knob and we stepped inside. The place looked as though it had been abandoned years ago. There was a thick layer of dust covering everything in sight, with the exception of a few footprints leading off to the right. We followed them into a dingy living room. The few pieces of worn furniture were thrown into stark contrast by the large, gleaming Telepoint in the center. Rift strode over and immediately began to punch in our next coordinates.

"So now that I'm 'in,' can you tell me the Atrium's actual location?" I asked.

Rift chuckled. "I'll save that little tidbit as a present for your Swearing-in Ceremony."

My eyes widened. "There's going to be a ceremony?"

"Of course," he said. "It's standard for all new recruits. Don't worry, though. It's nothing too involved. Just a declaration of loyalty before the local Commanders and then you'll be issued your tracker ID's and inked with your very own Circlet."

The thought of my own Circlet sent a shiver of excitement over me. I glanced down at my wrist and tried to imagine the design imprinted there.

"Here we go!" said Rift. He swept an arm toward the archway. "Ladies first."

I ducked in a mocking curtsey before walking through.

This transition was one of the more surprising. I had seen the Arrival Room from a number of angles during my time in the Atrium, but this was the first time I had stepped onto the dais at its bustling center through one of their central Telepoints. Rift appeared momentarily behind me. He stepped toward me and squeezed my arm. "Welcome home."

It took a moment for the full weight of that to hit me. From now on, *this* was home. The manor and my life within it had vanished the moment I had stepped through that archway.

Rift raised an eyebrow. "How does it feel?"

I looked around the busy room. Some of the darkly-clad figures were manning computers with looks of deep concentration. Others were hurrying to other sections of the Atrium on their own tasks. Whatever their assignment, it was obvious that every person here was dedicated to their task. They were making a difference.

I turned back to Rift. "It feels right."

Rift grinned.

"About time," said a deep voice from behind me.

I turned to face the Commander. "Good to see you again, Kade."

"And you, Miss Croft. Or should I say Reynolds?" he asked.

"I think I'll just go with 'Ambry' for now," I replied.

"Ambry it is then." He turned to Rift. "Everything go smoothly?"

"All according to plan," said Rift.

"Good. In that case, let's get you both outfitted for your mission. Torque and Ming are already prepped."

Rift nodded. "Lead the way."

We followed Kade down a tunnel I didn't recognize and into a brightly-lit room. Torque was waiting for us, along with the slight Asian woman who I recognized as Ming. Across the room from them was a solitary Telepoint. "Do you have Telepoints all throughout the Atrium?"

"No," Kade replied. "It would be too difficult to monitor the people coming and going, and we prefer to keep close tabs on everything that happens here. We brought this one in specifically for your send-off. Best if this mission remains a secret beyond the people in this room."

I frowned. "Why? Do you suspect a mole in the Resistance?"

"Hardly. But it's best to be cautious nonetheless.

Ambry, I believe you've already met my Second-in-Command," he said, gesturing to Ming.

"You're Second?" I repeated. I'd never given Ming a lot of thought in my brief interactions with the woman, but now I took a good look at her. She stood with her hands clasped behind her back, her feet shoulder-length apart. A soldier's "at ease." Yes, there was definitely a militaristic air about her. "Nice to see you again, Ming."

"Nice to have you on board, Miss Croft," she said, returning the nod.

Kade walked across to a table lined with an assortment of weapons, from handguns to knives to air rifles. He picked one up and inspected it. "Have you used a gun before?" he asked.

For some reason, it took me a moment to realize he was addressing me. I shook my head. "I've had training in hand-to-hand combat, but there would have been no point training us with weapons we're forbidden to use."

"Then stick to what you know. But, in case of emergency…" Kade held up one of the guns. "It's pretty simplistic. Make sure the safety's off, aim, and pull the trigger," he said, mimicking each action. "This model can either be set to stun or to kill. Flip this switch here to change the setting," he said, indicating a button on one side.

"Setting on white, out like a light," quoted Torque with a grin.

"And the other?"

"Setting on red, target dead," Rift said as he holstered

his own weapon.

Swallowing, I eyed the gun with a nervous respect. Only Officials were allowed to carry guns. I had never even seen one up close.

"Stick to the white setting today," Kade said to the others. "This mission should be quick and quiet. Leaving a trail of bodies behind will only draw more attention to ourselves." He turned back to me and held out a thin, black vest. "Go ahead and put this on—under your jacket so it won't be seen."

I took the vest and shrugged off my jacket. "Bullet proof?" I guessed.

Kade nodded. "It disperses the impact of the standard ammunition used by Officials. It'll protect you from a shot to the torso, but I can't promise it won't hurt."

"You'll also need this," said Rift. He held up one of the tiny blue capsules I'd seen during my last visit to the Atrium. "May I?" he asked, gesturing to my watch.

I unhooked the watch and handed it to him. He inserted the capsule into a small hidden compartment in the back before handing it back to me. "These each have about ten seconds worth of freeze-time," Rift said. "If you hold the three buttons simultaneously, it activates the opening sequence."

"Just these three buttons?" I repeated, pointing to the ones he had indicated. "I thought the opening sequences on time capsules were supposed to be complex?"

"They are," Rift replied. "Which is why we

programmed the entire thing into the watch mechanism to be activated by a more simple combination, like the Officials do. The actual sequence is too lengthy and complicated to do manually if you're in a pinch."

"Which is what you're likely to be in if you have need of it in the first place," added Torque. "All right. We've got the toys. Now what's the plan?"

Kade pointed to an island on the map slightly northeast of French Polynesia. "Now that we know where Bellanger is hiding, Cody will be able to hack into his security feed and override the cameras with a loop."

Rift grinned at me. "I wasn't bluffing when I said he was the best."

"What about the guards on premises?" asked Ming.

"They make their rounds every half-hour. Our plan is to go in immediately after one of those shift changes, giving us about twenty-five minutes to get in, get Bellanger's piece of the Anagram, and get out," Rift replied. "From our satellites, we know that there are typically two guards on duty next to the Telepoint itself, so we'll be sending a friend in to herald our arrival." He held up a gold sphere the size of his fist. "This little beauty should knock out anyone within a ten yard radius."

"Aren't there guards inside as well?" I asked.

"Most likely. That's where the watches come in. Each of ours has one small capsule inside, which gives us a total of just under a minute of freeze time if we link up before activating them."

"So we just have to be touching?" I asked. I had heard of the basic premise before, but I'd never seen it in action. Supposedly, a time capsule would freeze everything except the person, unless someone else was touching them. Then they would be exempt from the freeze too.

Rift nodded. "As long as we link up for the activation itself, we'll all be able to move freely for the duration of each freeze."

The watch gave me far more comfort than any gun could have. It wasn't even a contest. Ten seconds of stolen time could mean the difference between a bullet in the head and a perfect escape.

"All right. We know what we need to accomplish. There's just one problem I see with this plan," said Torque. "How are we supposed to *find* Bellanger's piece of the Anagram within twenty-five minutes? Not including the time it takes us to get in and get out, of course."

"Good question," Ming said. "We've had Noelle from tech up all night sifting through the back-up records from Bellanger's security footage—which reminds me, I should have someone bring her a coffee. She saw him open a hidden safe behind a portrait in his office a few weeks ago."

"Did you get the combination?" Torque asked.

Rift shook his head. "It's not a combination at all. The safe only opens with a small key that Bellanger appears to keep on his person at all times."

"So we need Bellanger in order to open the safe." Torque rubbed a hand over his face. "Great. So no matter what, at least one person will know we broke in."

Rift nodded grimly. "Sorry to disappoint you. On a positive note, we doubt he'll put up too much of a fight if we level a gun in his face."

"And you're positive that his piece of the Anagram is in that safe?" Ming asked.

"No," Kade admitted. "But right now, it's our best hope of finding it. Based on what you overheard yesterday, it sounds like the longer we wait, the more time he'll have to add to his security system. So your job once you've entered the villa is to find Bellanger and get that key."

"Any other questions?" Rift asked.

"Yeah," said Torque. "When we get back—assuming we survive—should we check into an insane asylum immediately or wait for a professional diagnosis?"

Rift rolled his eyes.

"Then it sounds like everything is in place." Kade typed in the coordinates, and the Telepoint in the corner flared to life. *"Buena suerte."*

....

Two Officials lay sprawled on the ground. The last rays of the South-Pacific sunset gleamed off of their silver uniforms as we stepped out of the Telepoint. "Looks like our little friend did her job," said Torque. He picked up the golden sphere and pocketed it.

I raised an eyebrow. "She?"

"Don't ask," Rift said. "Remember, we stick close and move fast. We need to be within a couple steps of each other in case one of us has to activate a capsule."

Next to me, Ming gave a curt nod. She was all business. "Then let's move."

The four of us broke into a run, heading for the villa. "How do you know where we're going?" I asked Rift as we ran.

"I memorized the floor plan. Bellanger's office is in the farthest corner of the villa."

"Figures," said Torque. "Couldn't make it easy for us, could he?"

The western wall of Bellanger's villa was made entirely of glass. Perfect for creating a panoramic view of the ocean from the comfort of his living room. From the looks of things, the room inside was empty.

We vaulted up the marble steps and jogged through as quietly as possible while still maintaining some speed.

Being careful to stay near one another, we checked several side rooms. There was no one in sight. And while I was glad that we'd managed to avoid Bellanger's guards, we still needed the man himself to get what we came for. "Let's try the office," Rift whispered to us.

We followed him down a hallway lined with beautiful, illuminated pieces of art. I recognized a handful of them from the Art History course I took a couple years ago at Honoratus. It wouldn't surprise me if they were the originals. Rift paused outside the door at the opposite end and motioned for silence. "*Ready?*" he mouthed.

Torque, Ming, and I nodded.

Rift opened the door and leveled his gun as he stepped inside. The rest of us moved quickly to follow.

Humphrey Bellanger sat reclining behind his desk, the stubby remnants of a cigar poised halfway to his mouth.

"Don't move," Rift ordered.

For someone about to be robbed, Bellanger looked remarkably unfazed. "Not even to put down my cigar?" he asked in a gruff voice.

Rift's expression remained unmoved.

Bellanger chuckled. "I get it. One false move and you shoot me. Well, whatever you're planning to do with me, boy, I'd rather not burn my fingers." Slowly, he lowered his hand and planted the cigar on an ashtray at the edge of his desk. Smoke curled lazily into the air around his face. "Now, how can I help you?"

"Are you always this courteous to intruders?" Rift asked.

"I am when they have guns trained on me."

The corner of Rift's mouth lifted. "Very wise. Perhaps we can avoid killing you after all."

"What a comfort." Bellanger's eyes roamed the rest of our group until they finally fell on me. "Well, well. Ambrosia Croft. Not the person I'd expect to find breaking into my home. How did you come to find yourself in such… *diverse* company?"

I swallowed. I had known from the start that Bellanger

was bound to recognize me. Not that it mattered... after this mission, my disappearance would force me into hiding one way or another. At least this way my family would know I'd chosen a side. And thankfully, Cody's manipulation of the security footage would prevent anyone other than Bellanger from seeing the others' faces.

"Enough, Bellanger," Rift interrupted. "Open the safe."

Bellanger pursed his lips and tilted his head. "And what safe would that be?"

"The one behind the Matisse over there."

"Ha. Good eye, boy. Though you do realize that will require my getting up?"

Rift motioned with a jerk of his gun toward the painting.

With a great deal of effort, Bellanger hefted himself out of his chair and lumbered across the room. He gave a cursory glance at the weapon in Rift's hands before reaching into the pocket of his pants and pulling out a small key. He then pulled on the left side of the painting, which consisted of several impressionistic trees in a colorful background. It swung open like a small window. Sure enough, a lockbox was set into the wall behind. Bellanger inserted the key and opened the small metal door.

"That's enough. You can have a seat, but keep your hands up," Rift said.

Bellanger returned obediently to his chair.

Rift nodded to Ming. Without a word, she strode

across to the safe and began to sift through its contents. "This it?" she asked, holding up a silver object. This one was thin and cylindrical, far less complex-looking than the one procured from my father's study.

"Does it have the Timekeeper seal on it?" Rift asked, his eyes still on Bellanger's mocking face.

Ming turned the object around in her hands. "Yes. At the base."

"Then that's it," Rift said. "Let's get out of here."

We began to backing toward the door, but Bellanger spoke again before Rift could turn the handle. "I know you, don't I?" His watery eyes were fixed on Rift.

Rift halted so fast that I nearly ran into him. "Excuse me?" he asked, frowning.

Torque took a step toward Rift, casting a nervous glance at Bellanger. "He's baiting you, mate. Don't let him get under your skin," he said.

It was obvious that Rift gave the man more credence than Torque did. Still, he turned back toward the door.

Bellanger issued a low whistle. "My god. It's been years. You were what, thirteen?"

Rift spun back to face the portly man. All the blood had drained from his face. His stony expression could have vaporized ice.

I took an involuntary step back. Even as an initial captive of the Resistance, I had always felt safe with Rift. Maybe it was because he had chosen to help me on that rooftop when he could have saved himself the trouble and left me to the wolves. Maybe it was because when Kade had decided they couldn't risk trusting me, he had made a different call.

But the person standing next to me wasn't the Rift I knew. This was someone different. Someone dangerous.

It was the first time I had looked at Rift and felt afraid.

Rift's hands shook as he raised his gun at Bellanger and cocked the safety. "Talk," he commanded. His voice had taken on a low and menacing tone.

Bellanger's face split in a mirthless grin. "About what, exactly? The day we met, perhaps?"

Torque put a hand on Rift's shoulder. "Rift, we have to go. Now," he whispered low enough that Bellanger wouldn't be able to hear. "We've only got ten minutes before the guards change shifts and this gets a hell-of-a-lot more complicated."

Rift jerked out of Torque's grasp. "I said *talk!*" he bellowed at Bellanger.

Suddenly two opposing doors to the study flew open, and silver-clad guards began to rush toward us.

"Ambry, grab hold!" Torque yelled.

I clamped a hand onto Torque's upper arm just as he reached for Rift—

—and time stopped.

It was the first time I had experienced the power of a freeze capsule firsthand. I don't know what I'd expected, but the utter stillness almost left me with a sense of vertigo. The only sound was of our heaving breaths.

"He must have triggered a silent alarm. I couldn't wait for Ming," Torque panted.

"Go," Rift said to him. "Get Ambry out of here. I'll stay back and get Ming."

"There's no way I'm leaving without you," Torque argued. "Now stop wasting our time!" He didn't wait to hear Rift's response, but began firing stun blasts in rapid succession at the closest guards.

I winced, thinking of the unpleasant surprise awaiting them when they regained mobility.

Rift growled and turned to me. "Ambry, help me get Ming."

I swallowed and hurried with him toward the slight Asian woman. She had been frozen in the act of raising her own gun, her face tight with determination. Rift and I ducked under her arms and began to drag her toward the door we had entered through. "Be ready!" Rift said. "This could end any—"

The room snapped into motion. The six guards that had either entered the room or broached the doorways collapsed in twitching heaps.

Behind his desk, Bellanger's jaw fell open.

Ming stumbled trying to get her feet back beneath her. Once she had regained her footing, her knives were in her hands and at our throats before she realized who we were. "Sorry about that. Force of habit," she said.

The cool metal of the blade left my neck just as more guards began to pour through the opposing door.

"Grab hold again," Rift ordered us.

Ming and I obeyed, clasping his forearm above his watch.

"Torque!" he called. "Get over here!"

Torque started toward us, but all of a sudden a gunshot rocked the room. His back arched, and he crumpled to the floor. The Official standing in the doorway behind him turned his gun toward us—

—and once again, everything went still. "Torque!" Rift rushed to his friend.

I clapped a hand to my mouth. "Is he alright?" I asked finally.

Rift lifted Torque's shirt. "He'll be fine," he said, looking profoundly relieved. "The shot caught him in the back, so the vest took the worst of the impact. If anything I'm just worried that the fall might have knocked him out."

"We won't know until time resumes," Ming said from where she was removing a fallen Official's gun. "We can't get out of here dragging him with us. Plan?" she demanded.

"Get in close," said Rift. "Ming, the second things start again, hit the switch. We have to hope Torque will be conscious."

The words were barely out of his mouth when the room lurched back into action.

But rather than the immediate re-freeze I'd anticipated, I suddenly found myself on my feet with no memory of standing. A muscular arm had me in a choke-hold, and I could feel the barrel of a gun pressed to my temple.

I took in the scene before me. Torque still lay motionless on the floor, but Ming—like me—had been dragged to her feet. A dark-skinned Official had taken her knife and now held it firmly against her throat. Rift was standing a few feet away from me with burly Officials on either side of him holding his arms. The handcuffs around his wrists clattered as he tried to wrench himself out of their grasp.

Now that he was out of immediate danger, Bellanger had resumed his relaxed attitude. "That was quite a show you put on," he said as he stepped around his desk. He strode toward Rift until only mere inches separated the two of them. "Good to know this guerrilla group of yours has obtained some of the capsules."

Rift said nothing, but his breathing intensified as the aging Timekeeper leaned in to stare him in the eyes. It was almost as if Bellanger were searching for something. After a long moment, he leaned back and frowned. "It really is you then, isn't it?"

Rift stiffened.

Bellanger laughed and slapped his thigh, which rippled with the impact. "Well, I'll be damned," he said, his watery eyes widening. "Been a long time, hasn't it boy?"

"I think I'd remember meeting you," Rift said coldly.

"You'd think so, wouldn't you?" A cold sneer spread across Bellanger's sagging face, deepening the lines of old age so that he looked like a grinning bulldog. "But then, I suppose memory loss runs in your family, doesn't it?"

Another bout of fierce, sudden anger flashed in Rift's eyes. He lunged at Bellanger and grabbed the front of the older man's white silk shirt with manacled hands before the Officials could react.

The two initial guards grabbed him by the shoulders and tried to pull him off of their boss, but two more guards were forced to step in to assist their comrades in restraining him. They barely managed to pry Rift's hands away from Bellanger.

"What do you know about my family?" Rift snarled as he was yanked backwards.

I stared in horrified fascination. I'd never seen Rift lose control. He exuded a savage, unadulterated fury that rivaled even my father's worst explosions. It was like a simmering pot had suddenly boiled over, steam and scorching water spewing in all directions. He looked as though he could rip Bellanger's throat open with his teeth.

While the guards were distracted by Rift's outburst, I saw my window and went for it. I raised a foot and jammed it back into the knee of the Official behind me.

My attack must have taken him by surprise because he dropped the gun in his effort to remain standing.

Rift took advantage of the guards' confusion. He jabbed an elbow into the stomach of one and whipped back his head to knock out another behind him. Freed of their grasps, he spun and threw the chain of his handcuffs around the third guard's neck, tightening his hold. The guard coughed and spluttered until he finally slumped to the floor.

Across the room, Ming was a whirl of motion as she fought two more guards. With no weapons of her own, she spun tightly and kicked the gun out of one Official's hands before flipping a second guard over her shoulder. He grunted as he hit the ground. She sent a savage kick to his ribs for good measure.

Another new guard ran at me. She began to raise her gun—

That's when ten years of training at the Academy kicked in. Ducking her gun arm, I caught her in the gut with my fist. She doubled over in pain. I took the opportunity to knock the gun out of her grasp. It skittered across the floor, landing near Torque's still-prone form. Before she could recover, I bent down and swung a leg in a low arch causing her legs to fly out from under her. She crashed to the floor, whacking her head against the marble tiles. She didn't move.

Rift had dropped to a crouch beside the guards who had held him and was searching their pockets. He straightened up holding a key, which he inserted into his cuffs. The first one clicked open and he had almost moved on to the second when a guard approached him from behind.

With a running leap, I jumped onto the encroaching guard's back and tackled him to the ground. The Official struggled beneath me as Rift managed to free himself of the second handcuff. He sprinted for his own gun and fired a stun blast at the legs of the guard pinned beneath me. The guard jerked and fell still.

"Thanks," I breathed as he pulled me to my feet.

Before he could respond, a cry of pain caused both of us to turn. Ming was on the floor clutching her thigh at the feet of the last remaining Official. He was a massive man with broad shoulders, his biceps bulging against the sleeves of his uniform. Ming looked up at him as he raised the bloodied knife again.

Rift sent a stun blast into his chest.

The colossal guard gritted his teeth as the shock racked his body, but he didn't fall. He turned to look at Rift, and his grimace twisted into a sneer. With a yell of rage, he brought down the knife…

But another stun blast caused his arm to freeze inches from Ming's neck. His enormous body contracted, and he collapsed with a *thud* that shook the room.

Satisfied, Rift turned to face the other side of the room, but the Timekeeper was nowhere in sight.

No! I thought, my eyes scanning the room wildly. *Did Bellanger escape in all the chaos?*

But Rift didn't appear concerned. He holstered his gun and rounded the desk. I watched him reached down. There was a yelp of pain, and then he was yanking Bellanger up and shoving the rotund man into his chair. The Timekeeper must have retreated behind his desk for the duration of the fight. He obviously hadn't expected his guards to be overcome by a handful of Rebels. Now his blasé expression melted into terror as Rift grabbed him by his collar. "Please, don't hurt me!" he begged. "I —I know the secrets of your past! I can help you... just don't hurt me!"

I stared down at the pathetic man cringing in Rift's grasp as his insinuations coalesced in my mind.

Rift had been Wiped.

"I don't make promises I don't intend to keep," Rift muttered. "So I wouldn't count on leaving this room unharmed. But if you want cling to your miserable life, I'd advise you to start talking. Now."

I gaped at the vengeful person before me. This wasn't Rift. I'd never seen him harm anyone unless it was in an effort to protect others. But then again, what did I really know about Rift? What did *he* even know about *himself*? I took a tentative step forward and reached toward him. "Rift, please, this isn't you," I whispered.

"Stay out of this, Ambry!"

Stung, I let my outstretched hand fall back to my side.

Rift turned back to Bellanger. He pressed down so that the old man began hacking and gasping for air. "Tell me what you know about my family or I swear, they'll be picking up pieces of you from Paris to Shanghai," Rift spat. He was shaking.

For some inexplicable reason, Bellanger laughed. "You want to find your family?" *Click.*

That's when I saw the barrel of a handgun pressed firmly into Rift's abdomen.

"You can join them in death," Bellanger finished.

Rift's eyes widened.

"*No!*" I screamed.

The sound of the gunshot exploded through the room. But when Rift staggered backward, it was Bellanger that slumped to the floor, a bullet hole marring the white silk of his shirt.

I stared down at the old Timekeeper's unseeing eyes before swiveling around.

Torque—battered and blood-stained—stood behind me, the gun in his hands still aimed at the body now lying limp on the floor.

When I turned back, Rift was staring down at the blood pooling across Bellanger's chest in mute, wide-eyed shock. Seconds passed like hours before he finally turned to me. "You."

"Rift, what…?" I started.

But his eyes weren't focused on mine. He pushed past me, advancing on Torque. "You *idiot!* What were you thinking?"

Though stunned, Torque's gaze held no shred of remorse. "I was thinking that he had a bloody gun leveled at you!" he snapped. "What did you want me to do, let him send a bullet through your spleen? If I'd only stunned him, the jolt might've caused him to pull the trigger!"

"He knew about my family, and now he's *dead!*" Rift bellowed, closing in so that he was inches from Torque's face. In his rage, he seemed to tower over him.

"As dead as you would be too if I hadn't shot the bastard!" Torque bellowed back.

"Stop!" I cried, shoving myself between them and forcing them back at arms length. "You can't do this right now! Rift, please, we have to get out before more guards come," I insisted.

Rift's heart hammered beneath my palm. His face was splotchy and red with rage, but the reality of our danger penetrated his blind fury. He wiped a hand over his face and looked back to where Bellanger lay sprawled on the carpet, then back at Torque. His anger began to melt into mere helplessness, and I was shocked to see tears brim in his eyes.

Slowly, tentatively, I reached out to take his other hand in mine. It felt hard and calloused.

He looked down numbly to where my fingers threaded with his.

"It's done, Rift," I whispered. "We have to get back to the Atrium."

He didn't say anything. He didn't even nod to acknowledge that he'd heard me. Instead, he dropped my hand, crossed the room to pick up Bellanger's piece of the Anagram from where it lay on the floor flecked with blood, and began to walk toward the door of the suite,

Torque and I exchanged a brief, worried glance before helping Ming to her feet and following.

CHAPTER SIXTEEN

Alarms rang out as the four of us ran through Bellanger's house. "Ming, you're the only one of us left with any juice!" Rift shouted over the screeching noise. "Can you buy us some time?"

"Gladly," Ming said with a grimace. "Everybody link up." She reached for her wristwatch as Rift and Torque grabbed hold of her arm.

And once again, everything stopped. Except for us.

The sudden silence was even more startling than the alarms. I doubted that I'd ever get used to the world coming to a complete halt—birds motionless in midair outside; guards in the distance, their pumping arms and legs now frozen. Some had begun to pull guns from their belts while others were crouched, already taking aim.

We, on the other hand, didn't pause for a moment. Rift led the way, dragging Torque along while Ming and I hobbled behind them. I made the mistake of looking down at her leg; the gash in her thigh oozed dark blood, and it looked as though whoever had stabbed her had cut deep enough to reach the muscle. Maybe the bone.

The Telepoint loomed ahead of us through wall-length glass windows. "Door's that way!" I yelled to Rift, jerking my head to the right.

"No time to be picky!" he called back. And without slowing, he and Torque crashed through the window. Glittering shards of glass showered down around them as they tumbled onto the grass outside.

I slowed in shock.

"Keep going!" Ming urged me. Her voice was tight with pain. "They're fine!"

Sure enough, Rift had already hauled Torque back to his feet and was only yards from the sleek archway. Ming and I reached the window, jumping down onto the lawn just as the last of her watch's power was depleted.

The noise resumed. "Hey, freeze!" bellowed the closest guard. A dozen more followed close on his heels. They were still a good distance away, but their sudden motion made it look as though they'd been propelled forward from their frozen positions like stones from a slingshot. They would be on us in seconds.

"Like hell we will!" Torque bellowed. He and Rift had reached the Telepoint and Rift was already punching in coordinates. With a grunt of pain, Torque lifted his gun and fired. One of the guards crumpled, but others sent a flurry of bullets back in response. I heard one whizz past only inches from my ear as the Telepoint ahead flared to life.

"Come on!" Rift shouted.

I tried to move faster, but it was hard to compensate for Ming's added weight, and the extreme loss of blood was starting to make her lose consciousness. "*Go!*" I screamed, stumbling as Ming finally went limp.

Rift shook his head furiously. "Not a chance!" He spun to face Torque. Before his friend could react, he shoved him forward into the portal.

Torque's shout of protest was cut short as he vanished through the Telepoint.

Rift sprinted toward Ming and I, ducking under her other arm. Together, the two of us ran toward the glowing archway, Ming's feet dragging in the over-watered grass. Adrenaline surged through me, heightening all of my senses. I gritted my teeth and forced my legs to move faster—faster—*faster.*

More shots rang out. Ming's body jerked, and I heard Rift cry out in pain. He staggered, but quickly righted himself.

My stomach plummeted. "Were you—?"

"Just move!" he yelled.

And then I felt the tingling sensation, and the faint fizzing warmth of the Telepoint's embrace.

"We need a medic!" Rift shouted as we stumbled into the Arrival Room of the Atrium.

Dozens of heads whipped towards us. Several Rebels took off down the corridor to the left, presumably to find Dmitri or one of the other physicians.

Rift and I lowered Ming to the ground. I was shocked to see blood streaming from the base of her neck. Her chest rose and fell in shallow, labored breaths.

Rift tore a strip from the bottom of his shirt and pressed the dark fabric over the bullet hole, then took my hand and placed it where his own had been. "Hold it there," he commanded. "I've got to find Kade."

"You've got to find a medic for yourself first," I said sharply, though I did hurry to apply pressure to Ming's wound.

Rift looked down to the point just above his left hip where blood was seeping through the fabric of his shirt. "It barely caught me. Probably didn't even go deep enough to penetrate muscle."

I gaped at him. "You were *shot!* Now's not the time to be stubborn!"

Fortunately, Kade's face appeared in the midst of the growing crowd before Rift could rush off. The dark-haired Commander wore a worried frown. "What happened?" he demanded.

"Bellanger triggered a silent alarm," said Torque.

"We got his piece of the Anagram, but we had a run-in with some Officials before we could escape."

Dmitri appeared next to Kade, his medical bag in tow. "Move aside," he ordered.

Everyone—Kade included—hurried to make room for the medic. He knelt down beside Ming and motioned for me to move my hand. I was quick to oblige.

Her breathing had slowed even more...*was* she even breathing? Without thinking, I found myself reaching for Rift's hand. He clasped it in his own, his worried eyes not leaving Ming and Dmitri.

The seconds dragged on until Dmitri finally shook his head and stood. "She's gone," he said. "There's nothing I can do. I'm sorry."

Gone? I thought blankly. But we got her back. How could she be gone?

Several of those still standing around her raised hands to cover their mouths. Tears welled in the eyes of some while others began to weep openly. It took me a moment to remember that she had been their Second-in-Command.

Kade sank to his knees beside her. Next to me, I felt Rift's hand slip away.

All I could do was stare down at Ming's lifeless body. I had never seen someone die before. Were it not for the two pools of blood staining her chest and leg, I might have thought she was asleep.

I shivered and rubbed my arms; it felt uncomfortable standing there as a relative stranger, unable to fully understand or enter into their grief.

Dmitri put a hand on Rift's shoulder. "You ought to be heading to the Hospital Branch by the looks of it," he said, his tone gentler than I'd ever heard it.

"I'm fine for now," Rift murmured. "The bullet grazed me. I'll stop by the Hospital Branch after I speak with Kade."

Dmitri stared at Rift for a long moment from where he knelt, then turned to Kade. "What do you think, Commander? "

It took Kade a moment to realize Dmitri had spoken to him. When he did, he got to his feet and gave a curt nod. It reminded me of my father's response back when his own father had died: he was a leader first and foremost—his grief would have to wait. "I'll speak with him first."

It took all the restraint I possessed not to smack Kade across his stupid, stoic face. Talking could wait! Could he not see *bullet wound* in Rift's side? He'd already lost one friend that day…

Dmitri clearly shared my opinion, but he shook his head with a sigh. "Suit yourself. At least keep pressure on it." Several more maroon-clad medics arrived with a stretcher and began to lift Ming's body. Dmitri turned to help them ease her on, and within seconds they were gone.

Rift pressed a hand to his side and held it there, wincing. He turned to Torque once he had gritted his way past the pain. "What about you?"

"I'll manage," Torque said. It was disconcerting to see

him so somber.

"Then let's talk," said Kade. "I want to know what the hell happened on that island."

Rift, Torque, and I nodded.

. . . .

We followed the Commander until we reached the dark corridor Avienne had pointed out to me on my first day in the Atrium, the one criss-crossed with green beams of light. Kade's fingers flitted over the keypad to the right of the door. The light beams abruptly vanished and the corridor lit with a soft, more welcoming glow. Kade led the way to another door at the far end. This time, he merely inserted a key in the handle to unlock it.

Once we were inside, Kade shut the door firmly behind us. "You have it then?" he asked.

Rift nodded. With the hand that wasn't holding pressure over his wound, he pulled out the silver cylinder from his jacket and offered it to Kade. "I haven't had a chance to take a good look at it yet."

"Understandable." Kade took the cylinder gingerly. "But the Anagram can wait. What is it you're so hell-bent on telling me before you'll accept medical treatment?"

I was happy to hear the disapproval in his voice. At least he didn't agree with Rift's blatant disregard for his own health.

Rift's jaw tightened. "It's Bellanger. He was...there."

"Well, that's hardly new information," said Kade, crossing his scar-mottled arms.

"No." Rift closed his eyes. "He was *there*, Kade. The day I…" He cast a glance toward me. It was full of shame. "The day I forgot."

Something in me lurched toward him. All of his cryptic references to his past now made perfect sense. All this time, he hadn't been holding back out of a desire to shut me out. In some ways, he knew as little about himself as I did. What could have happened—what could he have *done*—to warrant the loss of his memories? Based on the age Bellanger had alluded to, Rift had spent the past six or seven years not knowing who he was or where he came from. What had life been like for him knowing he might have a family somewhere looking for him, but no way to find them? Or not knowing if they were out there in the first place…

I wanted to run to him, to take his hand and tell him it would be all right. But what sort of assurances could I offer? From everything I'd been taught, a Wipe was said to be impossible to reverse.

Kade stared hard at him, his mouth parted. "Did he talk?"

"He would have." Rift swallowed, clenching his eyes shut once more. "He's dead."

"Dead?" Kade's arms fell to his sides. "How…"

Torque took a step forward. "I shot him."

Kade massaged a hand over his face and took a deep breath. "We've been searching for clues to Rift's past for

308

seven years, and you bury the first legitimate lead we've had?"

"It's not as though I didn't have a reason." Torque jerked his head toward Rift. "The guy had a gun shoved in his gut."

Kade looked at Rift, but the latter didn't look up. "Well, as much as I hate to say it, it was probably for the best. There may be people still on the lookout for you, or at least for who you *were.* If Bellanger had lived to talk…" Kade trailed off. "Did you manage to find out anything at all before planting a bullet in him?"

Taking a deep breath, Rift finally opened his eyes. "He said my family is dead."

There was a long, fragile silence that all of us seemed hesitant to shatter. Eventually, Torque spoke up. "Well of course he'd say that, mate. He wanted to hurt you. He'd have said anything."

"You can't know he was lying," Rift whispered. Whether from the pain of his injury or the pain of the thought, it was obvious that talking was taking him a great deal of effort.

"And you can't know he was telling the truth," Torque countered.

Kade nodded. "Torque's right, Rift. I wouldn't trust a word the rat said."

But his friends' assurances had little effect on Rift's countenance. The light in his eyes had dimmed, and none of us had the faintest idea of how to stop it from going out altogether.

When Rift didn't respond, Kade stepped forward and put a hand on his shoulder. "This isn't over yet," he said. "I gave you my word a long time ago that I would help you get your life back, and I plan on making good on that promise. But in the meantime, I officially order you to march yourself straight to the Hospital Branch. Torque, Ambry, make sure he doesn't wander off."

Torque nodded. "Will do. Let's go, mate."

Rift said nothing, but allowed Torque and I to shepherd him out the door and down the hall. As we walked along, his hand brushed mine. I caught the tip of his finger as it passed.

This time he didn't pull his hand away. Instead, he allowed it to slide into my own.

I held onto it tightly as we walked, as though the connection might serve as a lifeline to hope.

....

After Torque and I dropped off Rift at the Hospital Branch (the silver-haired medic woman who admitted him insisted we wait outside while she stitched him up), I wandered aimlessly down the corridor.

This place was my new home, but I still knew so little about it. How many tunnels interconnected here, buried beneath the earth? I didn't even know where *"here"* was. It might have been Istanbul or Antarctica, and I had no way to tell the difference.

310

I had just turned the corner when I nearly ran straight into Avienne. "Watch it—oh, it's you," she said when she recognized me. She instantly perked up. "Where are Rift and my brother?"

"Rift is getting stitched up in the Hospital Branch. I think Torque is still waiting outside."

Her perfect brow furrowed. "Getting stitched up? What happened?" she asked.

I folded my arms and sighed as a wave of exhaustion stole over me. It had been a trying day to say the least. Could it really have been just this morning that I said my last goodbye to Prewitt? He had looked so broken as I walked away from him. And when he had ran to hug me one last time... *No. I can't think about Prew right now. I have enough to worry about.* "Long story short, it turns out Bellanger and Rift were old acquaintances."

The blonde Rebel paled. "You mean from—before?" she asked carefully.

I nodded.

"So you know about Rift's...past now?"

"I know he was Wiped," I replied. "Although that's pretty much the extent of what I can claim to know about Rift."

She shrugged. "That's about the most anyone can claim to know about him."

"You and Torque seem to be exceptions to that rule," I noted.

Avienne shrugged. "Maybe Torque is, but Rift has

never opened up much to me."

That was a surprise. I had thought both Avienne and her brother were in Rift's confidence. I guess being Wiped and not knowing who was responsible for it must have made it difficult for him to trust people.

I looked up from my thoughts to find Avienne staring at me, her almond-shaped eyes narrowed. "What?" I asked.

"Nothing," she said. "It's just funny, I've been wondering the same thing about you."

I started. "What do you mean?" I asked.

"Why out of all the people here, would Rift choose to draw close to you? I mean, you're an Elite for starters," she said with evident distaste. "And you know almost nothing about what it means to be a part of the Resistance."

I could feel my eyes widening. "You think Rift... you think he's interested in me?"

"Please," she said, waving her hand. "I've seen the way he looks at you. I mean, if he'd looked at *me* that way when we met years ago..." she trailed off, raising an eyebrow suggestively.

My reaction must have been comical because Avienne snorted. "Don't tell me you haven't noticed."

"I... I mean..." I stammered. "Why would you think that?"

"He broke concentration in the middle of a sparring match to race to your rescue. He spent the next night watching over you like a bloody guard dog, he smuggled you out of the Atrium against the express orders of his

Commander, and he's been at your beck and call ever since." She shook her head. "Are you seriously going to tell me that all of this escaped your notice?"

I could only blink at her. In some ways, her litany of evidence *had* escaped my notice because all along, I'd simply attributed Rift's behavior to Kade's orders. He'd instructed Rift to take care of me in the Atrium, so of course he would jump to my aid when I was attacked. It also explained him acting the part of dutiful sentry following my re-hospitalization.

What it *didn't* explain was his complete disregard for Kade's ultimate decision to have me Wiped. Now that I knew he had suffered that same fate, it made sense that he'd be reluctant to allow someone else to undergo the process. Still, it would have only meant me losing a few days of my life, not my entire identity. I shook my head in disbelief. Could Rift's actions have really been motivated by something more?

But what about the night he had dropped me off near the manor? When I leaned toward him, he had pushed me away. I could still remember the way his mouth had tightened, the hard-set angle of his jaw as he held me at arm's length. "There have been some mixed signals," I murmured.

There was an awkward pause. From the time I had arrived in the Atrium, Avienne had been courteous, but never kind toward me. She had done her duty—as had Rift—in protecting me when Marius threatened to beat me to a pulp, but in a detached, unsentimental way. "You don't trust me, do you?" I asked. It was more observation than question.

She crossed her arms. "Would you, if the situation were reversed?"

"Probably not," I admitted. I shifted my weight from one foot to the other and tried to think of a polite excuse to slip away.

When I looked back at her, Avienne was studying me. "I may not trust you yet," she said, "but I do trust Rift, and for some reason he seems to think you deserve a chance."

"Do you think he's right?"

She tapped a long, delicate finger on her arm. "I haven't decided yet."

I nodded. "So where does that leave us?"

She shrugged, but with less annoyance. "I can't speak for you, but it leaves me willing to try."

I was about to respond when a voice called from behind. "There you are!"

I turned to find Rift and Torque striding towards us. Rift had changed out of his bloodied shirt and into a dark green sweater that set off the reddish tones of his hair. A smile tugged at the corner of his mouth. I was relieved to see him marginally more like himself. Or at least, the self I had come to know. "Better hurry up or you're going to be late," he said.

"Late?" I wondered. "For what?"

"You're getting your Circlet," he said, crossing his

arms. "Ready to become a proper Rebel?"

....

Kade stood before me with his hands clasped behind his back. "Repeat after me: I solemnly swear to uphold justice, seek truth, and remain loyal to the cause of the United World Resistance."

I held my hand aloft and bit my lip, trying to make sure I didn't forget the words. It was hard with so many eyes staring at me. Avienne, Rift, Torque, Juliet, Cody, and Mateo were all in attendance for my swearing-in as a new recruit of the Resistance.

From his place between Torque and Juliet, Rift smiled and gave me an encouraging nod.

I smiled at him in return, and some of my nerves settled. "I solemnly swear to uphold justice, seek truth, and remain loyal to the cause of the United World Resistance," I repeated in a loud, clear voice.

Kade went on. "And do you swear to protect the secrecy and integrity of our cause, no matter the cost?"

A bead of sweat found its way down my brow. "I swear."

"Good," Kade said. "Then as Lead Commander of the Atrium Sector of the UWR, I welcome you to our cause." He turned to the rest of the gathering and held up a fist. "United for justice!" he cried.

"United for truth!" shouted the rest of the group, each

person raising a fist. Then they all began to clap as they strode forward to congratulate me.

Torque ruffled my hair so that wavy blue strands temporarily blocked out my vision. "Atta girl!" he said, giving me a good thump on the back. He wiped away an imaginary tear from his eye. "Our little princess is all grown up," he sniffled.

"Congratulations, Ambry," said Juliet, slipping in to give me a quick hug.

"Thank you," I said warmly. "So if you and Cody are here, who's running the Command Center?"

"Oh, we have a dozen other tech people that can sub in as needed," said Juliet. "Turner and Noelle are covering for us. We couldn't miss your initiation."

At her side, Mateo nodded. "We all need something to celebrate today," he murmured. I was surprised to see tears in his dark eyes.

With a pang of guilt, Ming's lifeless body flashed through my mind. Her funeral was set for later that evening. Everyone in the Atrium was in mourning. Mateo, in particular, seemed to have been one of her closer friends. "I'm so sorry," I whispered.

Mateo didn't say anything, but smiled sadly before walking over to Kade.

As I watched him go, Cody tugged at my sleeve. "So you took my advice and decided to stay, huh?"

"I know," I agreed, smiling down at the boy. "I wish I'd known about all this when I was your age."

"No worries," said Torque. "You just have a little catching up to do is all."

"Psshh." Cody waved a hand with a look of grand superiority. "You really shouldn't compare her to me, Torque. I don't want her to feel intimidated."

Torque and I laughed as he puffed out his slender chest. "I guess you'll have to show me the ropes then," I said, tousling his sandy hair.

As our chuckles died down, Avienne stepped forward, pulling Kade in tow. She slipped an arm around his waist.

It was the first time I had seen them show any open sign of affection. "Congratulations, Ambry," she said. She opened her mouth, then hesitated. "I'm...sure you'll make a great addition to the team."

I gave her a courteous smile. It was obvious that she was trying her best to give me the benefit of the doubt. "Thanks, Avienne. I really appreciate that."

"Well, now that the pledge is finished, are you ready to get your ink?" Kade asked.

I felt my face break into a grin. "Absolutely."

Kade chuckled at my eager expression. "Good, because Mateo is all set up and ready to go."

The Commander showed me over to a long, tilted chair. It reminded me of a dentist's office. I sat down and laid my hand palm-up on the armrest.

Mateo took a seat on the stool next to me as the rest of the group ambled over to watch. Apparently, the Latino boy's talents extended beyond forging signatures. He pulled on a pair of hygienic gloves and held up a strange, pencil-like machine before pushing a small pedal at his feet. The bulky pencil-thing began to issue an ominous whirring noise. "Ready?" he asked.

I gulped at the sight of the needle at the tip of the machine. *I can do this*, I thought. If I could survive the mission to Bellanger's villa, I could handle getting a little tattoo. Swallowing back my fear, I nodded. "Ready," I replied.

Mateo lowered the device to the tender skin of my wrist. With steady precision, he began to draw the interlocking whorls of the Circlet.

I was prepared for it to hurt, but I hadn't expected just how *much* it would hurt. Surely this ought to be considered some form of socially-approved torture! Everything in me wanted to yank my hand out of Mateo's reach, but I gritted my teeth and forced myself not to move. It took all the self-control I possessed to keep the wrist he was working on relaxed.

Rift stepped around to the other side of my chair. "You okay?" he asked. His face was drawn with concern.

"Mm-hmm," I grunted. I clenched my eyes shut and reminded myself to take another breath.

Rift gave a low chuckle. "Needles aren't my favorite either," he said.

"It feels less like a needle and more like a knife carving into my flesh," I panted.

He laughed and shook his head. "Here," he said,

taking my left hand and prying the fingers open. "Focus on squeezing my hand instead."

Rift's palm slid into my own. As Mateo began yet another whorl of the design, I wrapped my fingers around his and squeezed with everything I had.

"Ow, geez!" he cried.

"Sorry!" I yelped, easing up my grip.

"It's all right," he cringed. "I guess I wasn't prepared for you to take me up on the offer with so much enthusiasm."

I would have blushed, but all the blood in my body was rushing to my extremities. The normal response to this much pain in the human body was fight or flight. Yet here I was, trapped in a pseudo-dental chair while some guy I barely knew sliced away at my skin. *What would my mother and father think if they could see me now?*

The thought gave me a weird burst of pleasure.

"Hey, I've got a good distraction for you," said Rift. "I still need to give you your present."

"My present?"

"Don't you remember? I said that at your Swearing-in Ceremony, I'd tell you the location of the Atrium."

For a split second, I almost forgot the pain streaming from my lower right arm. A dozen possibilities flew through my mind. Were we hidden away beneath a jungle somewhere? Or buried under some third-world metropolis?

Rift took a deep breath, drawing out the suspense. "We're in a cavern system in the Altai mountains," he said.

319

I waited for him to say more. When he didn't, I laughed. "I know you may think the Academy would have made me some kind of incredible geography buff, but where exactly are the Altai mountains?"

Rift gave me a wide grin. "Siberia."

Siberia? The word triggered a vague memory…one of Orelia standing with hands on her hips the night of the Gala, telling me not to get any ideas about the cute servant boy she'd seen me talking with. *"Unless you want Father to have him teleported to Siberia…"*

And here I was, teleported right there with him. *Oh, Orelia,* I thought. *If you only knew.* I squeezed Rift's hand tighter.

"Almost halfway there!" said Mateo over the noise of the machine. "It'll be visible for the first half hour or so."

"You mean you're not done yet?" I demanded.

"You got this far," Rift reminded me. "You can make it the rest of the way."

I nodded and refocused my energy on relaxing my other wrist.

Out of nowhere, a loud siren began to wail overhead.

A dozen heads snapped toward the hallway. "The alarm!" Avienne shouted. She, Torque, and Kade were already pulling out their guns.

"We've got to get to the Command Center. Now," said Kade. "Everybody move!"

The pressure of the needle immediately lifted as Mateo rushed to turn off the machine. "What's going on?" I asked Rift as he yanked me to my feet.

"Security breach," he said sharply. "We've got to hurry."

I blanched. "Security breach? But I thought you said that nobody knew our location?"

Rift's expression was bleak. "Apparently, somebody just figured it out."

CHAPTER SEVENTEEN

We ran in a tight group down the hall with Kade at the lead. He raised his wristwatch to his mouth. "Talk to me, Noelle! Where's the breach?" he demanded.

"Southeast tunnels," replied Noël's voice over the frequency. She sounded frazzled. "They're coming in fast."

"Who is *they*?" asked Rift as we ran.

"Who do you think?" she said sharply. "Officials. Dozens of them."

Kade brought us all to a halt as Rift swore under his breath. "How the hell did they get our location?"

"It doesn't matter right now. If they know where we are, then the entire compound has been compromised,"

Kade said. "Noelle, make the call. We have to evacuate the Atrium."

"Evacuate?" I interjected. "You're going to try to move over five thousand people?"

"It's an eventuality we had hoped to avoid," Rift muttered.

Kade began shouting orders. "Torque, find Marius! We need to secure the time capsule cache and get them and the rest of the weapons to Sector B. Juliet, you and Cody head for the Archives and make sure everything is either smuggled out or destroyed!"

People broke off as they received their orders. "Avienne, head for the Arrival Room and *get everyone out of here*," Kade said. "You know the drill; contact Sector B and let them know they've got a whole host of visitors incoming. They can redistribute our people from there as necessary. Mateo, head to the Hospital Branch; Dmitri will need all the help he can get."

Avienne and Mateo sprinted down the corridor just as Noelle swore over the wristwatch frequency. "Kade, we've got a problem."

"You think?" he snapped.

"No, I mean another problem," she said. "Someone is trying to hack into our Grid."

Rift and Kade froze. This time, Rift answered her. "How much time do we have?"

"Not long," came Noelle's grim response. "They've already broken through the first set of firewalls. If they take down the others, they'll be able to get in through *our own Telepoints*."

Kade's eyes widened. "Rift…"

But Rift was already sprinting away toward the Command Center, leaving Kade and I standing alone in the hall. I turned to him. "How can I help?" I asked.

"You want to help?" Kade's narrowed eyes turned on me like icy flames. "Start by explaining how after decades of total obscurity, our location is discovered on the same day *you* join us?"

"You don't seriously think I had anything to do with this?"

"I don't know what to think, but it seems like quite a coincidence!"

"Kade, I have no idea how they found us! I didn't even know where the Atrium was until about five minutes ago, and you all have been with me every second since then!" I insisted. "Ask Rift yourself! There's *no way* I could have fed that information out that quickly!"

Before I could react, Kade shot out a hand and grabbed my wrist.

I yelped. The skin around my half-finished tattoo stung as he searched for the small incision where my tracker had been removed. He found the cut just above the interwoven semi-circle.

"See? It's not there," I said sharply.

Kade frowned. "And you left it at the Academy this morning?"

"I watched McCullough pocket it right after he cut it out of me! He said he'd give me an hour and then destroy it. I swear, Kade," I said, willing him to believe me.

Anger and frustration roiled over the Commander's care-worn face, and I could tell he was desperate for someone to blame.

But that someone wasn't me. I met his stare with defiance. This was my home now too, and I wanted to protect it just as badly as he did.

A muscle worked in Kade's jaw. finally, he shoved my wrist away. "We'll see," he said in a low voice. "I'll talk to McCullough. For now, you can help by going after Cody. Do you remember where the Archives are?"

I nodded.

"Then hurry. Rift is going to need his help."

Without another word, I turned my back on him and sprinted down the corridor to find Cody.

....

Sirens wailed overhead as I burst into the Archive Room. Half-a-dozen heads jerked up from their harried work.

I spotted the boy's shaggy blond hair across the room near some filing cabinets. "Cody, you've got to come with me!" I shouted.

The young tech dropped the box of files he was holding and vaulted across the room. "What happened?"

I doubled over and took a gasping breath. "Someone is—hacking into the Telepoint Grid! Rift needs your help," I panted.

Cody turned to look at his mother.

"Go! We'll be fine here," Juliet assured him.

Nodding to her, Cody ran to meet me at the door and the two of us sprinted back toward the Command Center. "How could they have beat my system?" he demanded.

"Well, it is the Global Government," I said breathlessly. "They do have a few resources at their disposal."

"Yes, but someone *still* would have had to smuggle some sort of transceiver with a remote signal into the Atrium…"

All of a sudden, screams echoed from down the hall ahead. The end of the corridor suddenly became enveloped in smoke. "The Arrival Room!" Cody cried. "They must have broken through!"

I could feel the blood drain from my face. "Then we're out of time. We've got to find Rift and get out of here. Some of the Officials may have time capsules!"

"I know a roundabout route to the Command Center. This way," said Cody, angling off down a hallway to our right. We barreled past several doors before turning left down another corridor. "It's right up ahead!" he called.

Suddenly, the door in front of us burst open. The person behind it lifted their gun, aiming directly at us.

Cody and I skidded to a halt. "Rift! It's us!" he

shouted.

I was relieved to see that it was indeed Rift holding the gun. He lowered his weapon and ran to us. "It's too late," he said. "I tried to hold them off, but they've already bypassed our security."

"They've set off smokescreens in the Arrival Room," Cody said. His voice was growing more and more panicked. "It's probably a sleeping gas. Maybe even a neurotoxin. Pretty soon the Officials will come through themselves."

"We have to get everyone out." Rift dug into his pocket and handed each of us a small blue capsule the size of a large pill. "Another ten seconds each. I keep a few handy in case of emergency."

I hurried to slip off my watch and insert the capsule into the hollow space on the back as Cody did the same. "What do you want us to do?" the boy asked.

"Take the back way to the Hospital Branch, Cody," said Rift. "They have an emergency Telepoint stashed there. Help Dmitri and the other medics to get the patients to safety."

Cody took a deep breath and nodded before racing off. I watched him disappear around the corner with admiration. Not only was the kid brilliant for his age—for any age—but he was also incredibly brave.

Once Cody was out of sight, Rift turned to me. "Take this," he said over the noise of the blaring alarms. He pulled one of the two guns from his belt and handed it to me. "Go back the way you came and find Torque or Avienne. They'll get you out of here."

I looked down at the gun in my hands. "But aren't you coming too?"

Rift shook his head. "I'm going to the Arrival Room. If I can destroy the central Telepoints, it ought to give the others enough time to escape."

"You're *what?*" I demanded. "Rift, the Officials will be here any minute! You can't go back there!"

"If I don't, it could cost us hundreds of lives!" he insisted.

I holstered the gun in my belt. "Then I'm coming with you," I said.

His eyebrows drew together. "I can't let you do that."

"I'm not letting you go alone!"

"Ambry, you're a member of the Resistance now, and with Ming gone, I'm Second-in-Command in this sector. This isn't a request: it's an order," Rift said firmly, his voice taking on an authoritative tone.

I drew myself up as tall as I could, although the top of my head still only managed to reach his nose. "Well, since I only have half of the Circlet, you should probably count on me listening about half the time," I said.

"Ambry, I don't have time for this!"

I crossed my arms.

Growling, Rift ran his hands through his hair. "Fine!" he snapped. "But we have to move fast!"

We raced back to the main corridor, following the cries coming from the Arrival Room. The smoke had already begun to settle to reveal dozens of prone figures scattered across the floor. Others held cloths pressed over their noses and mouths and staggered through the room issuing muffled cries for help.

Rift knelt down next to the closest person, a woman with a pixie-cut who looked to be in her forties. He pressed two fingers to her neck. "She's dead. The gas must have been toxic," he said grimly.

Suddenly, masked figures in silver began to erupt from three of the Telepoints.

Rift fired stun blasts at the first two Officials. Each one seized up before collapsing to the ground. "Ambry, watch out!" he yelled.

I fumbled with my gun as the Official in front of me raised his own weapon.

"Duck!" cried a familiar voice.

I instinctively dropped to a crouch. A stun blast streaked through the air above my head and straight into the Official's chest. Looking up, I caught a flash of white hair and an arm covered in tattoos. "Torque!" I cried.

He took two more shots, and the two Officials crumpled.

"About time!" shouted Rift as he aimed another blast at a newly-materialized Official and ran over to me. He grabbed my arm and pulled me behind one of the thick pillars surrounding the Telepoint dais.

Torque dove into a roll, springing back to his feet behind a neighboring pillar a couple yards away. "Well it would have helped if you'd told us what you were planning!" he shouted back. "If it weren't for Cody, we would have had no idea which way you were headed!"

"We didn't tell him where we were going!" Rift said over the din.

"I know," Torque called in between shots. "But when you didn't show at Sector B, he guessed you'd pulled the hero card and headed straight into the thick of things!"

Rift laughed as he sent another blast into the fray. "Kid doesn't know me at all, does he?"

An Official appeared around the side of the pillar. "Look out!" I yanked on Rift's sleeve, pulling him toward me just as a bullet chipped off the edge of the pillar exactly where his head had been.

The guard who had fired it suddenly seized up and fell twitching to the ground. "Nice shot!" I called to Torque.

"Thank you," breathed Rift. He was so close that I could practically feel his heart beat against mine.

Something more than adrenaline burned in my veins. "Don't mention it," I whispered.

Rift turned toward Torque. "We have to get to the consoles!" he said. "I'll use my capsule! Can you get over here?"

Torque gave a swift nod. Holstering his gun, he backed up a step before vaulting into a spinning flip. He arced through the air and landed on his feet directly beside Rift, grabbing hold of his arm.

And once again, all of the noise and motion came to a

silent, screeching halt.

"Stay with me!" Rift ordered as we sprinted for the nearest Telepoint, ducking beneath the outstretched arms of an Official who had been in the act of raising his weapon. Rift reached the console and began to punch in numbers with a fury.

Torque and I could only stand on either side, watching. "What are you doing?" I asked.

"Using the emergency override codes," he said, his eyes never leaving the console. "I have to force the archways to self-destruct."

"Self-destruct?" I repeated incredulously. "As in *blow-up*?"

"Which is why we need an exit strategy," Torque cut in.

Sweat began to bead across Rift's brow. He hissed under his breath and smacked the machine. "I need more time!"

"We'll use mine," I said. "Grab on!"

No sooner had the words left my mouth than everything jerked back into gear. I immediately held down on the two opposing sides of my watch.

Frozen once more.

"I think I'm getting whiplash," I said, holding a hand to my forehead. The room spun slightly.

"Vertigo," said Torque. "It's natural when you're stopping and starting time in rapid succession."

Rift had resumed his typing. "Almost there... got it!"

he cried triumphantly.

"How long do we have?" Torque asked.

"The whole line of them will blow thirty seconds after the reboot," Rift said. He grabbed my arm and began dragging me toward the edge of the dais. "Come on! We've got to get out of here."

"Wait!" I exclaimed. "Can't we use these portals to get out before they self-destruct?"

Rift shook his head and continued to pull me along. "Now that I've entered the code, they're out of commission. We'll use the emergency Telepoint in the Hospital Branch. Get ready to—"

...Lurch...

Motion, noise, chaos.

It exploded around us in a maelstrom of speed and sound.

"Go!" Rift shouted, shoving me forward.

I stumbled and righted myself. Looking back, I saw that Torque and Rift were right on my heels, their arms and legs pumping as they broke into a sprint—

And then, suddenly, they weren't.

They weren't there.

I stared around in confusion. *What—?*

I wasn't standing anymore. I'd been shoved to the ground, but I had no memory of it.

A groan nearby caught my attention. It's owner rolled over and pressed a hand to his snowy head.

"Torque!" I said, moving to stand.

Torque turned to me. Suddenly, his eyes widened. He leapt to his feet and ran straight at me, tackling me to the ground.

We crashed to the floor as another round of bullets ripped across the wide pillar. "One of them must've used a capsule of their own!" Torque said.

"Where's Rift?" I asked, scanning the room wildly.

Torque swore. "Whoever opened that capsule must have grabbed him."

Fear clawed at my stomach. "We've got to find him!"

"First, we've got to get out of this room before the whole thing gets blown to pieces. Get ready," he said.

Right, I thought. *Self-destruct sequence.*

"Stay close to me," Torque commanded. "We go on my mark. One, two, *three!*" Torque sprang forward, sending a succession of blasts in the direction of the incoming bullets.

The Officials who had been firing at us dove for cover. I tried to see how many of them were left, but it was all I could do to keep up with Torque.

We were almost to the main hallway when an explosion from behind rocked the floor beneath our feet and catapulted us forward. My legs flew out from under me, and I felt my body slam into the floor. Pain exploded down my right arm as debris rained down across my line of vision.

Next to me, Torque coughed roughly and staggered to his feet. Thick clouds of dust floated down around us. "Are you okay?" he asked.

I bit my lip and tried to take a deep breath, but wound

up in my own coughing fit. When I finally caught my breath, I shook my head. "I think my arm may be broken."

"Here," Torque said, slipping under my other arm and hoisting me to my feet. "We've got to find Rift. They can't have dragged him far, even with the added time."

He started off down the hallway and I hurried to match his pace, cradling my arm as I ran. With every pounding step, I winced at the pain that shot up and down from my elbow to my wrist. "Do you think they know about the emergency Telepoints?" I asked.

Torque's reply was cut off by the appearance of another figure down the hall. "Avienne!" he shouted.

His sister's head snapped towards us. She looked particularly pissed off. "Where have you *been*? And what is it about 'evacuate' that you don't understand?" she demanded.

"I came back to look for Rift," Torque said as we ran to meet her.

"So where is he?" she asked.

"We think the Officials got him," he panted. Blood was seeping from a cut on his temple, the red radiant against the white of his hair. "We have to hurry. If they manage to haul him out of here, we may never find him. Which way did you come from?"

Avienne paled. "The emergency Telepoint in the Commanders Only Area. I didn't see him down the southern corridor."

"Then they probably went east," Torque said. "Come

on!"

Still cradling my arm, I ran as quickly as I could to keep up with the Guerriers. Each footstep sent a jarring reminder that one or both of the bones in my forearm were likely broken.

The Hospital Branch appeared on our right. "It's still in lock-down, and it looks like the doors haven't been breached," said Avienne.

Torque smacked a hand to his forehead. "The tunnels," he said. "That's how they got in."

"Then they could already be through one of the portals by now!" Avienne exclaimed. She burst into a sprint with Torque close on her heels. I hurried after them, abandoning all hope of protecting my injured arm. I let it hang limp at my side and pumped my left arm as fast as I could. If we lost Rift…

If *I* lost him…

We rounded the end of the eastern corridor with Torque at the lead. *We're headed into the same tunnels that Rift used to break me out,* I realized as we ran. I could smell the same metallic-earthy scent as I had the night he'd helped me escape.

Just as I'd suspected, a row of motorbikes appeared as we entered into a wider segment of tunnel. "Ambry, go with Torque!" Avienne called as she leapt onto one and pressed her wrist to the ignition. The bike purred to life.

I hurried to obey her, hopping on another bike behind her brother. Torque had already started its engine. I tightened my one-armed hold around his waist as he spun in a tight circle and sped us off down the tunnel.

Lights on either side flashed by faster and faster as we accelerated. "The archways are just ahead!" shouted Torque. His voice echoed down the rounded tunnel.

Suddenly, he swerved us to a halt. Avienne had skidded her bike to a stop ahead of us. "What are you—?" he started.

"Quiet," she whispered. "Do you two hear that?"

Over the sound of the engines, I could just make out more echoes bouncing down the tunnel from up ahead. I squinted in the low light. A bike lay discarded near the far end. Several figures were stumbling away from it. "It's them!" I exclaimed. "They're almost to the first Telepoint!"

"They still have to program it!" said Avienne. "If they used our coordinates, they'd wind up in the middle of nowhere!"

We hurtled down the tunnel with new intensity, mine and Torque's bike now outstripping Avienne's. Ahead of us, I could now see two Officials dragging what looked like an unconscious Rift toward one of the silver archways. The taller of the two turned toward us. He raised a gun.

"Hang on!" shouted Torque. Shots rang out. Torque angled us sharply to the right, then left again. We wove back and forth, sparks flying from the bullets that bounced off the tunnel walls. I looked back to see Avienne making the same weaving pattern.

The shorter Official allowed Rift to slump to the

ground while he started up the Telepoint. The archway lit up, flooding the tunnel with an eerie glow. We were only seconds away. The Official who had fired at us turned and sprinted to help his companion. Together, they hefted Rift up and moved toward the Telepoint.

"We're going to make it!" I shouted to Torque. He evened out our path so that we were now speeding in a straight line directly for the archway, with Avienne close behind.

But as Rift and the shorter Official disappeared into the portal, the taller one held back just long enough to fire one last, calculated shot directly at us.

It hit the bike's front tire. Torque swerved, but it was too late. The bike slammed into the ground, and Torque and I were flung from the vehicle. My body slammed into the ground and rolled and rolled to a stop.

Slowly, I blinked my eyes open. Avienne's bike must have collided with ours when it crashed. The Guerriers lay a dozen feet from one another. Neither moved.

With a great effort, I raised my pounding head and turned just in time to see the second Official's boots disappear through the gate only feet away from me.

"Rift!" I shouted. *But of course, he can't hear you,* I thought.

They took him.

I staggered to my feet. My right arm was completely useless and my vision had begun to go dark. *Just a little further,* I thought as the world around me blurred and faded.

All that was left was the light of the archway. I lifted my left hand and reached toward it…

My legs buckled beneath me, and the light disappeared.

CHAPTER EIGHTEEN

The first thing I became aware of was the pain.

It clawed into my arm and pounded in my head, coaxing me to fall back into the bliss of unconsciousness. *"Go back to sleep,"* it throbbed in rhythmic succession.

Honestly, it didn't seem like such a bad idea…

No, my mind urged sharply. *There's a reason I have to wake up.*

Ah, but the pain! What could be so important that I should have to endure *this*? So much easier just to keep my eyes closed and let it disappear again…

Disappear.

Like Rift had disappeared through the Telepoint.

Rift!

....

My eyes flew open. I was lying with my cheek pressed against a cold, linoleum-tiled floor in what looked like an office supply closet.

Dark spots appeared across my vision as I rose unsteadily to my feet. I leaned back against the wall and took several deep breaths until they faded. My head felt as though someone had inflated it with air and then taken a safety pin to it. Once another wave of dizziness passed, I staggered across the room and wrestled with the doorknob, but it was no good. I was locked in. "Okay, think," I whispered, clenching my eyes shut. "What would Rift do if he were here?"

Easy, I thought. *He would start by looking around for something useful.*

Careful not to bump my injured arm against the shelves, I began to scour the room for anything that might serve as a tool to escape. My options turned out to be slim. After digging one-handed through several boxes of office supplies, the most promising tool I found was a miniature stapler, which might do for a makeshift weapon in a pinch.

The door behind me creaked open. I wrapped my fingers around the stapler and turned to see an Official entering. His expression was unreadable.

"Where am I?" I demanded.

He ignored my question. "You need to come with

me," he said.

When I didn't move, Stern-Face grabbed hold of my left arm and yanked me out behind him. He marched me down a brightly-lit hallway lined with wide windows.

As we passed the glass panes, I could see what looked like technological laboratories. Men and women in white lab coats scurried to and fro fidgeting with various mechanical gadgets and scribbling on clipboards.

He shoved me through a door to the left. "In here."

"Wait!" I cried. "You can't just leave me in—"

The door slammed in my face.

—here." I sighed, letting my head fall forward against the door.

"You know," said a voice behind me. "I have a great deal of empathy for how you must have felt the day you woke up in the Atrium."

I swiveled around. Rift lay in a bed, bound by thick plastic straps. He smiled wanly at me.

"Rift!" I exclaimed. I hurried over to him. "Are you okay?"

"I'm fine," he assured me. "I just don't prefer the Globe's particular brand of hospitality."

I shook my head. Unbelievable. Captured and bound by his enemies, and he was still making jokes. "Come on. We have to get you out of here." I grabbed the end of the closest strap with my uninjured hand and tried to loosen it, but the strain exacerbated the raw ache throbbing in my other arm. Now fiery jolts of pain shot between my elbow and wrist. I bit back a yelp, but the wince on my face must have been telling enough.

Rift's eyebrows drew together in concern. "Are you hurt? What happened?"

"Torque and Avienne and I were trying to stop them from taking you, and we may or may not have totaled a couple of your bikes," I said apologetically.

He smiled. "Thanks for coming to my rescue," he said as I continued to tug at his bonds.

"A lot of good it's doing you. I can't—even—get—these—loose…"

The door behind us opened. Rift and I turned to see two people enter. The first was a neatly-dressed woman with deep auburn hair pulled into a tight bun. Spectacles were perched atop her thin nose, and she wore a distinctly smug expression.

Behind her stood my father.

I gazed at him in shock. He stared back, frozen in the doorway.

"Ambrosia Croft," said the woman, taking a seat in the corner. "I don't believe I've had the pleasure. It's a pity we have to meet under such circumstances."

"Dad," I whispered, ignoring the woman.

At my address, my father clenched his hands into fists. He said nothing.

I licked my lips, which had suddenly gone dry. "Dad, please. I…"

At the word "please," Titus began to take several slow

steps towards me. "After everything you've done, Ambrosia—after everything you've put me through, you *still* play the victim." He paced in front of me. When he spoke again, his voice shook with contempt. "Are you going to tell me that this was all some sort of misunderstanding?" he whispered. "That you were forced to leave the Academy under duress... that you were threatened and dragged to Bellanger's island as a captive? That you didn't *fight against* the guards?"

I lifted my chin and met his glare. "No. I don't deny any of it."

He stared at me for a long moment. Suddenly, his hand flew. It struck the side of my face so hard that spots appeared in my vision. I stumbled back against the side of Rift's bed and gasped, unable for a moment to raise my head.

"*Stop!*" Rift cried in outrage. From the corner of my eye, I could see him writhing against his restraints. "Don't touch her!"

"You *dare* rebuke me, boy?" bellowed Titus, rounding on Rift. "She is *my* daughter! And I'll do with her whatever I damn well please!"

"If you want to hurt someone, hurt me," Rift insisted. "I'm the one you're after."

"You'll get your turn," he snapped. He turned back to me and raised his hand once more.

"After everything you've done," Rift said, "can you blame her for her choice?"

Titus' hand froze, but his eyes didn't leave my face. "I blame her for believing your lies," he whispered. "For turning against her own society…her own family."

"Family?" I said, looking up at my father. "How can you call yourself my family when you've never even claimed me for who I really am? You wanted 'Ambrosia Croft'— ideal student, obedient daughter, dutiful addition to the Elite society. Someone you could be proud of. But somehow, you got stuck with me instead. Ambry. Mediocre student, constant disappointment." A tear slipped down my cheek. I had dreamt so many times of how good it would feel to say these things to my father's face, but the words tasted stale in my mouth. "I've always failed to meet your standards. Even when I tried everything to please you, it was never enough." I shook my head.

Titus' eyes followed the movement of my blue tresses.

I laughed. "Right. Of course. All you've ever seen of value when you looked at me was a scientific anomaly." I gripped a handful of my hair. "Another rare gem in your collection."

My father lowered his hand. His composure slowly trickled back. "I won't waste my energy arguing with you, Ambrosia. It's clear that these rebels have compromised your clarity with their lies. Who knows what they've told you. It's fortunate for us that Mr. Lindstrom had the presence of mind to plant the tracker we gave him in your backpack before you left the Academy."

It felt as though someone had leeched all the blood

from my face. My entire body went cold. "Prewitt?" I whispered.

"Since your behavior continued to become more and more erratic, we gave him the extra tracker along with instructions to plant it on you if he sensed you might put yourself in harm's way," said Titus. "Fortunately for us, his instincts proved correct."

I thought back to when Prew had chased me down the hall and thrown his arms around me. He hadn't wanted one last goodbye... it had been a cover for slipping the tracker in my bag. Our last goodbye—but not in the way I'd thought. He wasn't letting me betray him.

He was betraying me. To protect me. He had been so worried that I was putting myself in danger. He would have known I could never forgive what he'd done.

I had to remind myself to breathe. Even so, my inhale was shallow and shaky. *Prewitt is the reason the Atrium was attacked,* I thought. How many people had died down there, all because my friend had tried to protect me one last time?

"Regardless," my father was saying, "things will go back to the way they were once you return to the manor."

My mouth opened in confusion. "Are you really that delusional? How could you honestly think I'd go back with you? I finally know the truth, and I don't want anything to do with you or your plans," I spat. "Nothing you could ever say will change that."

To my astonishment, my father seemed unfazed by my reaction. "I don't doubt you," he said. "And you'll find that I have no plans of engaging you in a battle of willpower. There are other ways of rectifying the situation."

"What are you going to do, Dad?" I challenged. "Torture me? Throw me in the Catacombs with all the other people who've pissed off the Forum? Well, you can try whatever you want. I'll *die* before I go back to that life!"

"Oh, I don't think that will be necessary," spoke the auburn-haired woman from her seat in the corner of the room. She had remained silent for the duration of my tirade, but now she stood with a surprising air of authority. "The sad truth, my dear, is that we can do whatever we like to you, and tomorrow you will still be praising us for rescuing you from the clutches of the underground Dreg cult that captured and tortured you for information." Her thin lips twisted in a sneer.

Icy-fingered horror gripped me. *Of course.*

Their choices weren't limited to convincing me or disposing of me. All they had to do was erase the last several weeks of my life, and I would revert back to the oblivious girl I'd been before.

I turned to Rift, but he looked just as helpless as I felt.

"In the meantime, I think it's best to keep you close at hand," the woman continued. "You are about to witness one of the most innovative pieces of technology since Imhoff's invention of the Time Harness."

As if on cue, several white-coated scientists entered the room pushing a cart. On the cart sat a simple-looking box with a series of wires protruding from one side. They wheeled the cart around to the side of Rift's bed. Rift eyed it apprehensively.

"What's that for?" I asked.

The woman crossed to the cart. "We need to perform a few procedures on your friend here."

"What is it you're trying to get?" asked Rift. "A kidney? A few thousand brain stem cells from a more highly-evolved life form?"

The woman's face remained impassive as she turned to him. "Information, actually."

"Information?" Rift repeated with a frown. "Then wouldn't an interview be more profitable for you than a bunch of scientific tests?"

"Not for the kind of information we seek. This," she said, caressing the metal box, "is a prototype our Research Specialists have been working on for quite some time. They're calling it a Memory Projector. It can scan and read the brain as it recalls memories, then project them onto a screen for observation."

Rift snorted. "Sounds impressive. Only one problem with this brilliant plan of yours," he noted. "Someone— maybe even your own intellectual miscreants—*erased* my memories."

Once again, the woman's thin, red lips stretched in an unsettling smile. "That won't be a problem. Contrary to popular belief, when a person is Wiped, their memories aren't completely gone."

Out of the corner of my eye, I saw Rift straighten up.

The woman's eyes narrowed. "I thought that might be of interest to you. You see, rather than removing memories altogether, the Wipe process actually buries one's memories in a deep level of the subconscious. Over time, the mental barrier separating the patient's active memories from those made dormant begins to deteriorate, creating what we call 'leakage.' Of course, it's unlikely that the victim of a Wipe will ever fully regain their memories, but traces may be resurrected." She gazed at Rift, pursing her lips. "Tell me, have you noticed anything unusual in your sleep patterns of late? Say, within the past six months?"

Rift didn't say anything, but his answer was apparent in the way he clenched his jaw. I suddenly remembered the morning in the Atrium when I had watched him wake up and scribble frantically in his battered notebook.

The woman grinned. "I thought you might. It appears that you have begun to leak, Patient D2."

Rift glared at her. "I told you not to call me that."

She went on as though not having heard him. "Now that you have entered the Leakage phase, we may be able to gain access to certain more prominent memories."

"Gain access?" I interjected. "What do you mean?"

"I hardly think the particulars of the process are relevant for you, Miss Croft," she said. One of the scientists who had wheeled in the cart had begun to adhere the box's wires around the circumference of Rift's head while the other held him still.

"So you're saying that there's something in Rift's

memories that you need?"

"Rift?" the woman repeated, looking at him. "Hmm. Appropriate name for you to have chosen, considering the break between this new identity you've created and the one you once had."

Rift said nothing, but continued to glare at her.

"The answer to your question, Miss Croft, is yes," she replied without taking her eyes off of Rift. "In fact, your friend here may hold within the recesses of his mind the key to our world's future."

I thought I saw Rift's eyes widen by a fraction, but he was keeping his face under tight control.

"Inspector," said my father in a disapproving tone. "Are you sure that Ambrosia ought to be remain here for this?"

Inspector? I turned to look at the rigid woman more closely. So that was why she acted so at ease with my father. She was one of the only people in the world who ranked almost equally with him. This must be the Globe's head Inspector, Dr. Kimberly Grey. It was well known that Inspector Grey was at the forefront of all high-level global investigations. It was rumored that she had never failed to close a case. But what was she hoping to gain from sifting through the last vestiges of Rift's memories?

Inspector Grey turned to my father. "I do. As I recall from what you've told me, Titus, your daughter has a nasty habit of slipping away. I'd prefer she stay where we can keep an eye on her. Besides, she's clearly injured. She won't be

349

able to do any harm." She turned to me. "Have a seat over there, Miss Croft," she said, gesturing across the room.

"I'll stay here, thanks," I said, dropping into a fight stance. I had no plans to move an inch further from Rift.

"Perhaps you didn't understand me," said the Inspector. She gave a curt nod to the Official who stood by the door. He immediately pulled a gun from his belt and leveled it at my head. "Move away," Grey said.

"No."

"Do you consider yourself to be in a position to defy me?" she demanded. "You are a renegade fugitive… a traitor to the Global Alliance. You will do as you are told or you *will* be shot. In fact, it may actually add to the backstory of your being rescued from the Rebels."

"Inspector, perhaps we could…" began my father.

"No, Titus," Grey snapped. I couldn't remember anyone talking back to my father like that. "You may be willing to tolerate to your daughter's disobedience, but I am not. The Forum—which includes you yourself—has employed my assistance in this matter, and your fellow Timekeepers will not thank you for hindering my work." She turned back to me. "This is your last chance, Miss Croft."

"Ambry, go," Rift insisted.

"I'm not going to stand by and let them dig through your mind," I said, gripping his arm.

"Don't be an idiot! They'll shoot you!"

"Three… two… one…" the Inspector counted. I

closed my eyes, bracing myself.

"Hold your fire!" my father ordered.

I opened my eyes to see the Official lower his arm halfway, glancing between Titus and Inspector Grey. Clearly he had never been torn between such equal levels of authority.

My heart was racing with adrenaline. *My pills,* I thought suddenly. *It's been at least a week since I last took one...* As a tightness spread through my chest, I was beginning to think I might have made a mistake when I spit the last dose out.

"Ambrosia," said my father. His voice was unsteady. He sounded uncharacteristically frightened. "Standing there won't stop this from happening. But if you move away now, we'll give you a minute to say your goodbyes." His expression was almost pleading.

I clenched my hand tighter around Rift's arm and turned to look down him.

"It's going to be okay, Ambry," Rift said softly.

"No it's not!" I said, tears slipping down my cheeks. The sting of Prewitt's betrayal mixed with the thought of never seeing Rift again left me feeling as though my sanity were slipping away. "I'm *not* going to say goodbye to you."

"Ambry, move away," Rift begged.

"But—"

"You can't stop this!" Rift exclaimed. I was shocked to see tears in his earthen eyes. "Please, Ambry. For me."

"Listen to your friend, Miss Croft," the Inspector

advised. She gave the slightest nod to the Official. Slowly, he began to move toward me.

I closed my eyes and pretended not to notice. Sobs wracked my body. Releasing Rift's arm, I reached my good hand across to the other even as the Official put a hand on my shoulder…

Grabbing the stapler from my right hand, I opened it and slammed it down on the Official's hand.

"*Gahhhh!*" He screamed in pain and stumbled away.

I whipped back to Rift and made one last attempt to yank the straps free.

"Ambry, watch out!" Rift cried.

The explosion of gunfire made my heart stop. My hand instinctively tightened on Rift's shirt.

And then everything went deathly still.

I looked around. The room looked exactly the same as it had before. If this was the afterlife that some people believed in, it certainly was anticlimactic. I glanced at Rift.

He blinked his eyes in stunned silence.

"What happened?" I asked.

"I have no idea," Rift said, staring past me.

Slowly, I straightened back up and turned around.

The Official, my father, and Inspector Grey were all frozen. Most astonishing of all was the bullet that hung suspended in midair only inches from my head. Was it my imagination, or could I actually see a bluish wake trailing behind it, like a trajectory from the gun? In fact, faint blue lines trailed from each of the petrified figures, as though marking their paths of motion leading up to the point time froze.

Rift gaped at me. "Ambry, how did you…?"

"I didn't do anything," I said. "I don't even *have* a time capsule with me!"

Rift's open jaw snapped shut as he transitioned from awe into action. "We have to move quickly. Grab that knife from the Official's belt."

I hurried to obey. Pulling the knife free, I began slicing through Rift's plastic bonds. Fortunately, Officials were in the habit of keeping their knives well-sharpened. Within seconds, he was ripping the wires off of his forehead and rolling out of the bed. He pulled me into a brief but tight hug, careful to avoid my bad arm. "Let's go," he said, taking my hand.

We dodged past the immobile figures—my father's face frozen in fear and shock, the Inspector's plastered with a look of stunned surprise—and burst through the door into the hall. "Which way?" I asked.

"No clue, but I want to put some distance between us and that room," Rift said as we hurtled down the hall. We skidded around the corner and paused to read a sign above. "The Telepoint is this way!" he said, heading straight.

And then in a swirl of movement, time resumed.

Rift didn't slow down. We barreled ahead past a group of stunned scientists and several Officials before it registered to them that something was off. "Hey! Stop!" one of them called as they began to sprint after us.

Running next to me, Rift laughed. "I'll never understand why they think we're going to listen when they say that!"

Alarms began to blare. The double doors down the hall ahead of us swung open to reveal a dozen Officials carrying impressive-looking weapons.

Rift threw out an arm and we skidded to a halt.

"Hands above your heads!" commanded the Official at the lead of the group. Her gun was aimed directly at Rift's chest.

Suddenly, the Officials at the back of their formation began to crumple. The one who had shouted at us barely had time to turn around before she too collapsed to the floor.

Beside me, Rift's face lit up.

Kade and a dozen other darkly-clad Rebels were cascading through the double doors, leaping over fallen Officials. When he reached us, Kade clapped Rift on the shoulder. "Couldn't just leave my Second behind," he said.

"But how did you find us?" I asked.

"Rift swallowed his tracker during the raid," Kade said.

Rift grinned at me. "Emergency protocol."

"Now let's get out of here before the whole damn Globe descends on us," Kade said.

Nodding, we fell into formation following Kade and a handful of others while another half-dozen Rebels fell in behind us. Together we all sprinted down the hall in the direction of the signs marked TELEPOINTS.

Two archways stood ahead. "Go!" Kade ordered, waving us through.

"They'll follow us," Rift said. "We don't have time to initiate a self-destruct. How are we going to stop them from getting into Sector B?"

Kade grinned. "The old-fashioned way." He reached into his pocket and pulled out a grenade. Shouts echoed down the corridor behind us. "Go on! I'll bring up the rear," he said.

Rift grabbed my hand and pulled me forward as the Officials began to shoot. I looked back to see Kade pull the clip from the grenade and drop it on the floor behind him. Suddenly, his face contorted in pain as a bullet hole ripped through his chest.

Rift turned his head in response to Kade's grunt of pain. "Kade!" he cried as he and I were enveloped in the portal.

CHAPTER NINETEEN

Rift gripped both of my shoulders and looked me squarely in the eyes. "Stay here," he commanded. He turned and leapt back through the portal.

"Rift!" I yelled.

The other members of our rescue team moved in around me, each one staring transfixed at the archway. Seconds ticked by so slowly that we might as well have been in a time freeze.

It was taking too long...

I was about to disregard Rift's order and jump through the portal myself when he suddenly emerged, Kade's arm slung over his shoulder. The Commander's body hung limp. "Get him to the hospital!" Rift shouted.

Several burly Rebels leapt to Rift's aid, carefully lifting

Kade beneath his shoulders and legs. They shuffled away, cutting a clear path through the small crowd that had gathered around us.

"Is he going to be okay?" I asked Rift.

"He will be," he said, but the look on his face was uncertain. He crossed his arms and watched Kade's prone body disappear from sight. "He has to be."

I let out a sigh and shook my head. "I still don't understand how we got out of there."

"Neither do I," he said, tapping a finger against his sleeve. I could tell that it was going to bother him. After a moment's pause, he let his arms fall to his side. "For now, I'll settle for just being glad we *did* make it out."

I smiled and took a deep breath to steady myself. Now that we were out of harm's way, I could actually take in my surroundings. I turned to look around the large room and gasped.

Similar to the Atrium's Arrival Room, it was dome-shaped and spacious. It could have fit both the ballroom and dining room from my family's manor comfortably at its center.

But the size of the room wasn't what caught me off guard. Whereas the Atrium had been nestled beneath hundreds of feet of rock and earth, this sprawling glass dome was surrounded on all sides by water. Several dozen small fish flitted out of the path of a giant manta ray as it floated by, flashing its white belly as it inspected the surface of the glass. Light from the distant surface above just barely permeated the water, lending it an ethereal glow.

I was about to stammer something stupid and awestruck to Rift when the crowd around us began to part once more, making way for a woman with wild lavender hair and skin the color of burnt caramel. Those around her gave a strange sort of salute—crossing their hands at waist level so their inner wrists touched, then placing their right fists over their hearts. She stopped just short of us.

"Gloria," said Rift, extending a hand.

As she clasped his forearm, I saw the Circlet materialize in white against her dark wrist. "Good to see you again, Rift," she said. "I'm sorry for the loss of your home."

Rift nodded. "Thank you, Commander. We all appreciate your hospitality while we get things sorted out."

"No problem whatsoever. Atlantis can easily accommodate twice the numbers we normally house," she said.

Atlantis. So we really were under the ocean. I glanced again at the schools of fish meandering along the glass panes. A part of me had almost wondered if it might be a clever holographic image projected onto the glass...

Gloria's green eyes fell on me. "And this must be the famous Ambrosia Croft."

Famous? It was strange to think that the people here already knew who I was. "Ambry," I said, shaking her hand awkwardly with my left.

"Your changeover caused quite a stir throughout the Resistance," Gloria added. "I know that there may be those who are... hesitant... about your presence here, but know that the majority of us have been encouraged to know that those in the higher ranks of the Elites—even family members of the Timekeepers themselves—are learning the truth."

"Um, thank you," I replied, not quite sure how to take her words. *Did that mean there were whole groups of people like Marius down here who were hell-bent on doing me in?*

As though sensing my unease, Rift put a protective arm around my shoulder. "Once they've had a chance to meet her, they'll see that her loyalty lies with the Resistance," he said.

"I'm sure they will," Gloria agreed. "Now, I suggest we get you both cleaned up at the Medical Unit. Francesca here will show you the way."

Rift and I nodded. He released my shoulder as we followed the short girl across the room. Now that his arm had left my shoulders, it was amazing how much I missed the comfort it had brought.

Large video screens were scattered along the walls of the expansive dome. Most featured a combination of smoke, fire, protests, or people screaming and crying in the streets. As we walked, I looked from the screens to Rift for explanation.

"Uprisings in various corners of the world," he said. "More and more people are starting to get frustrated with the Elites taking people down left and right with their superior weapons. They keep these running here twenty-four seven as a reminder."

We exited the dome and followed Francesca down a small glass corridor. When we entered the Medical Unit at the corridor's end, we were greeted with the sight of a hospital-gowned Torque engaged in a heated argument with Dmitri. "I don't need all this bloody fuss!" Torque growled, ripping the IV out of his wrist.

"What you need, Mr. Guerrier, is to understand that *I* and not *you* am the medical professional here!" Dmitri snapped. "You will leave when I decide you are fit to leave!"

Torque was about to unleash a reply when he caught sight of us. "I can't believe it. You're alive!" he cried. He strode forward to embrace his friend.

"Whoa!" said Rift, stepping back. "You may want to tie the back of that gown a bit more thoroughly..."

"Oh. Sorry about that," Torque said, re-knotting the string. "Ambry!" he exclaimed.

He was about to heft me in a crushing embrace when Rift stepped in between us. "Watch it, broken arm," Rift pointed out.

"Yikes," Torque said. "All I had was a couple hair-line fractures and a sprained ankle. Nothing a good sparring match won't fix," he added with a wink.

"What about Avienne? Is she all right?" I asked. When I had last seen the two of them, they were both lying unconscious in the dark tunnel.

"She should be fine," Torque assured me. "She's out cold right now. Dmitri says she's got a concussion and really just needs to sleep it off."

"All right. I think that's enough with the meet-and-greet," Dmitri said. "I'd like to treat my patients now." There was a depressed edge to his normally-sarcastic tone, and I could tell that the strain of the day had taken its toll on him. Dark circles framed his eyes. How many injuries must he and his team have treated after the ambush on the Atrium?

Rift must have picked up on the change too, because he allowed Dmitri to inspect him without comment or complaint while a sandy-haired woman with thick glasses went to work setting my arm. "How is Kade?" Rift asked as Dmitri checked his blood pressure.

"Don't know. The Atlantian medics have got him in surgery," Dmitri replied, still focused on his work.

"What happened to Kade?" asked Torque sharply.

"He got shot in the chest right before we made it here," Rift answered. "But he's alive," he said, seeing Torque's horrified expression. "It went a little wide, completely missed his heart."

Torque ran a hand through his white hair, making it stick up at all angles. "Whew. Thank God for that."

Once we were all bandaged and splinted up, Dmitri released us from his custody with only a single verbal jab. "I'm worried about him," Rift murmured, looking back toward the Medical Unit.

"Who, Dmitri? He'll be all right," Torque said with a wave of his hand. "Nothing he hasn't seen before. Anyway,

I'm going to go check on Kade. I'll come find you two later."

"Good idea. Let us know how he's doing," Rift said. When Torque had disappeared, Rift motioned for me to follow him. "Come on. Let's find somewhere we can talk."

. . . .

Rift paced in front of me. He had led us into a small side- room, one wall of which offered a panoramic view of the ocean outside. "Ambry, what happened when that gun went off ?"

"Um, well, time froze right as I nearly got shot in the head..."

"No," Rift said as waved his hands in front of him. "What happened to *you*? Internally. Did you feel anything?"

I thought back to the shock of hearing the Official's gun discharge. "Well, I remember how tight my chest felt leading up to it, and when it actually went off, I felt as though I couldn't breathe," I said. "It was almost like my heart stopped."

A look of comprehension dawned across his face. "You haven't been on your meds, have you?"

"No," I said, puzzled. "But what does that have to do with anything?"

But Rift was staring transfixed at my hair. "It has everything to do with it," he murmured. He met my eyes. "When did your parents put you on the medication?"

I thought back. It was hard to remember a time before the pills. "I was five," I said. "My mom says I had some sort of 'episode;' she says my blood pressure rose to a dangerous level and nearly caused my heart to fail, so they had to rush me to the hospital. The doctor diagnosed me with hypertension and I've been taking the pills ever since. Well, for the most part," I added.

"Do you remember the episode?"

I shook my head. "Which is weird, because you'd think a five year-old would remember something that traumatic..."

Rift's face broke into a wide grin. "Ambry, you don't have hypertension. That's not why you've been on those pills all your life."

I frowned. "What do you mean?"

Excitement bubbled all over him. "Don't you see? When you were five, something like *this* must have happened, something that made time freeze! Something must have made your heart speed up—an extreme adrenaline rush of some kind—and then *bam*, everything frozen just as if a time capsule had been opened!"

I stared at him blankly. Could it really be possible that *I* had been the source of the time freeze back at the Globe Research Facility? Then again, there was something odd about it. In my other experiences with time capsules, I had never seen those blue wakes...

Rift was still rambling as he paced. "And of course, your parents couldn't just let their child run around freezing time… who knows what kind of havoc a kid could wreak or what danger they could get themselves into with that kind of power? So they came up with an excuse for why they needed to slow your heart down—to prevent it from ever being able to reach a rate that would activate the time lapse. It even explains your hair!" he said.

I reached up and caught a tendril of it between my fingers. Glancing down at the blue strand, I could suddenly see the resemblance between its hue and that of the eerie glow of the time capsules. "That would explain why my parents spent so much time and money trying to figure out the mystery behind my hair. It wasn't about the color… it was about whatever happened when I was five."

"And it explains why your father was so upset when you tried to change it," Rift said. "He was worried it might have some negative impact on your ability! They obviously didn't want you to know about it or operate in it, but they also didn't want it to be destroyed."

"Yeah. My father would never want to let something that rare and valuable out of his sight."

Rift suddenly stopped his pacing and looked at me. "I'm sorry, Ambry," he said, taking a step toward me. "Between your father today and what Prewitt did…"

"It's fine," I lied, wrapping my good arm around my torso. I suddenly felt cold. And very, very tired.

Rift lifted a hand. He hesitated, then reached out and drew me into his arms. "It's not fine. Not at all," he said. "But hopefully the worst is over now."

I rested my cheek against his chest, marveling at how perfectly my head fit beneath his chin. With all the chaos of the raid, confronting my father, Prewitt's betrayal, and my brush with death in the Research Facility, standing there being held by Rift was like catching my breath in the eye of the storm. I didn't want to leave, to face the aftermath of everything that had happened. *If only we could stay tucked away here...*

"Commander?" spoke a deep voice.

Rift and I broke away to find a tall Rebel with a crew cut standing at attention in the doorway. He gave Rift the same strange salute that the other Atlantian Rebels had given Gloria.

It suddenly dawned on me that with Ming gone and Kade out of commission, *Rift* was the acting Commander of the Atrium Sector.

"Yes?" Rift asked.

"You're needed in the council."

"Thank you. Tell Gloria I'll be there in a minute," Rift said, dismissing the messenger with a nod.

It was strange to see others treat him with the same level of authority they normally addressed Kade. Rift had always been the easygoing one...the lower-level leader with enough clout to let him get away with bending the rules. Now, he was the one issuing them.

"Commander," I said, tasting the word.

"I know. Sounds strange on me, doesn't it?" he said.

"Not necessarily," I said. "I think you would make a

good Commander."

Rift smacked a hand to his chest and took two staggering steps backwards.

"I know, I know," I said, laughing. "Don't let it go to your head."

He chuckled, but it died quickly on his lips. Resolve replaced mirth. I could see a hardness settle in his eyes. Too much had happened in a single day...too many lives lost. Too many reminders of his own loss. And now he would have to step forward and help those who were left navigate a new course. "Come on," he said. "We have to face what's happened sooner or later."

I nodded as I followed him out the door. He was right in more ways than he understood. Today might have been the first day I had to face the consequences of my decision to join the Resistance, but it was only the beginning. I had thrown a boulder into the placid waters of my life, and I had a feeling the ripple effect would stretch farther into my future than I could begin to imagine.

But as Rift's calloused hand brushed against mine, it didn't seem so impossible. I looked up at his profile, determined and strong. He may not have known his past, but he did know his place in the present.

Whereas I had to figure out the opposite. All my life, I'd been told who to be. My prescribed identity had always overwhelmed and overshadowed me. Now I finally had the chance to discover my true identity for myself. But whoever I was, one thing I did know was that I belonged to this cause.

I was fighting for something greater than myself.
And I wasn't doing it alone.

Acknowledgments

I'm grateful to God for His ferocious grace and love,
as well as for imbuing me with a passion for stories.
Jesus, thank you for getting me to the end of this segment of
the journey.

Special thanks to my content editor, Stephen Parolini, for
unleashing his "Red Pen of Life and Death" upon my
manuscript and urging me—with great wit and wisdom—to
raise the bar; to Ashleigh "Beee" Dunne for designing the
phenomenal cover of this book; and to Chelsea O'Neil for
showing me the proper way to fix a dislocated shoulder.

Thanks also to my brave band of beta readers who provided
me with much-needed feedback: Grace (aka sister); Beee;
Josh; Danika; Kollin; Eilidh; and Fiona—
my number-one fangirl from start to finish!

Thanks, Sarah and Todd, for friendship and coffee
and snowy days writing on the yellow couch.

And of course, I must thank my wonderful parents not only
for their encouragement and support, but for cultivating a
love of reading in me from a young age. Thanks for letting
me look at books in my crib until I fell asleep.

About the Author

Jessie Biggs has always been an avid reader—especially of science fiction and fantasy—believing story to be one of the best mediums for communicating truth.
She graduated from Liberty University in Lynchburg, VA with a BA in Teaching English as a Second Language—a degree chosen far less for its practicality than for the chance to take both English *and* Linguistics classes.

She lives in Virginia surrounded by the Blue Ridge Mountains and incomparable community of friends.

Made in the USA
San Bernardino, CA
21 December 2016